MR. WONDERFUL

MR. WONDERFUL

MR. WONDERFUL

By
ALGERNON

Contains Mature Situations and Content – Discretion Advised

CHAPTER 1

"I cried at my own funeral!" recalls the former accountant for the Mongelli crime family. His real name is John Magi, but his clean, family-man image earned him his street name: Mr. Wonderful. He is the last one the crime boss would have expected to bring down the entire operation and extended empire. Now a single photograph flutters from his hand to the floor: a car smoldering amid a dense cloud of smoke and leaping orange flames. The crime boss, Mr. Wonderful's former number-one client, perished in the fire, the result of a high-speed chase with FBI agents.

"I watched in agony on a surveillance monitor as my wife attempted to comfort my heartbroken young daughter. Now after all these years, my nightmare is finally over," John Magi weeps as he hugs FBI special agent Michelle Ross. The tall, athletic woman, who is often dressed in the standard navy-blue slacks with matching jacket and white blouse, is almost ear to ear matched to John's height—even without the advantage of heeled shoes. John himself stands a modest five foot, ten inches tall. The 46-year-old first generation Italian-American grew up on the tough streets of Brooklyn, New York. In his prime, he was in pretty good shape. Although he is currently not in the poorest of health, more than a decade of limited activity coupled with meatball heroes and pasta dinners has produced a bit of a gut and spare tire. On the contrary, the attractive female with shoulder-length hair that he is hugging is rather physically fit—particularly for a woman who is herself in her early 40s.

Over the past 15 years, agent Ross has been John Magi's closest thing to a friend. His life in the special witness protection program was torturous, but Ross kept John updated on his wife and daughter—even providing him with surveillance photos of them from time to time. It is these photos, pinned on the inside of the wooden door of his bedroom closet in his small, barren apartment that kept him going all these years.

"Yes, well at least now you can get back to a somewhat regular life," replies agent Ross as she pulls away to escape the awkward embrace. Her eyes dance around the room, looking for something else to focus on. There are few options, as the room is conspicuously absent of the normal lifestyle comforts and collections.

Her statement brings the reality of the circumstances to light, and John Magi's countenance reflects it—the fact that there is a new man in the lives of his now ex-wife and daughter.

"Now John, you can't just barge in on them and say, 'Surprise honey, I'm not dead!'" agent Ross states as to discourage John from even thinking such a thing.

The sobering reality quickly extinguishes the tiny hope that John Magi had of returning to his old life and reclaiming the family he once cherished. The irony is that it was John's love for his family that convinced him to go along with the FBI's plan of faking his death, and entering this special witness protection program, in the first place.

"I know, I know! I just wish things could be different," exclaims a deflated John.

"We've been over this a million times … your former associates were more likely to believe that you alone died in that crash. No one would ever suspect that Mr. Wonderful would abandon his family to turn government witness. If we relocated the entire family, they would have never given up looking for you … all of you," states agent Ross.

"Well I did abandon my family, didn't I?" replies John. He made the decision a decade and a half earlier but still hasn't come to terms with it.

"It was the best thing for everyone. The best thing you can do for your wife and daughter now is to remain out of their lives. They've moved on, and so should you," agent Ross states in a firm tone.

John Magi is clearly conflicted within himself. He buries his face in his hands and lets out a muffled scream of frustration.

Agent Ross continues to try to reason with the former government's star witness. "You made the choice to …"

John Magi's interruption is immediate and abrupt.

"Choice? I wouldn't call it much of a choice, Ross! Either spend the next 60 years in federal prison, or testify against the most powerful mobsters in New York City," John spews with equal parts rage and sarcasm. "Oh, but if I do testify, my family and I will be hunted for the rest of our lives … unless they think I'm dead! I wouldn't call that much of a choice!"

Agent Ross has clearly had this particular conversation with this witness before. Her worn- out patience is evident on her face as well as in her tone.

"What do you want me to tell you, John? Huh? The fact is that your wife and daughter are still alive and doing well … not to mention YOU are still alive, and not rotting away in prison. I would say that under the circumstances, you came out on top here," replies agent Ross.

John shakes his head side to side and lets out a sarcastic half chuckle.

"I'm alive, but I wouldn't call this much of a life," John states with his eyes fixated toward his opened closet door. Agent Ross' eyes follow John's to a surveillance photo of his now 22-year-old daughter—a photo that agent Ross herself took and provided to him.

"Let them live their lives, John. It is the best thing for everyone," agent Ross suggests in a much softer tone.

She retrieves a large manila envelope from the kitchen table in front of them. She brought it specifically for this final meeting with

John. She offers it to him, but he refuses to even look at it ... or her. At his reaction, or lack thereof, she returns it to the table.

"So, I'm guessing no, you don't want a ride to the airport?" she asks, but gets no response.

"Well there is your new ID, backstory, and everything you will need for your last and final relocation. You know the drill," states agent Ross as she turns to exit.

The crashing sound of the table being violently overturned startles her and she stops in her tracks. After the brief pause, agent Ross continues to make her exit as she offers her final remarks ... with added sarcasm.

"Goodbye, Mr. Wonderful!"

The attractive, yet unapproachably tough federal agent exits the brick apartment building where John Magi has been hiding under a false identity. There is an indication of relief added to her already confident stride as she walks to a dark-colored sedan awaiting her arrival with the engine running. Perhaps the sense of ease and satisfaction that agent Ross possesses lies in the fact that they have successfully managed to keep a former mob affiliate and federal witness alive for all these years. Now, with the death of the last remaining member of the Mongelli crime family—the boss himself, Salvatore Mongelli Jr.—Ross and her team can finally close the book on this lengthy saga.

Agent Ross enters the dark-colored sedan on the passenger side, and plops her weight down in the back seat with exaggeration. Her partner, an African-American male, agent Steve Granderson, has a puzzled look on his face as he watches his partner through the rear-view mirror. He is suave, yet boyish and extremely charismatic. His hands are still on the steering wheel as he addresses Ross.

"Um, hello? This is not a taxi, Michelle," declares Granderson.

"Please, just drive! It's at least two hours to the nearest airport and I am experiencing a serious sweet-tea hangover. The sooner you get us to the airport, the sooner I can get on a flight out of the hot-ass South," replies agent Ross as she unbuttons her jacket and removes it. After throwing her jacket onto the passenger seat in front of her, she removes her shoes and flings them to the front passenger floor.

She then begins to unbutton her blouse. After undoing four buttons, she pauses and looks up as her eyes directly meet agent Granderson's in the rearview mirror.

"Excuse me!" huffs agent Ross as she clutches her blouse against her chest.

"What? Objects in the mirror are closer than they appear," replies agent Granderson.

"Cute, is this close enough for you?" asks agent Ross as she presses her tightly clenched fist against her partner's right temple.

"OK, gosh ... easy," replies a smiling agent Granderson as he adjusts the mirror up toward the roof—and away from Ross' reflection.

"Thank you," agent Ross offers as she continues to change into more comfortable and cooler attire.

"How did it go?" Granderson asks.

"I think he's a stubborn old fool that, against my better judgment, will totally go see his family," replies Ross as she continues her wardrobe change in the back seat.

"I don't think there's anything to worry about," states Granderson as he puts the car in gear and pulls away.

"I've been doing this long enough to know, there is *always* something to worry about," Ross replies as she sits in the back seat with her legs up as if she is lounging on her living room couch. "Wake me up if we pass one of those Country Smothered Biscuit places," she requests as she leans her head back and shuts her eyes.

From his second-floor apartment kitchen window, John Magi watches as the two federal agents drive away in the dark-colored sedan. He steps around the overturned kitchen table as he makes his way to the small, rusty refrigerator in the corner of the room. He grabs a beer and pops the can open. As he takes a swig of the cold beverage his eyes catch a glimpse of some of the spilled contents of the envelope left by agent Ross. He reaches down and picks up a partially dislodged airline ticket. He spits out the remaining drink from his mouth as he reads the destination of the one-way ticket.

"Seattle?"

CHAPTER 2

Heavy rain pounds against the window of apartment 3A. This typical Chelsea apartment building is unpretentious, with high ceilings and old hardwood flooring. The single tall window facing the street equally lets in plenty of light as well as street noise from bustling city traffic and pedestrians alike. Jamie Magi has not gotten used to the loud noises that come from outside, as well as those of her neighbors in apartment 4A above. She has to use noise-cancelling headphones in order to study for her senior year of college. To get some sleep, she has found that playing music from her Bluetooth speaker, which sits on her nightstand, is rather helpful.

The speaker is currently blasting reggae music—more so to conceal noise rather than keep noise out. Jamie Magi and her boyfriend Kyle have a committed sex schedule, and every Thursday afternoon, between her accounting class and his part-time job at the bar, the young couple makes love religiously. Their relationship is familiar enough to have a great level of comfort and understanding of each other's pleasure peaks, yet new and fresh enough that the level of intensity and excitement is well above average.

As the young lovers reach dual climax, they collapse into each other's arms—sweaty, flush, and winded—each of them grinning as they exchange expressions of mutual satisfaction and adoration. After catching his breath, Kyle reaches over to retrieve his pants from the floor next to the bed. He grabs a cigarette and lighter from his pocket, much to the disgust of his girlfriend.

"What the hell are you doing? Don't smoke that in here!" scoffs Jamie with a scowl.

"What? Everybody in this building smokes," replies Kyle defensively.

"Well not me, and definitely not in bedroom! Go out in the hallway," she replies.

Kyle reluctantly returns the cigarette and lighter to his pants pocket and drops them back down to the floor.

"I'm trying to quit anyway," he replies as he gets up and walks toward the bathroom.

Jamie smiles as she watches her naked man walk away. His confidence and raw male sexual energy completely turn her on.

"And put the toilet seat back down!" she yells playfully as he disappears around the corner into the bathroom.

Jamie also gets up and retrieves her underwear from the floor at the foot of the bed. After putting on her bra and panties, she puts on the short robe that she keeps hanging on her metal headboard. She then attempts to gather her long, dark-brown hair up into a ponytail, but the tiny rubber band pops. As she looks for another, she is distracted by notification alerts shining from Kyle's phone. She looks over toward the bathroom and then again at her boyfriend's phone.

Jamie tries not to have trust issues with men, but according to the shrink that her mother made her see back in high school, "the death of her father left damaging emotional scarring, blah-blah--blah." Basically, as a little girl whose father, the first man she ever loved, was so badly burned in an accident that they had to have a closed-casket funeral, which didn't really provide the closure she needed, Jamie Magi has trouble believing a man that loves her will always be around. As she reaches for her boyfriend's cell phone, the sound of the toilet flushing indicates that she will not have much time to properly inspect the device, so she abandons her mission … for now. Kyle emerges from the bathroom with a dark-colored towel wrapped around his waist. He offers his girlfriend a quick peck on the lips, followed by another on her neck.

"Don't do that unless you're ready to go again, mister," says Jamie flirtatiously.

"You're lucky I have to go to work," replies Kyle before planting a final passionate kiss on his girlfriend's lips. "Just going to take a quick shower," he adds, before retrieving his cell phone from the nightstand and carrying it to the bathroom with him.

"Want me to join you?" offers Jamie to Kyle's back as he quickly disappears around the corner and into the bathroom.

"Then I'll be late," he replies before closing the door behind him.

The playful smirk on Jamie's face indicates she is up to something sneaky. She disrobes as she tiptoes toward the bathroom. Her plot is interrupted by the sound of an incoming call to her cell phone as it vibrates loudly on her dresser. She can see the caller ID. It is her mother calling via video chat. She initially considers ignoring the call, but then decides to answer. She is a bit annoyed.

"No, I didn't forget, I was just about to hop in the shower," yells Jamie as she holds the phone screen up at her face.

"Well, hello to you too, dear," replies her offended mother, Katherine.

Mrs. Katherine West doesn't look a day over 35. In fact, people often mistake her and her daughter for sisters. She has aged very well, and her personal trainer, Cathy, helps the sexy housewife and mother to stay fit and trim. Katherine is just leaving a workout session and decided to video chat with her only daughter.

"That's not why I'm calling," Katherine continues. "I assumed you did not forget your stepfather's birthday dinner. I just thought I'd try one more time to convince you to bring that handsome boyfriend of yours ... the reservation is for four," Katherine says, as if trying to close a sales transaction. Her husband, Jerron, is a wealthy investor. After Katherine's first husband John Magi was killed in an automobile accident 15 years ago, Katherine met Jerron on a blind date, and they completely hit it off. He is everything that she could possibly want in a mate. The loving couple has been married for six years now. Jerron is a tall and very handsome man who treats his wife and stepdaughter like royalty.

"Sorry, Mom, not going to happen. Kyle has to work and couldn't get anyone to cover his shift, remember we had this conversation?" Jamie replies with a little too much sass for her mother's liking.

"Just thought I'd ask once more. No need to bite my head off," replies Katherine with an exaggerated sigh.

The tone of this conversation is a bit tenser than either lady would like. Jamie smiles genuinely as she realizes that her mother actually approves of someone she is dating—which hasn't always been the case.

"Seems like you really like this one, huh?" asks Jamie playfully.

"What's not to like? He's tall, handsome, he absolutely adores you ... and most of all, he is a great kid from the old neighborhood. His father and your dad were good friends," Katherine replies with a smile.

The subject of Jamie's father creates a bit of awkwardness. After a brief pause, Katherine continues.

"If your father were alive, he would like Kyle for you, too," she concludes.

The mother and daughter share a giggle in the moment.

"Well, we've just gotten to the exclusive dating level, so don't jinx it," replies Jamie jokingly.

"I won't ... just saying," offers Katherine before realizing that she has an incoming call. "Sweetie, I have to take this call. I will see you at the restaurant," she concludes as she abruptly ends the video call.

As the call ends, Jamie's screensaver appears. It is a photo of her and Kyle, taken on her birthday a few months ago. She smiles every time she sees the goofy image, and ponders the memory of that day. Her eyes then move to the eight-inch by five-inch photo in a frame on her dresser. It is of her and her parents, taken back on her seventh birthday. This image brings up a mix of emotions, since it is one of the last memories that she has of her father.

As Jamie stares listlessly, caught up in the emotional moment, Kyle playfully grabs her from behind and lifts her off of her feet.

He gently throws her down onto her bed. This startles her, as she didn't hear him exit the bathroom and enter the bedroom. He then removes his towel as he addresses his half-naked girlfriend.

"I think we may have time for a quick …"

Jamie abruptly cuts him off as she jumps up and runs toward the bathroom.

"You snooze, you lose," she interjects while removing her panties in midstride. "I have to meet my mom and stepdad downtown, and I still have to pick up his present," she yells over her shoulder as she disappears into the bathroom.

Kyle has no response as he is left standing alone—in the nude, in his girlfriend's bedroom. Within seconds the bathroom door opens. Jamie soon emerges and pokes her head around the corner to address Kyle.

"Babe, don't forget I'm stopping by your place tonight when I leave the restaurant. I need to grab my textbook for class in the morning. Don't lock the top lock, because my key only opens the bottom! OK, have a good shift," she says and blows a kiss toward him before disappearing back into the bathroom.

"You got it!" replies Kyle.

He gets dressed, removes the cigarette and lighter from his pocket, and then prepares to leave. Before he exits, he pauses. He is thinking hard about something. He looks at the cigarette, and then toward the bathroom. He sparks the lighter and holds it up to the cigarette's tip.

"Don't tell me I can't smoke. I'm a grown man. I'll smoke wherever the hell I choose," mumbles Kyle to himself.

As he takes a big puff and holds it in, he can hear the shower stop running. He chokes on the smoke as he quickly tries to escape the apartment before Jamie emerges from the bathroom.

CHAPTER 3

The room is filled with applause as the jazz trio holds out its final note of another popular standard. The small platform stage set up in the corner of the classy downtown restaurant has played home to many iconic jazz musicians since its inception back in the early 1930s, some of whom are memorialized with plaques and photos that decorate the walls—autographed by the artists themselves. The room is dimly lit and decorated with contemporary furnishings, which gives a modern twist to the old elegance. The three musicians exit as they break in between sets. Seated in the table closest to stage right is Jerron West. The strikingly good-looking man with a perfectly straight smile and impeccable hair is celebrating his birthday with a lavish dinner. His very pretty wife, Katherine West, and his equally attractive stepdaughter, Jamie Magi, accompany him. It was Katherine who planned the evening and chose this particular restaurant because of Jerron's love of jazz ballads. Both Jerron and Katherine are fully decked out in their visibly expensive attire and jewels. The wealthy man and his wife are sporting several carrots in diamonds, between his watch and her necklace and earrings. As they continue to enjoy the ambiance and the spectacular dining experience, a very attentive server keeps their glasses filled with exquisite red wine. Now that the live music lends over to soft pre-recorded background music, this creates the perfect atmosphere for intimate conversations.

While Jamie sips her wine, she periodically glances down at her cell phone that lies flat on the empty seat next to her. She also watches her mother interact with her stepfather. Katherine lovingly caresses her husband and her eyes sparkle as she looks at the man and love of her life. Jamie can see that what her mother and Jerron have is something special. She cannot help but wonder if she will ever find such intimacy and love—with Kyle, or any man in her lifetime. The 22-year-old has dated all types of guys during her college experience, but she still doesn't believe that she has ever felt what her mother seems to have with her husband.

As the table is cleared and prepped for the dessert portion of the meal, Katherine stares intently at her daughter—trying to give her a nonverbal reminder. Jamie notices this and follows her mother's eyes as they motion toward the small gift bag on the floor to her right. After getting the not-so-subtle hint, Jamie reaches over and retrieves the bag.

"So, Jerron, here is a little something from me. It's not much, but I want to thank you for being awesome … a wonderful man, and a father figure to me. Happy birthday," declares Jamie as she leans over and gives her stepdad a hug and kiss on the cheek.

"Why, thank you so much, kiddo," replies a smiling Jerron.

Katherine gives her daughter a smile and a wink to show her approval of the kind gesture.

"Wow, this is so thoughtful, Jamie. Thank you," Jerron continues as he opens the gift bag to see its contents. He pulls out an engraved leather tablet case that bears his initials: J.A.W.

"You're welcome. I'm glad you like it," Jamie responds.

Elegant dishes of tiramisu, New York cheesecake and crème brûlée arrive and the party of three continues with the indulgent meal. After coffee and a final glass of wine, they call it a night. Katherine and Jamie wait at the table as Katherine pays the tab, while Jerron goes outside to give the ticket to the parking valet.

"Thanks for coming out, sweetie … and the gift is perfect. It means a lot to him that you see him as a father," says Katherine to her daughter in almost a whisper.

"Father figure," Jamie corrects her mother.

"Yes, well all the same, thank you," concludes Katherine.

The brief moment of awkwardness is broken up by a text message from Kyle to Jamie's phone. Jamie smiles after reading the text and then reads it out loud to her mother.

"*Hey, again, I'm sorry I could not make the party. Please send my apology, and happy birthday Mr. West.* That's from Kyle," states Jamie.

"Aw, that is so sweet. I like that boy. Don't forget to give him the dessert we saved for him," replies Katherine.

Jamie holds up a small to-go bag to display to her mother, and then the two women exit the restaurant.

When the ladies meet Jerron outside in front of the valet parking booth, he is still waiting for their car to be pulled around. Katherine leans into her husband's chest, and he wraps his arms around her. With adoration, Jamie watches the loving couple as they embrace.

Jamie is not the only one watching. Across the street, about a half block away, there is another pair of eyes closely watching this birthday party of three.

Jamie begins to feel awkward as her mom and stepdad kiss. She turns her attention to her phone. While looking at the photo of her and Kyle on her phone, she gets the idea to surprise him at his job.

"Hey, you guys. Thanks again for inviting me to celebrate with you. I'm going to swing by the bar and take Kyle his dessert," announces Jamie to her mom and stepdad.

Mr. and Mrs. West are completely into each other and their passionate exchange of affection—they don't even hear her. No longer wishing to play the role of third wheel, Jamie steps off of the curb and into the street with her left hand extended. Almost immediately, a yellow taxicab pulls to a complete stop in front of her.

"Good night!" yells Jamie to the distracted lovers as she gets into the back of the cab. Jamie gives the driver the address to the bar where her boyfriend works, and then turns her attention to her phone to check her social media for anything she may have missed while at dinner.

*   *   *

After the short drive through the city, the taxi pulls up to the bar. Jamie pays with her credit card, and then makes sure she has all of her belongings before exiting the vehicle.

The cab pulls away, and Jamie stands outside of the bar with her phone to her ear. She is calling Kyle to let him know that she is outside. She feels as though walking in unannounced will appear as if she is trying to spy on him, and she doesn't want Kyle to see her as "that girl."

Jamie tries a second time to call Kyle, and after four rings, it goes to his voicemail again. She figures that he is busy working. As she is trying his phone a third time, resigned to leaving a message, a female employee of the bar comes outside to have a smoke. Jamie decides to ask the other employee for assistance.

"Excuse me, after your break, can you ask Kyle Woodard to come outside?" asks Jamie.

"Kyle? Oh he's not working tonight. Corey is filling in for him tonight because he had an important dinner with his girlfriend's family," replies the girl as she continues her cigarette.

Jamie's heart is in her throat. She cannot believe that Kyle lied to her. She is fuming but hides her emotions in front of this stranger.

"Oh, I see. Well, thank you," offers Jamie as she walks away.

A single teardrop races down her face as she walks rapidly to the corner to hail a taxi. As a cab pulls up, she violently tosses Kyle's dessert into a green metal trashcan on the corner. She gets into the cab and gives the driver the address of Kyle's apartment as her destination.

As the yellow New York City taxicab weaves through bottle-necking traffic to enter the Williamsburg Bridge, a visibly upset Jamie sits in the back seat frantically calling Kyle's phone, her breath deepening with each unanswered ring. Eventually she decides to stop calling. She reasons with herself—for there must be a simple explanation. She soothes herself with thoughts of talking things through at Kyle's place.

When the cab finally makes it over the bridge into Brooklyn, Jamie has calmed herself quite a bit. By the time the cab pulls up to Kyle's apartment building, Jamie is completely in control of her emotions.

After paying her fare, she exits the cab and walks up the front steps of the building. She opens the door to the lobby and quickly walks across the black-and-white tiled floor to the elevator. The elevator light indicates that it is all the way up on the top floor, but Jamie has no patience at this point so she takes the stairs.

Once on Kyle's floor, she almost tiptoes down the hallway to his front door. When she reaches the door, she presses her ear against it in an attempt to hear any activity. However, all she can hear is the blaring loud television set of one of the neighbors. Jamie takes several deep breaths before deciding to enter the apartment.

She quietly slides the key into the bottom lock, and turns it. She doubts that Kyle even left the top lock open as she requested. She opens the door quickly and turns on the light in the doorway. It doesn't appear that Kyle is home. In fact, he left her textbook out on the table by the front door with a note on it. Jamie opens the note and reads it: *Babe, have a good night and don't fall asleep in class tomorrow. Love you.*

Jamie is confused. She doesn't know what to do next. Should she confront Kyle directly? Should she wait for him to come clean? She doesn't know if she can trust him at this point. She decides to just go home and sleep on it, then deal with it in the morning.

Just when she steps toward the door, she hears a key enter the lock and turn. She is frozen and cannot even take another step. The top lock is turned into the locked position and she hears the soft thud of a failed attempt to open the door. Jamie figures that Kyle must have forgotten he left the top lock open for her. The top lock then slides back to the unlocked position. Jamie doesn't know what she would do if Kyle opens the door and is with another woman. She doesn't even want to have that conversation, so she quickly turns off the light, and ducks into the closet by the door. The doorknob turns and the door flies open. Kyle is alone and in a rush. He drops his bag by the door and his keys onto the table, and then runs down the hall to the bathroom. Jamie can hear urine flowing heavily into the toilet, so she decides to sneak out. She silently steps out of the closet and over Kyle's bag. She exits quickly and quietly, then races down the hall to the stairwell.

Once she makes it to the lobby, she darts out to the sidewalk, around the corner and out of sight.

CHAPTER 4

Early in the morning, as is her routine, just as the sun peeks out along the Jersey coast, FBI Special Agent Michelle Ross is completing her morning run. Her brightly colored running shoes match her head-band and fitted workout top. Her skin-tight three-quarter spandex pants accent her toned legs and plum-shaped buttocks. Almost every passing male takes a gander at the extremely fit agent's rear end and she can sense it. This much attention from the opposite sex offended a much younger Ross, but since passing 35, she welcomes it. She knows that she is well respected for her brains and intelligence by her male counterparts on the job, so it is a welcomed sense of ease to feel male appreciation in a non-work environment. She had to get comfortable with allowing herself to feel sexy and feminine.

She pants and tries to slow her breathing while checking her workout progress on her electronic sports wristwatch. After taking a mental note of her new best time, Ross takes her usual walk along the promenade to her favorite coffee spot.

After her first cup of coffee, followed by a hot shower, agent Ross gets dressed in her signature navy pantsuit and white blouse. Even with the jacket unbuttoned, Ross' hourglass figure seems al-most exaggerated by her confident walk as she enters the lobby of the Federal Bureau of Investigation's New York office.

Once she arrives outside of her office, she is met by her boss and supervising agent, Stewart Howard. Agent Howard is an older gentleman nearing retirement. He has aged well in spite of the long hours, vigorous work, and mental pressure that accompany his high--ranking position. He has somehow managed to keep his full head of hair, which is now all completely grey and neatly trimmed. His facial age lines perfectly accent his dimples. His redheaded Irish parents have blessed him with a gracious number of well-placed freckles. Agent Howard's height and strikingly broad shoulders indicate that he once sported quite the physique. Agents Ross and Howard seem to have a student-teacher relationship, as well as mutual respect as they greet one another in the office hallway.

"Good morning, agent Ross," offers a polite and semi-formal Howard.

"Good morning, sir. I see that you got my report," replies Ross, referring to the file folder held by her supervisor.

"Yes, I was just about to call you. Now that you have closed that case, I was thinking you should take that vacation I've been trying to get you to take," states Howard.

"I haven't taken a vacation since, ..." replies Ross, as Howard cuts her off in midsentence.

"You haven't taken a vacation since you were promoted to my team," he interjects.

The two share a smile with brief eye contact. Howard soon diverts his attention past Ross as he ends the interaction.

"Take a vacation, Ross ... that's an order," Howard demands playfully as he hustles to catch up to another male agent by the elevator.

"Yes, sir," replies Ross underneath her breath as she watches Howard and the other male agent disappear behind the closing elevator doors.

Agent Ross walks into her office and sits in the cushioned, black leather chair at her medium-sized cherry maple desk. While logging onto her computer, there is a knock on her opened office door. It is her partner, agent Granderson, and he is displaying a small envelope.

"Well, looks like somebody scored a pair of tickets, two rows right behind the Yankees' dugout for tomorrow night's game," Granderson gloats.

Agent Ross appears initially excited as her eyes light up.

"No way! Against Boston?" replies Ross.

"That's right," declares Granderson as he waves the envelope in the air. "Get ready to boo the Dead Sox."

Ross' expression quickly turns from excitement to disappointment, and Granderson picks up on it.

"Well, have fun," replies Ross as she turns her attention back to her computer monitor.

Agent Granderson steps into the office and looks around outside before closing the door to get privacy.

"What? Is this because of what happened that night in San Diego?" Granderson asks in a whisper.

"What ALMOST happened," clarifies Ross in an even softer whisper.

"Well, if it didn't happen, what's the big deal with two coworkers going to a ball game?" replies Granderson.

Ross shakes her head and continues to work at her computer. Granderson, who refuses to be ignored, walks around Ross' desk and leans against it, almost seated upon it. This close physical proximity clearly makes Ross uncomfortable as she rolls her chair back about two feet.

"Look, whatever happened, almost happened, doesn't matter. Blame it on the California sunset, but we're two adults here …" continues Granderson, who is corrected by Ross.

"Two adults? Two agents who work together in a professional capacity," she barks.

Granderson tosses the envelope with the tickets onto Ross' desk and holds his hands up at shoulder height as a sign of surrender.

"You know what, I give up. I know you love the rivalry, go and enjoy the game," offers Granderson as he stands up and walks toward the door.

"Wait, I can't take your tickets, Granderson," replies Ross as she stands to her feet, picks up the envelope and extends it toward her partner's back.

"Consider it a gift for closing a successful case," replies Granderson as he walks out of the office, leaving the door opened behind him.

Ross lets out a sigh and sits back into her chair. That exchange almost felt like sexual foreplay—or at least her body has reacted to it as such. Her face flush—palms sweaty. She cannot deny the tension, but fears navigating to the point of no return. As she stares at her computer monitor, she doesn't even realize that she is fanning herself with the envelope when a young, full-figured female assistant enters her office.

"Agent Ross, would you like me to turn up the air conditioner?" asks the assistant.

"Oh no, that's OK," replies an embarrassed Ross.

"Very well, NYPD counter terrorism is here for your nine o'clock," she states.

Ross can now see three men standing in her doorway looking into her office.

"Yes, send them in," replies Ross as she places the envelope in her desk drawer, stands and gathers herself.

•   •   •

"I was so embarrassed," exclaims Jamie Magi as she sits up in her bed, still in her pajamas with a cup of tea in one hand and her smart phone in the other. She is video chatting with her friend, Montez Bloom. The two of them have been friends since meeting at the library during Jamie's sophomore year. Although she doesn't attend the same school as Jamie, the two keep in touch regularly, and Jamie always confides her deepest concerns with her non-judgmental friend. Montez is an athletic African-American female, with short hair and flawless brown skin. She listens intently as Jamie shares all the details of last night.

"I feel like such an idiot. I don't know what to do ... Should I confront him, pretend not to know, and wait to catch him in a lie? ... This is weird," continues Jamie, pausing only to carefully sip her hot beverage. "I mean, look at me ... I missed class this morning, haven't slept a wink, and for what? ... A misunderstanding?"

As if in the role of counselor, Montez discerns that her friend's rant has reached the point where intercession is needed.

"Damn Jay, girl, I don't really know what I would do in your position, but if you suspect he's cheating on you, just wait for him to slip up. Men are dumb, and they always get caught," offers Montez.

"I don't want to look like the psycho chick that was hiding in my boyfriend's closet trying to catch him with another female," cries Jamie.

"Girl, nah, you don't have to tell him you were even at his apartment. Just pretend like everything is cool, and eventually he will tell on himself. Trust it," replies Montez confidently.

"You think?" asks Jamie skeptically.

"Girl, have I ever steered you wrong?" asks Montez.

Jamie smiles and coyly shakes her head "no." Almost on cue, a text message comes in from Kyle.

"Speak of the devil," announces Jamie to Montez as she reads aloud the text message. "*Good morning sunshine – smiley face kiss – I hope you are not sleeping in class – lol – see you later?*"

"Oh, he has no clue that you're on to him. Play along, girl," suggests a seemingly excited Montez.

"OK, OK..." replies Jamie as she reads aloud her reply text. "*Hahaha. I am not sleeping in class. Missed you at dinner last night,*" replies Jamie as she shares a chuckle with Montez.

Within a matter of seconds there is another incoming text from Kyle. Jamie reads it to Montez: "*Sorry I had to work.*"

Both Jamie and Montez roll their eyes.

Jamie continues to read: "*I will make it up to you tonight. I have a big surprise for you.*"

The two ladies have very different interpretations of that last text.

"Aw, you think he was out getting me a surprise, and that's why he lied about having to work? Oh-my-gosh ... what if it's an engagement ring?" asks Jamie with a huge, child-like grin.

"Or … what if it's a sonogram of the baby he's having with some skank he's been seeing behind your back?" replies Montez with a sassy attitude.

"No, don't even play like that, Monty. I will break his neck," replies a deflated Jamie.

"Girl, I'm just saying. I mean, how well do you even know Kyle?"

Jamie takes an exaggerated breath before reading aloud her reply text to Kyle: "*I like surprises. I can't wait. See you later – smiley face kiss.*"

"There you go, girl, play along," instigates Montez.

The girls share a few laughs before ending their video chat session. Jamie then gets out of bed, determined to salvage the rest of her morning in a positive way. She grabs her yoga mat from underneath her bed and heads up to the rooftop of her building—her favorite place to practice yoga.

Now dressed in her yoga pants and sports bra, Jamie unrolls her green yoga mat and places it onto the black finished rooftop deck. She sits on her mat facing the Empire State Building—a view that she has loved for as long as she can remember. While meditating and manipulating some rather tricky yoga poses, the pretty, young Italian girl from Brooklyn seems to get lost in her movements. The stress of the last 12 hours seems to melt off like the trickling beads of sweat from her body.

The time flies by during Jamie's yoga session. After more than 90 minutes, she rolls up her mat, lets her hair down and exits the roof—all while a pair of eyes on a higher roof across the street follows her every step.

CHAPTER 5

Frank's Famous Deli in midtown Manhattan had been John Magi's favorite lunch spot for years—ever since his father, Michael, took him for hot dogs back when he was a young boy. Hands-down the best pastrami sandwich on the East Coast. Today, John Magi sits in an Irish pub, a block down the street from his favorite diner. John is having a beer-and-peanuts lunch on a squeaky bar stool in the far corner—away from the window and door. With a baseball cap pulled down low on his forehead, the former mob accountant shifts nervously every time the front door opens.

Against the advice of his former FBI handler, John used some of the cash he made doing odd jobs down South to buy a bus ticket to New York City. His presence back in the big city shall remain undetected as long as the homeless man, who flew to Seattle in his place with his ID, stays out of trouble.

Although the feds are confident that the last of the Mongelli crime family is deceased, John is not taking any chances. He is maintaining a very low profile and not visiting any of his former hangouts—after all, he *is* a dead man. Not 100 percent convinced by the FBI's assessment regarding his former mob connections, and their complete dissolution—John could not stay away from his family. In spite of agent Michelle Ross' objection, John Magi is here for one purpose: to reclaim his family.

Using information that he gathered over the years from Ross and her team, John was successfully able to track down the address of his wife's new Long Island home—one she shares with her wealthy new husband.

· · ·

John replays in his mind the moment he stepped off the bus yesterday, and then boarded a Long Island Rail Road train to see Katherine. He vividly recalls the moment he first laid eyes on her—for the first time in 15 years. She was even more beautiful than he remembered. As John crouched down in the bushes outside of the home that she shares with her husband, his heart flooded with anguish—for she had completely given her heart to another man. For years he beat himself up, imagining Katherine making love to someone else. Giving her body to another man is something he can get over ... but her heart?

While spying outside his wife's home, John discovered where they were planning to have dinner last night. That was the break he needed to see his daughter—his baby girl—all grown up now, and as pretty as her mother. Seeing his wife and daughter outside the restaurant last night with the new man in their lives was more than John could handle. He regrets his decision to come back home ... to no home at all. Now John sits alone, drowning his pain and sorrow in tepid beer and salty peanuts. At best, he can keep an eye out and watch over his family from a distance as they go on with their lives ... without him.

The pale-skinned Irish bartender is a heavyset woman with her enormous cleavage bursting out of her black, low-cut dress. She approaches as John chugs the last of his mug.

· · ·

"Would you like another there, handsome?" she asks.

John appears tipsy as he stares into the bottom of his now-empty mug. He lets out a burp, slams the clear plastic mug down onto the bar along with a few crumpled dollars, and stumbles to the front door. He puts on a pair of dark sunglasses and pulls the

MR. WONDERFUL • 25

baseball hat down as far as possible before exiting the bar and heading down the street—his next move unknown—even to him.

"Where do you want to go, Barbados or Costa Rica?" asks Katherine West.

She is eating a chicken salad sandwich and fresh fruit with Jerron in the kitchen of their stately Long Island home. As the couple enjoys the lunch Katherine prepared and flawlessly presented, they discuss plans for a vacation.

"Totally up to you, baby. Just as long as I can play golf," replies Jerron as he chews.

"Well, both places have lovely courses ... but remember, it's a *family* vacation, so you're not going to be golfing the entire time," states Katherine firmly.

"Speaking of family, did you talk to Jamie about inviting Kyle to come along?" asks Jerron.

"I was going to bring it up once we finalized a place and which weeks we want to go," replies Katherine.

Their conversation is interrupted by the ringing telephone. Jerron gets up and picks up the cordless phone from the granite countertop.

"Hello ... Hello?" answers Jerron before hanging up the phone. "That is like the third time today that has happened. Why do we even have a home phone? Who still has a home phone?" he continues.

Jerron rejoins his wife at the table and they continue to discuss their vacation plans over lunch.

*   *   *

After lunch in the cafeteria, which consisted of a smoothie and spinach wrap, agent Michelle Ross waits for the elevator back up to her office. When the elevator doors open, Ross allows others to exit before getting in and pressing the button to her floor. As the doors begin to close, a hand reaches in, causing the doors to reopen. That hand belongs to agent Steve Granderson, who steps into the elevator for what just may be the most uncomfortable ride ever. Neither

Ross nor Granderson speaks, but they both wish someone—any-one—else would join them for the long ride upstairs.

After what seems like an eternity, Ross decides to break the painfully awkward silence.

"Look, I don't want things to be weird between us, ..." states Ross.

"Well, let's not make it weird, then," Granderson snaps back.

"I just don't want, ..." replies Ross as she struggles to find the right words.

"What the heck, Ross? It's just two coworkers going to a sport-ing event outside of work! It's not like a romantic candle-lit dinner," interjects Granderson.

"Not to mention it's the Yankees and Red Sox," chimes in Ross.

The two partners share a smile that seems to have shattered the awkwardness.

"Sorry if I overreacted earlier," offers Ross.

"Yeah, you were kind of a jerk," jokes Granderson.

The elevator stops and the doors open. The two agents step off as the doors close behind them.

"So, second row behind the dugout? How did you score those seats?" asks Ross.

"C'mon, I never reveal a source," replies Granderson.

"Oh, it's like that?" asks Ross, almost flirtatiously.

Granderson walks off smiling and Ross goes in the other direc-tion to her office.

*   *   *

When Ross walks past her assistant's desk, she notices her assistant's eyes following her. It is only then that Ross realizes she is grinning ear to ear. She immediately loses her smile and returns to serious--professional mode.

As she enters her office, Ross is surprised to see her boss, Agent Howard, standing near her desk with another male agent. The man that Ross has never seen around before is bulky and intimidating, with dark eyes and large, beefy hands. Howard is holding the file containing Ross' final report on the John Magi/Mongelli family case.

"Sir, I didn't know we were having a meeting ... I'm sorry, am I late?" asks a confused Ross.

"Agent Ross, this is agent Chad Evans," states Howard.

The newly introduced agents shake hands. Ross can feel the incredible, almost super-human strength in the hand of agent Evans.

"Agent Evans has been working with the Seattle field office. There have been some developments in the Mongelli case," states Howard.

Ross is confused and waits for clarification. Howard plops the file containing Ross' final report down on her desk before continuing.

"According to your report, you and agent Granderson put the witness, John Magi, on a plane to Seattle, is that correct?" asks Howard.

Ross looks at both Howard and Evans in an attempt to see where this is heading before answering. Just as she is about to respond, agent Granderson bursts into the office. He doesn't notice that Ross has company since his head is buried in his handheld tablet.

"Ross, guess what? That night, the Yankees are retiring McLean's jersey ..." Granderson blurts out before looking up and realizing that Ross is not alone.

"Ah, agent Granderson. Come on in, this involves you, too," orders agent Howard in an irritated tone.

Granderson looks at Ross as if she could somehow telepathically clue him in as to what is going on.

"Agent Granderson – agent Evans," offers Howard as he introduces the two male agents. "Now that we're all familiar, agent Ross was just about to tell us how you and she put a high- security federal witness on a plane to Seattle," continues Howard—his eyes now piercing through his prized agent, Ross.

"Well, we didn't actually see him to the airport ..." explains Ross, looking awkwardly at Granderson, who is currently avoiding eye contact with anyone in the room.

"Please explain to me exactly what that means, Ross," orders Howard.

"Well, as is the custom, I gave the witness a package containing his final relocation and ID. I then offered transportation to the airport. Mr. Magi declined that offer, and even grew violent," recalls Ross.

"So you assumed that he packed up his stuff and boarded a flight?" asks Howard while looking at both Ross and Granderson.

Granderson continues to avoid any eye contact with his irritated supervisor.

"As the lead on this team ..." explains Ross.

That declaration gets Granderson and his ego's attention and he perks up to hear what she is going to say next.

"... and as the lead agent, I take full responsibility for maintaining eyes on the witness. I will get on the next plane out West," continues Ross.

"There is no need for that ... Because John Magi never got on that plane to Seattle," states Howard.

Ross and Granderson are confused.

"But the airline confirmed that Magi was on that flight," Ross declares.

"A man got on the plane using Magi's ticket, but it wasn't him," explains Howard.

"I don't follow," states Ross while looking at the hulking agent Evans, who has yet to utter a single word.

"There was a hit on John Magi. He was followed from the Seattle airport. Apparently he got into a car with someone holding a sign with his name. He was then shot to death in the back of the car and dumped off the highway. Only problem is, that wasn't John Magi that got off the plane," explains Howard.

After getting over the initial shock of such developments, Ross begins to try to figure out what went wrong.

"Well, sir, that file has remained sealed, and only agent Granderson and I knew the whereabouts of that witness. That's why no one could get to him in 15 years. Only his final location was posted in my final report as his case was closed," states Ross as the gears in her brain continue to turn. "This means that there is a mole, a rogue agent or agency personnel that ..."

Howard cuts her off.

"Not so fast, Ross. Before we start pointing fingers and digging into the lives of reputable agents, let's figure out where Magi is now. Whoever attempted to kill him may already know that they got the wrong guy," states Howard.

"I think I know exactly where to find John Magi," declares Ross.

CHAPTER 6

Jamie Magi sits on a park bench near the lake in Central Park as the sun begins to set, and the street lamps illuminate. The evening temperature drops slightly, so she puts on the light jacket that she carried with her. She nervously shakes her leg as she awaits the arrival of her boyfriend, Kyle, who has a special surprise for her. This is the first time she is seeing him since finding out that he may not be completely honest with her, and she desperately wants to know exactly what he is hiding.

A short distance away, John Magi keeps a watchful eye on his beautiful daughter. Perched like an eagle, he sits anxiously on a metal rail along a running path up on the hill, periodically checking his surroundings. The protective father watches intently as a young man approaches Jamie. John can tell by their greeting that they are romantically involved. He watches carefully, wishing he could hear their dialogue.

When Kyle approaches Jamie in the park, she stands up to greet him as he comes in for a hug and a quick peck on the lips. Jamie is still on autopilot, and responds naturally as she is accustomed. However, in the back of her mind she is unsure she even really knows this man that she has been dating. Kyle can pick up on the slight discomfort that is coming from Jamie and questions it.

"Hey, what's wrong?" asks Kyle.

"Oh nothing, just tired, that's all … so what's the big surprise?" she replies, attempting to change the subject and get right to the point.

"Well, I said it's a surprise, so you will just have to wait," replies Kyle. He sits on the bench and tugs at Jamie's hand, urging her to sit next to him—she does.

"So when do I get to find out the surprise?" questions Jamie, now a tad annoyed.

Kyle picks up on her irritation and continues to torture her further.

"I will give you three guesses," he offers.

Jamie is not in the mood for this game but plays along.

"You won the lottery?" she guesses.

"I wish, but nope," Kyle replies. His smile indicates that he is enjoying this game—Jamie, not so much.

"OK, you decided to join the circus?" Jamie guesses.

"Ha, my family is already a circus, so no. One more guess, come on, what did we talk about being on both of our bucket lists?" hints Kyle.

Jamie is now actually thinking seriously, but comes up empty. She takes a stab at something random.

"Hiking the Grand Canyon?" she guesses.

"Well, I guess we did talk about that, too," replies Kyle.

Kyle finally decides to let Jamie in on the surprise. He reaches into his inside jacket pocket.

.   .   .

As John watches the interaction between his daughter and this young man, his instincts from the days of old impulsively take over. He trusts no one. As the young man reaches into his jacket pocket, John's entire body tenses up, and without a thought he is off the rail and on his feet.

Kyle pulls two tickets out of his jacket pocket.

"Yankees – Red Sox game," Kyle offers to refresh Jamie's memory.

Jamie smiles as she recalls the conversation the couple had about attending a game between the historic rivals at the famous stadium.

"Ah, yes! Awesome!" she replies as she leans in to give Kyle a hug.

Though she displays genuine gratitude, there are still some looming questions she has for her boyfriend, and she doesn't quite know how to start the conversation.

*   *   *

John Magi realizes that he is running down the hill full speed when he notices that the young man with his daughter is not pulling a weapon. He continues to run, but off in the direction away from the unsuspecting couple. He reaches a bench near a water fountain and stops. He pretends to take a drink, but his eyes remain fixed on the bench just a few yards away, where Jamie is embracing the young man.

*   *   *

After they hug, Kyle and Jamie stand and begin walking. With their fingers intertwined, the good-looking young couple strolls casually along the path—in the direction of John Magi.

*   *   *

When John notices this, he stops drinking from the water fountain and begins walking away from them. He maintains a slow, steady pace, matching theirs, even slowing a bit to allow them to get within earshot.

As Kyle and Jamie stroll along the path, they are unaware that Jamie's father—whom she believes to be dead—is just a few short feet in front of them. There is a strained vibe between the young lovers as Jamie tries to bring up what's really bothering her. She contemplates not bringing it up at all, but then decides to just ask a related question, to see where the conversation leads.

"So, you missed a great dinner last night ... how was work, anyway?" she asks.

She looks over at Kyle to see his reaction. She is already fully aware that he was not at work as he claimed, but now she wants to see how easily he lies to her face. She would feel better if he struggles with his dishonesty, which would indicate the ability to feel guilt.

"You know, the same crap ... professional losers and sloppy drunks," he replies jokingly, offering nothing else.

Jamie drops her head as she accepts the fact that she is in a romantic relationship with a professional liar. She seeks resolve in that but still wonders what he is hiding ... why the deceit? She decides to play dumb and let him fall into his own trap at a later time. She can no longer pretend that she is not extremely hurt, but doesn't want to cry in front of Kyle. She struggles to choke back tears. Kyle picks up on it.

"Babe, what's wrong, you OK?" he asks.

"I think I'm coming down with something. Do you mind if we call it a night?" she replies.

"No problem. Do you need something?" Kyle offers.

"No, I think I just need to get to bed," Jamie replies.

She pulls her hand away from Kyle and starts walking in the opposite direction. Kyle turns and follows her.

"Wait up, I'll ride in a cab with you ... make sure you get home safely," he offers.

"No, it's OK. I may be contagious or something," she replies as she continues to walk, even increasing her pace as she feels the tears building up.

Kyle also picks up his pace in an attempt to catch up and walk with his girlfriend.

. . .

John realizes that the couple is no longer behind him. He pretends to stop and stretch while looking back. He sees Jamie walking away and the young man in pursuit. John decides to follow them from a safe distance as they head toward the park's main entrance.

By the time John reaches the entrance, he catches a glimpse of Jamie getting into a yellow cab and the young man closing the door as he bids farewell. When the cab pulls away with Jamie inside, John observes the young man take out his cell phone and make a call. John follows the young man as he walks down the block toward the subway.

From the distance between him and the young man walking briskly ahead, John cannot hear the conversation. Uncertain if it is just his paranoia, John is taking no chances. He doesn't trust this kid and intends to keep close tabs on him.

The young man ends his call before dashing down into the subway station. John follows as the rumbling of an approaching train fills the stairwell. The young man swipes his metro card and then enters through the turnstile just as the number seven train comes to a screeching stop. The doors open and passengers exit and enter the cars as the dispatcher announces this stop and the next. John makes a couple of failed attempts to swipe his metro card before deciding to hop the turnstile. He runs toward the train and slips in just as the doors close. He is not in the same train car as the young man he is following, but he can see him one car up ahead.

John has questions about this kid: Who is he? And what is he up to? He has every intention of getting answers to these looming questions.

After passing several stops, the young man exits the train. John also gets off the train and follows the young man up the stairs to the street. Once outside, the young man walks across the street and enters a building on the corner. John casually walks over to the building and peeks inside the window. He observes the mystery kid as he joins a small group of others—both male and female—as they play on several pool tables.

John discreetly watches from outside as he wonders what other games this kid is playing.

CHAPTER 7

"How can you talk about a game at a time like this?" questions agent Michelle Ross.

She and agent Granderson sit in the back of a surveillance van near the home of Katherine and Jerron West. Also present is another tech agent, Patrick Ling, who is monitoring the phone line connected to the large Long Island house. Ross believes the first place John Magi will visit is here to see Katherine.

"It's a stakeout, what else do you talk about? So do you think we will snag any foul balls?" asks Granderson to an uninterested Ross. In his failed attempt to lighten the mood, he can see that Ross is focused solely on the mission at hand. The team's initial belief that the entire Mongelli crime family had been eliminated is now a definite uncertainty, with the attempted hit on John Magi. Only the FBI knew of John's existence and whereabouts. No one from the Mongelli family has seen him in 15 years. Ross thinks it is possible that the unidentified man who flew in John's place could have been mistaken for John to someone who hasn't seen him in a very long time, or that the hit was executed by someone who had never seen him before—a hired gun. What disturbs Ross even more is the fact that someone tipped off the killer or killers as to what flight John Magi was to board … information tightly guarded within the department. Who, other than the feds, knows that he is still alive? Who out there still wants Magi dead? What information does he possess that is worth killing for? Is the Mongelli crime family still operating? And how was that flight information leaked? These questions haunt Ross, as she now needs to locate the former federal witness, and protect his family, who may all have targets on their backs.

Ross has worked with agent Granderson long enough to trust him, but she thinks anyone can be bought if the price is right. She feels a sense of partner loyalty toward Granderson, but doesn't want her boss to start accusing her of any wrongdoing. If it comes down to her partner being the mole, she has no doubt she will turn him in to her superiors.

"What is the plan here, Ross? Are you going to let these people know that their lives may be in danger?" asks Granderson.

"Good idea ... Hey Mrs. West, your deceased husband, who's not really dead, is on his way here to see you and your new husband ... oh and there are mobsters that want you all dead," replies Ross mockingly.

The other agent in the van chuckles but maintains focus on the phone lines.

"I think they have a right to know," responds Granderson.

"I smell a huge lawsuit when she finds out the government faked her husband's death and now her life is in jeopardy," replies Ross, more as a thought out loud than a statement.

She won't admit this, but her life would be simpler had John Magi gotten on that plane and been killed. Then at least any unsettled scores between him and the Mongelli family would be settled, and maybe they would let Katherine and her family live. Now there are more targets to protect. In a best-case scenario, they locate John and find out what information or secrets he has kept from the FBI, and who wants to kill for it. For now, they will wait for John to attempt contact with Katherine and intercept him before he gets to her, or someone else gets to him.

. . .

Outside Jamie Magi's apartment, agents Howard and Evans sit in a dark sedan. They are keeping an eye out for any sign of John Magi. If he comes to pay his daughter a visit, they will bring him in for further questioning, and place him back in special protective custody.

· · ·

Upstairs in her apartment, Jamie sits on her couch staring aimlessly at her television. She is very distracted by the many thoughts running through her mind. It seems like less than 24 hours ago she had the perfect boyfriend. He was attractive, funny, terrific in bed, and loved her dearly ... or so she thought. Now it all seems very uncertain. She is not sure if any of it was real. The man she loves during her senior year of college is supposed to be the one she settles down and starts a family with. But who exactly is Kyle Woodard really? Can she even trust him? If he can lie so easily to her face, he is not someone she wants to be with.

Her cell phone rings. It is Kyle. She ignores the call and sends it to voicemail. She doesn't possess the strength or energy to have the breakup conversation tonight.

Soon after the call from Kyle, she receives a text from him that reads: *Just checking on you. Hope you're feeling better and getting rest. Love you.*

Jamie shakes her head in disbelief. Suddenly nothing appears authentic anymore.

· · ·

Outside the SoHo pool hall, Kyle has a cigarette as he finishes sending a text message to Jamie. He takes one more drag before dropping the cigarette to the ground and stepping on it. He slides his phone into his rear pocket and turns to walk back inside to rejoin his friends. He is punched in the ribs and grabbed violently from behind and put into a tight chokehold. He struggles to catch his breath after having the wind knocked out of him. He is then dragged around the corner and forcibly slammed to the ground behind a group of large dumpsters. His attacker maintains the strong grip around Kyle's neck and pins him down with his body weight. Kyle kicks and squirms in a futile attempt to escape. The assailant loosens his grip around Kyle's neck so he doesn't lose consciousness, and so that he can speak.

"Please, take me wallet and my phone ... whatever you want, don't hurt me!" pleads a frightened and distressed Kyle.

John Magi still has his street scrap from growing up in the tough streets of Brooklyn. Although he may have lost a step or two due to father time, his brute strength is still there.

"What's your name, and who do you work for?" demands an adrenaline-fueled John.

"Kyle ... Kyle Woodard! I work part-time as a bartender ... please just take my money," begs Kyle.

John's initial reaction to the name is almost to let him go. He grew up with Kyle's father back in the old neighborhood. He hasn't seen Kyle since he was about seven ... the same age Jamie was before he went away. He is still not sure of Kyle's intentions so he doesn't let him go.

"What were you doing with that girl in the park?" asks John.

Kyle's eyes open wide. He can't believe this lunatic has been following him and Jamie. This gives Kyle some fight. He almost throws John off of his back, but the scrappy, experienced John latches on even tighter.

"You've been following us? You better not hurt her ... I swear!" threatens Kyle.

Kyle's reaction and protective spirit of Jamie put John's suspicions to rest. He can tell that this young man has a genuine concern for Jamie's safety and wellbeing. Added to the fact that John knows that Kyle comes from a good family, the overprotective father feels that he can actually trust the kid.

A woman looking down from an apartment window above the dumpsters yells down toward the wrestling men.

"Hey! Get off of him! I'm calling the police!" she barks in a heavy New York City accent, before returning inside to make good on her threat.

John releases him, but pushes Kyle's face down to the ground so that he doesn't get a look at his face. He then jumps off of the much lighter young man and makes a dash down the block and out of sight. The last thing he needs is to be picked up by the police and turned back over to the feds.

Kyle struggles to his feet and holds his face that is now slightly bruised. He reaches for his phone to call 9-1-1, but it is gone—swiped by his attacker during the struggle. He limps in to the pool hall to alert his friends that he was just mugged by a man who stalked him from the park.

* * *

FBI agents Howard and Evans observe as Jamie rushes outside her apartment and frantically hails a taxi, then quickly jumps in when it comes to a stop. The two men look at each other as they are both thinking the same thing. They follow closely behind the cab as it takes Jamie to a nearby hospital, where she gets out and races to the emergency room. Evans, the driver, stays with the car and Howard goes inside to inquire as to what is going on.

* * *

In the van outside of the Wests' residence, agent Ross receives an alert by agent Ling, who is still monitoring the phones, about an incoming call to the home landline.

"What number is it coming from?" inquires Ross as she places headphones on to listen in.

"Call is coming from a mobile phone registered to a Kyle Woodard," reports the agent.

Ross looks at Granderson to see if the name is familiar. He responds negatively with a shrug of the shoulders. They all listen in as the phone rings, but there is no answer.

"Come on … pick up Katherine … this may be your dead husband calling from beyond the grave" utters Ross, almost prayer-like.

"I don't think anyone is going to answer," states Granderson as he points out toward the side van window.

Ross looks and sees that Jerron and Katherine are exiting their garage and leaving the house.

"Quick, let's tail them," orders Ross as she and Granderson scramble to the driver and front passenger seats.

*   *   *

John Magi is in a bathroom stall in a small bar. The door is locked and he is seated on the back of the bowl with his feet up on the toilet seat. He has Kyle's stolen cell phone to his ear.

"Come on Katherine ... pick up!" he utters, almost prayer-like.

He gets the couple's answering machine and hangs up in frustration. He takes a deep breath as he contemplates his next move.

*   *   *

When Jerron and Katherine West pull up to the hospital, so does the van carrying Ross, Granderson, and agent Ling. Katherine exits the car and hurriedly walks into the emergency room entrance, and Jerron drives around to the parking garage. Ross orders Granderson to pull the van next to the parked sedan where agents Howard and Evans are sitting. Ross rolls the passenger-side window down as they pull next to her supervisor's car.

"What the heck is going on here?" Ross inquires of Howard.

"Jamie Magi's boyfriend ... Kyle. Some nut case followed him from the park down to SoHo, stole his cell phone, and roughed him up a bit. Friends called Jamie, Jamie called Mommy, and now we've got a party," replies Howard.

"Kyle? Kyle Woodard?" asks Ross.

"Yeah, that's him," replies Howard.

Ross and Granderson immediately jump out of the van and run toward the hospital.

"It's John Magi ... he's here!" announces Ross over her shoulder to Howard.

Howard and Evans also exit their vehicle and follow behind Ross. Agent Ling, who was just brought along for his technical skills, and is not fully up to speed on the case, remains in the back of the van looking confused. This short, chubby agent is not just out of shape ... he is also clearly out of the loop.

CHAPTER 8

The decision had to be made to inform Katherine West that she is not actually a widow. Ross feels it would be best to break the news to her alone, outside the presence of her husband Jerron and daughter Jamie. Mr. West is sitting in a waiting area along with Kyle's cousin and two of his friends.

Katherine is confused as to why the FBI wants to talk to her. She simply came to the hospital in support of her daughter's boyfriend. She is not a witness of any crime. She is asked to join special agent Ross in a small chapel area at the hospital so that they can speak in private.

*   *   *

Jamie stands by the stretcher that Kyle is on. Only a curtain separates them from other patients here in the trauma unit. Kyle has a cracked rib and some bruises, but will be released soon.

"Thanks for being so awesome, babe," Kyle says weakly to his girlfriend.

Jamie forces a half smile. Kyle can tell that she has something on her mind.

"What's wrong? You've been distant all night," asks Kyle.

Jamie decides to come clean.

"Look Kyle, when I heard you had been rushed to the hospital, my heart dropped. I love you ..." declares Jamie.

"I love you, too," interjects Kyle.

He can tell that there is a "but."

"Uh oh ... what is it?" he inquires.

"I went to the bar last night to surprise you with dessert from the restaurant," she explains.

Kyle closes his eyes and grimaces as he realizes she knows that he has been lying to her.

"Look, I can explain," Kyle states.

A single teardrop slowly rolls down Jamie's face as she prepares herself for another lie.

"The truth is, I am flunking out. My advisor said that the only way that I can graduate on time is if I take night courses to make up the credits I need. I was embarrassed so I just told you I was working," he explains genuinely.

Jamie is relieved by this reality—it's not another woman.

"I know we have plans and talk about graduating together and then getting our own place. I didn't want that to change so I'm working my tail off and taking night classes," he continues.

"Babe, you don't have to be ashamed or embarrassed. You can tell me anything," Jamie replies as she buries her face into Kyle's chest, careful to avoid his injured rib. She is crying uncontrollably at this point. "I love you so much," she declares.

As the young couple basks in the moment of high emotions, the attending physician slides back the curtain. Jamie lifts her head and wipes the tears from her cheeks.

"Mr. Woodard, good news ... here is a prescription for some pain meds," the doctor announces, extending her hand. Jamie takes the slip of paper, gently pressing down on Kyle's arm to keep him still. "You will be very sore tomorrow, so get plenty of rest. The nurse will be by with your discharge papers," declares the doctor with a smile.

She exits and slides the curtain back as she visits the next patient.

"I'm staying at your place tonight so that I can take care of you," insists Jamie.

Kyle smiles in agreement.

The young lovers' deep, emotional moment is broken up when agents Howard and Evans slide back the privacy curtain at the foot of Kyle's stretcher. The intimidating presence of agent Evans makes Kyle a bit uneasy. A few beads of sweat are forming on the clean--shaven head of the tall, bulky, pale-skinned man. Standing next to him is the seemingly gentler agent Howard. Judging this duo merely on their physical dispositions, it is easy to tell which one will be playing the role of good cop. Agent Howard opens with a question, more so for positive identification than a greeting.

"Kyle Woodard?" he asks.

"Yeah, that's me," replies Kyle nervously.

Jamie can sense Kyle's growing anxiety, so she grips his hand tighter, and even uses her other hand to sandwich his into hers.

"We just have a few questions to ask you about what took place earlier tonight," states Howard.

"I already told the other detective everything," Kyle replies.

"We are fully aware of the statement you gave to the police ... we're with the FBI. I'm agent Howard, and this is agent Evans," announces Howard as he displays his federal badge.

"FBI? Why is the FBI getting involved in a street mugging?" asks a confused Jamie.

"Ma'am, can you please excuse us? We would like to speak to Mr. Woodard alone," requests Howard.

Jamie looks at Kyle to see if he is OK with that request.

"This is my girlfriend. Anything you say to me, you can say to her. We have no secrets," Kyle responds as he pulls Jamie even closer to his stretcher.

Howard and Evans make eye contact, but show no emotion. They are both pretty mechanical.

"OK, well we just need to clear up a couple of details," Howard says reluctantly.

He clearly does not want to reveal that Kyle's assailant is possibly Jamie's "dead" father ... especially not in her presence.

"I already told everything I remember about the entire incident to the detective," restates Kyle.

"So you've never seen the man who attacked you before tonight?" asks Howard for clarity.

"Before tonight? Hell, I didn't see him tonight, either. The punk jumped me from behind," Kyle replies before realizing that his girlfriend has only heard his embellished version of events ... he adlibs a bit now as well. "He must've hit me with some sort of weapon," he adds for the sake of his ego.

Howard tries not to roll his eyes at Kyle's feeble attempt to appear macho in front of his girlfriend.

"So you never got a look at him at all? Did he say what he wanted ... any demands during the assault?" asks Howard.

"No, he sucker punched me in the ribs and then grabbed me from behind. He didn't ask for my money ... I mean, I didn't even know he took my phone until I went to call 9-1-1," recalls Kyle.

Jamie suddenly grows anxious as she begins to overthink things. She rattles off whatever questions pop into her mind.

"But why is the FBI involved? Is Kyle in danger? Is there some guy from 'America's Most Wanted' out there mugging people?" asks Jamie.

Before Howard can respond to her, the chubby and semi-winded agent Ling rushes into the room and approaches agent Howard.

"I got a lock on the GPS inside the stolen cellphone," whispers Ling to Howard while using a handheld tablet to block the others from reading his lips. "It's currently located at a bar not too far from here." He continues as he displays the address to Howard.

"Thank you for your time. I hope you feel better soon," states Howard to Kyle before the three agents hustle out of the room.

Jamie and Kyle give each other the same puzzled look. They don't know what to think of that unusual interaction.

"Perhaps we should both just crash at my mom's place out on the island," Jamie suggests to Kyle. "If the FBI is hunting someone in the city ... getting out of the city may be wise."

• • •

In the hospital's chapel, agent Ross sits with Katherine West. The air is silent and peaceful, absent of the mechanical blips and beeps that fill the rest of the building. They sit in the front of the chapel on a hard wooden pew. It is nearly dark, with the hospital's fluorescent lights filtering in through stained-glass panes flanking the entryway at the back of the room.

Ross has just hit Katherine with the news that her first husband, John, is still alive.

"What kind of twisted game are you playing here? Are you for real? You think joking about somebody's dead loved one is funny?" spews Katherine.

This is exactly the sort of reaction that Ross expected.

"Mrs. West, this is not a game. I assure you that John is still alive. He spent the past 15 years in a special witness protection program. For years I have personally been keeping him up to speed on how you and Jamie are doing," states Ross.

Katherine is still in shock and needs further explanation.

"No way! I don't believe you. John would never put us through that," replies Katherine.

"I'm afraid he did it *for* you ... and your daughter," Ross says.

"What? *For* us ... what the hell does that even mean?" asks an offended Katherine.

"Your husband ..." states Ross before Katherine stops her.

"My husband? My husband is outside in the waiting area," states Katherine with a firm tone of correction.

"Yes, well, John ... your husband at the time, got into business with some very dangerous people that he helped the government put away. That decision put him, you, and your daughter at risk of deadly retaliation," explains Ross.

Katherine holds her head in her hands. She is absorbing this unbelievable version of events.

"But I saw the car, there's no way he survived that ... and the funeral ... we had funeral," Katherine states, and her voice shudders slightly. Water begins to fill her pretty brown eyes, reflecting colored light from the stained glass and splintering her confusion into a thousand tiny prisms.

Ross reaches into her inside jacket pocket and pulls out a handkerchief. She offers it to Katherine.

"Thank you," replies Katherine as she dabs her eyes. The response is automatic and does not relay true appreciation.

"The charred body you saw at the morgue was a corpse donated from the university's biology lab. John had a very tough decision to make, Mrs. West. If the people he testified against thought for a moment that John was alive, they would never have stopped hunting him … and you," explains Ross.

"Yeah, but John was just an accountant," states Katherine. Her voice shudders again. She's not sure if she is trying to convince the agent or herself.

Ross doesn't respond verbally, but Katherine can tell by her look that there was much more to that job title than John was letting on.

"So, wait … even so, in a witness protection situation, doesn't the FBI relocate the entire family?" asks Katherine.

"Not in this case, or similar," Ross explains. "The people we were dealing with would have hunted you all to the ends of the Earth. They never would believe, however, that John would abandon his wife and young daughter."

That point further upsets Katherine and full tears begin to stream from her eyes.

"That was the only way to convince them that there was no point in going after you or Jamie … if John was killed," continues Ross.

"So, John's death—or whatever we're calling it—was supposed to be some sort of mob hit?" questions Katherine.

"Yes. We intercepted information of a hit put out on John because photos surfaced of him meeting with an informant. They were going to kill him, and make it look like an accident. So, the night before the hit was to go down, our team of explosives experts defused the bomb set to go off on John's car, and swapped an identical vehicle in its place. The dummy vehicle was designed with a fire-proof cab, and only an exploding hood and trunk. We discovered that John's original vehicle was rigged to explode when he passed a trigger point ... sort of like an invisible electric fence. That trigger point was the intersection where, as you know ..." Ross doesn't need to replay the scene entirely for the already upset Katherine. "That intersection was chosen because of the cameras as proof of the executed hit. There was a man responsible for making sure John got into his car that morning and following him from the office to the intersection as well. We had to make it look real," continues Ross.

"I don't know what to believe. Where is John? If he is alive and everything that you're saying is true, let me see him," insists Katherine.

"Well, that's just the thing. We are hoping he contacts you," Ross replies.

"Why would he all of a sudden contact me ... after all these years?" questions Katherine. She is gripping Ross' handkerchief with white knuckles.

"We recently learned that the last person who was a viable threat to John was killed after his car slammed into a tree during a high-speed chase with a team of our agents. We informed John that we were terminating his program. He was given his final location, however there was an attempted assassination set up the moment he was to be released from the FBI protection program. Now we believe that there is someone out there that still wants revenge for John putting away the entire crime family and their associates," explains Ross.

"What? So there are dangerous people out there that want revenge against my dead husband, who really isn't dead, and now the FBI is looking for him to, what ... fake his death so he can go away for another 15 years? Am I all up to speed now?" replies Katherine. Her voice is sharply loud and aggressive in the quiet, somber chapel. She stands to exit the room, but then pauses.

"You tell John that as far as I'm concerned, he can stay dead!" she adds hotly.

Again she turns to exit, and again stops to add something else.

"And you better not say a word of this to my daughter. She lost her father once, and I will not allow him to devastate her further!" states Katherine as she storms off—for good this time.

Ross stands alone in the hospital chapel, staring at the door. Now walking in is her partner, agent Granderson. He stops in the entryway with his hands out, gesturing for details of the conversation with Katherine. He obviously witnessed the upset woman rushing past him.

"Well, how did it go?" asks Granderson.

"Ah, it's not every day you get to tell a woman that her dead husband is alive after 15 years ... I think she took it pretty well," Ross replies sarcastically. She exhales sharply and straightens her blazer in annoyance.

"Speaking of the living dead, Ling tracked Kyle's stolen phone to a bar not far from here. The boss is already heading over."

Ross runs past Granderson, who follows closely behind.

CHAPTER 9

Supervising agent Howard races out of the dark-colored sedan before it even rolls to a complete stop. The driver—agent Evans—puts the car into park, and quickly rushes behind agent Howard. Agent Ling, who is not a field agent, remains seated in the back seat of the car, while the other two agents enter the Bantry Bay Bar.

Inside the poorly lit establishment, several patrons sit at the bar, and others are scattered at high-top tables. The jukebox blares heavy rock music. The agents in suits stick out like two sore thumbs. After surveying the faces all around the room, they discover that John is no longer there. Howard, who now has agent Ling's tablet in hand, can see that the GPS from Kyle's phone is still giving off a strong signal. Howard asks the heavily pierced woman behind the bar for the location of the bathroom. Unspeaking, she points a finger to the back stairs.

Agents Howard and Evans cautiously walk downstairs to the basement, and along the graffiti- clad hallway toward the two bathroom doors in the back. As they reach the doors, Howard uses his cell phone to call the number of Kyle's phone … they hear it ringing on the other side of the men's room door. Howard lets it keep ringing as he gives Evans stern instructions.

"He lunged at you … you had to shoot," orders Howard with a facial expression as blunt his tone.

Evans nods affirmatively, draws his weapon, and enters the bathroom. Howard closes the door behind him, and stands guard outside so that no one enters.

As Evans enters the men's room with his gun aimed at the three partially opened bathroom stalls, he quietly creeps toward them. The muffled music upstairs continues to pound against the ceiling. The phone stops ringing before Evans can determine which stall the ringing came from. The large, muscular man kicks open the first door, which is empty. He then quickly checks the middle stall, but it too is empty. Evans readies his weapon before kicking open the final stall closest to the wall.

⋆　　⋆　　⋆

Agents Ross and Granderson rush into the Bantry Bay Bar. They approach the bartender, who has obviously assessed that they are accompanying the other two men dressed just like them. She automatically points to the back. Ross and Granderson race to the back toward the stairs to the basement.

When they reach the stairs, they meet Howard and Evans. Howard holds up Kyle's phone as he continues to walk toward them. They can see his shoulders held rigid, his brow lowered with irritation.

"He knew we would track the stolen phone. He ditched it in the bathroom," Howard states as he brushes past Ross and Granderson, and Evans follows closely behind him. Granderson can see the disappointment on his partner's face. The past 15 years of Ross' life have been spent convincing John Magi that she would do everything in her power to keep his family safe. Now with an unknown enemy out there, and John's whereabouts unknown, the confidence she once spoke with is uncertain.

"We'll find him, partner," offers Granderson warmly.

Ross reacts with a forced smile, but the worry in her eyes cannot be masked. She walks in the same direction of the exit, and Granderson follows.

⋆　　⋆　　⋆

When Ross and Granderson exit the bar, agents Howard and Evans meet them on the sidewalk.

"OK, you two go back to the hospital and keep a tail on the family. Any contact from John Magi, I want to be the first to know about it!" orders Howard to Ross and Granderson.

"You got it," replies Ross.

Evans walks to the sedan and gets in the driver's seat. Howard begins to walk to the car but then turns back to Ross and Granderson.

"Oh, and take the nerd ... he's useless," states Howard referring to agent Ling.

Howard walks to the car and gets into the front passenger seat. Ling gets his tablet from Howard and exits the back seat of the car. Howard and Evans peel off in a hurry. Granderson and Ross walk to their surveillance van—agent Ling follows them.

"So I guess I'm with you guys!" states Ling.

.   .   .

"Sure, you can stay with us," says Katherine to Jamie.

"Kyle, too ... so he doesn't have to be alone tonight?" asks Jamie.

"Sure! We have plenty of room," Jerron chimes in.

As the three of them talk in the hospital waiting room area, a nurse in scrubs rolls Kyle over in a wheelchair.

"Oh my goodness, Kyle ... you poor thing," gasps Katherine sympathetically.

"Aw, Mrs. West, it's nothing too serious. I can totally walk, but they say it is hospital policy that they take me out in a wheelchair," states Kyle.

"Well, you're coming home with us, and Jamie is going to take care of you," offers Katherine.

"Thank you, and thank you, Mr. West," offers Kyle.

"Don't mention it, kid," replies Jerron. "I'll go get the car and meet you guys outside," he continues before exiting toward the parking garage.

.   .   .

As Jerron pulls the car around to the front entrance of the hospital, agents Ross, Granderson, and Ling watch from a safe distance, parked in the surveillance van. Katherine gets into the front passenger seat of the Wests' vehicle, and Jamie and Kyle get into the back seat. Once everyone is loaded in and buckled up, their vehicle pulls away and heads toward the Midtown Tunnel. Agent Granderson follows behind in the surveillance van, from a safe distance. The florescent lights that line the length of the tunnel cascade yellowish beams that dance throughout the cab of the van as agent Ross checks her work emails from her smart phone. Agent Ling sits quietly in the back of the van completely uninterested, as the lack of intellectual stimulation appears to be nauseating to the brainy technical genius. He tools around on his tablet—manipulating its various settings, and exploring other functionalities. When they exit the tunnel, they approach a toll plaza several lanes wide. The vehicle belonging to the Wests bears to the far left lane, which is reserved for drivers with pre-paid transponders installed. This lane also leads directly to the interstate heading east, toward Long Island. Agent Granderson also takes this lane, keeping up with the vehicle he is discreetly following. He flips the windshield wipers to a low setting as raindrops begin to fall against the van.

∗   ∗   ∗

The raindrops trickle along the rim of John Magi's baseball cap as he jogs along the cobblestone streets in the West Village. As the rain continues to intensify, he decides to head down into a nearby subway station to escape the deteriorating weather. With nowhere to go, and running low of cash, John will aimlessly ride the number one train line … at least until his clothes and shoes dry. As he waits on the subway platform, he can see a family of three—father, mother, and a sleeping child in a stroller. That image instantly, as it has for as long as he can remember, brings up memories of the life he and Katherine once shared with their precious little angel, Jamie. He squints as he tries to focus his eyes, because momentarily he can swear that he is, in fact, looking at himself across the tracks. The smiling man shares a moment of affection with his lady as their bodies shelter their sleeping child. John is still gazing at what almost seems to be a mirage painted in his mind by the guilt of leaving his family, and the pain of seeing a new man in his place. John snaps out of his apparent trance when the train barrels down the track and screeches to a stop. He gets on the train and finds that there are plenty of seats available in the train car he boarded. This scenario would make for excellent sleeping conditions, had it not been for the air conditioner blowing frigid air onto his soaking wet body.

•   •   •

"Your mom has a great body," giggles Kyle to Jamie as they sit on the couch.

He is looking at a photo of Katherine and Jerron that is framed over the fireplace.

"Um … gross?" replies Jamie, wrinkling her nose in disgust.

"You know what I mean, for an older lady, she stays in good shape," explains Kyle.

"Tell you what, I will just assume that is the pain medication talking and that I don't have to worry about my boyfriend trying to hit on my mom when I'm asleep," replies Jamie.

"I can only imagine that you will still be hot when you get old," says Kyle.

"OK, did you just say that my mom is hot?" asks Jamie.

Realizing that he is only digging himself into deeper trouble, Kyle pretends to suddenly fall asleep.

"Don't even try it," Jamie jokes as she gives him a playful nudge with her elbow to his side. This causes him to grunt and grimace in pain.

"Oh, I'm sorry babe … did I get you in the ribs?" she asks out of genuine concern. Jamie gently kisses Kyle on the cheek repeatedly, as if her kisses have magical powers to alleviate his pain. As she continues to do so, Katherine comes down from upstairs. She is dressed in only a short, white silk robe. Jamie stops kissing Kyle but stares at him intently to make sure he is not checking out her very attractive mother.

"So I got both of your rooms ready," announces Katherine, declaring her position as both ethereal image and wonderful hostess. She picks up on the weird vibe between Kyle and Jamie, but presumes it has to do with the sleeping arrangements and responds accordingly. "What, you didn't think I would allow you two to sleep in the same bed, did you? No grandchildren-making under this roof," she jokes.

Jamie and Kyle look at each other and laugh, however this is an inside joke that will remain just that.

"No, it's fine, Mom ... We'll just sneak into each other's room when you and Jerron are asleep," Jamie jokes.

"She's kidding, Mrs. West. Thank you for your hospitality, and allowing me into your lovely home," offers Kyle.

Jamie shoots Kyle a humorous look, as if to suggest that he is a suck up.

"You're welcome any time, Kyle. Make yourself at home. See you kids in the morning," says Katherine before returning upstairs to join her husband for bed.

"Good night," reply Kyle and Jamie simultaneously.

Now alone with her boyfriend, Jamie starts kissing Kyle passionately. She is obviously trying to seduce him. Kyle, on the other hand, wants no part of this risky action.

"Girl, are you crazy? Your folks are right upstairs," he says as he pulls away.

"So you don't like my body as much as my mom's?" Jamie jokes with a mixture of sexiness and silliness.

The young couple shares a laugh and then Jamie gets up off of the couch.

"I'm going to take a shower. Mom left a towel on your bed and some of Jerron's shorts and a shirt. I hope they fit," she says before exiting to go upstairs.

Kyle finds pleasure in watching his girlfriend's butt as she walks away and up the stairs ... she finds pleasure in knowing this.

. . .

Outside the Wests' home, agents Ross, Granderson, and Ling sit in the van, waiting to intercept contact from John Magi. As Ling listens to the direct landline to the house, he continues to work on his tablet, while Granderson and Ross try to figure out John's next move.

"Listening to the landline only is not going to help us at this point. I'm sure John was smart enough to get his daughter's cell phone number from the boyfriend's phone. That's the line we need to tap into," states Ross.

"Yes, we're working on that but it will take some time. Cell phone carriers create tons of red tape in cases like this," Ling replies.

Ross' cell phone rings. She looks at the caller ID. "It's Howard," she announces before answering.

"Did they locate Magi?" asks Granderson anxiously.

Ross responds to his question only with a raised index finger, indicating him to hold on while she answers the call from their supervising agent.

"This is Ross" she speaks into her phone. She listens for a moment before responding. "Are you sure? OK, will do ... OK, bye," she says before hanging up.

"Well?" asks Granderson.

"No sign of John Magi ... Howard wants us to go home," she replies.

"Seriously?" replies Granderson.

"Yeah, seriously?" echoes Ling sarcastically, as he is clearly not happy on this stakeout.

"That was the order. He thinks Magi already left the city and most likely won't be coming here. We will meet in the morning," adds Ross.

"Yay!" cheers Ling under his breath as he quickly begins to pack up the surveillance equipment.

Granderson briefly stares at Ross, who is very nonchalantly scrolling through emails on her phone. He then shrugs his shoulders, starts the van, and drives away.

As the surveillance van rolls off past the home of the Wests, in its place arrives another vehicle ... a dark sport utility vehicle driven by agent Howard. He rolls to a stop and parks in nearly the exact spot his team was just occupying. He then makes a call on his cell phone.

"I'm in place. Let's be sure to end this tonight," he says into his phone before hanging up.

Agent Evans presses "end call" on his cell phone. He is sitting in a parked car outside of Jamie Magi's apartment building. He reaches into the glove compartment and retrieves a silencer. He calmly attaches it to the end of his firearm. Whatever is going down tonight will definitely not be deemed standard procedure.

*　　　*　　　*

John Magi walks along the city sidewalks as the streetlights glisten off the still rain-soaked pavement. He keeps his head down and walks briskly. Is his judgment still sharp in spite of being cold, exhausted and hungry? He has very little cash remaining and has to use it wisely. He has enough for a one-way ticket aboard the Long Island Rail Road. That can get him to Katherine. If he executes that plan, how can he get her alone to explain to her where he's been all these years? If he stays in the city he can see his daughter, but how can he be sure she will even recognize or remember him, after being away since she was so young? He does not have enough money to do much else—so getting all the way out to Seattle is not even an option. Whatever John Magi decides to do tonight ... he can somehow sense that it will significantly affect everything.

CHAPTER 10

Agent Michelle Ross is still in the midst of her regular morning run when an incoming phone call interrupts the music in her headphones. As she continues to run, she crosses her right arm and lifts it up to eye level in order to see the caller ID ... it displays the name Ben Marshall. She presses the "accept call" option on the screen to answer.

"Yes?" she speaks out loud into the air as she maintains her steady pace.

She smiles and looks up before starting to laugh.

"Not that it's any of your business, but no ... I'm just working out," she replies.

After a listening pause, she continues to speak.

"Oh really, and what's the occasion?" she asks with mildly flirtatious curiosity.

Whatever is being said on the other end of the call has the usually stern agent blushing like a high school girl at her favorite boy band's concert. However, her countenance shifts as she realizes there is a conflict.

"Oh ... I can't that night. Going to the game," she says with a slight grimace.

After a pause she smiles again.

"Sure, some other time ... any other time is fine with me. OK, let me know when. Bye," she says before ending the call.

Ross increases her pace and continues to run along the river as her workout music resumes.

*   *   *

A group of joggers runs past John Magi as he sits on a park bench in Washington Square Park. John stretches and yawns, as it is apparent that he most likely spent the night here in the park. After making the decision to use the little cash he had remaining to purchase a back-pack from a 24-hour drugstore, John slept off the cheap booze he lifted from a nearby bodega. In fact, his reasoning for the purchase of the backpack was so that he can shoplift food, hygiene products, and other items needed to survive on the streets, and easily remain mobile.

Hangovers from the cheaper booze seem to be worse than with the more expensive stuff. John looks for a place to relieve himself before heading to find a cup of black coffee.

*   *   *

A fresh pot of coffee brews in the kitchen of the Long Island home of Jerron and Katherine West. Jamie Magi and her boyfriend are the overnight guests who are joining her mom and stepdad for breakfast. As the foursome discuss the events of the night prior, they partake in a spread of breakfast favorites prepared by Katherine. The lovely hostess is delighted to have people to cook for other than herself and her husband. Her bubbly energy resonates with every compliment to her famous specialties: fresh-baked banana bread, fluffy goat cheese omelets and perfectly crisped bacon. In spite of the disturbing news that she received from FBI agent Ross, Katherine West hides her uneasiness quite well. By all appearances, she is the perfect hostess.

"Anyone else care for more coffee?" asks Katherine pleasantly. She gets up from the table and makes her way over to the counter that houses the coffee maker, and all of the other extravagant kitchen appliances. When she reaches the counter, the cordless phone rings. With the glass coffee pot in one hand, she reaches over and removes the phone from the charging base, and answers the call with the same politeness she has maintained throughout the morning meal.

"Hello?"

Almost immediately she drops the coffee pot into the kitchen sink. The crash of broken glass startles everyone else, but Katherine seems to be in a daze. Jerron hurries over to his wife.

"Hey, are you OK, did you get cut?" asks the handsome, concerned husband.

Katherine quickly hangs up the phone, and places it face down on the counter. She begins to rinse the coffee out of the sink and carefully remove shards of broken glass.

"No, I'm fine, just clumsy, that's all. Go back and finish your breakfast, I'll clean this up," she responds nervously.

Jamie and Kyle continue eating. Jerron, sensing the sudden uneasiness in his wife's tone and demeanor, questions her about the call that seemed to upset her.

"Who was that on the phone?" he inquires.

"Oh, just some stupid automated call. Probably trying to sell us a cruise or timeshare," she replies.

Before she can finish her answer, again the phone rings. She quickly tries to answer, but Jerron beats her to it. She looks on nervously as her husband answers the phone.

"Hello?" answers Jerron while looking at his wife.

Katherine can tell that Jerron didn't quite buy her story about the caller that freaked her out.

"Hello?" answers Jerron again, this time with a firmer tone.

The caller hangs up, and so does Jerron. Katherine looks on nervously, awaiting a response from her husband.

"I guess it was just a ring back from that automated telemarketer," replies Jerron as he returns the phone to its original charging base.

Katherine lets out a sigh of relief as Jerron returns to the table, and rejoins the two youngsters enjoying their meal. As she stares down at the remnants of dark coffee swirling into the drain, she can't help but imagine it as a symbol of her current life as she knows it, washing away. After that phone call, she knows that there is a conversation that needs to take place, and a past issue that must be addressed.

*   *   *

As agent Ross walks to her office, one of the office assistants alerts her.

"Agent Ross, there is a Katherine West here to see you. She says it's urgent," states the assistant.

Ross looks in the direction of her closed office door as the assistant reads from a note.

"*I was contacted by a ghost!* She said that you would know exactly what that means," adds the assistant.

"Thank you," offers Ross before heading into her office to meet with her unexpected visitor and closing the door behind her.

*   *   *

"It was like hearing the voice of a ghost," declares Katherine. She is visibly upset, her face ashen, as she sits in Ross' office, sharing the details of the phone call she received from her "dead husband".

"Tell me exactly what he said, Mrs. West," says Ross.

"Katherine, please don't hang up ... it's me, John," Katherine replies.

"Anything else? Did he mention where he was, or wanting to meet?" asks Ross.

"No. I was in such shock. I just froze," Katherine replies. "Then I panicked at the thought of my husband finding out that my dead ex-husband is back, so I just hung up the phone. I think he called back, but when Jerron answered, the caller hung up ... I mean, my daughter was right there, a few feet away. What if she answered the phone?" She grows increasingly upset at that last thought.

Ross offers a tissue box from her desk to Katherine, who takes two with which to wipe the tears that are beginning to form. There is a knock on the door, and then it opens and agent Howard enters the office. He closes the door behind him.

"Mrs. West, this is agent Howard, my supervisor whom I believe you've met at the hospital," announces Ross.

Howard steps in and shakes Katherine's hand, before taking a seat next to Ross—across from Katherine.

"So Magi reached out this morning. Agent Ling traced the call coming from a pay phone at the bus station," states Ross as she keeps her boss up to speed.

"Well, let's not assume that because he called from a bus station it means he is leaving the area," replies Howard in response to Ross.

"Did he say where he was, or where he was headed?" asks Howard directly to Katherine.

"No, I hung up before he could say anything," replies Katherine.

"Mrs. West does not wish to communicate with Magi, nor does she want him contacting their daughter," interjects Ross.

"Mrs. West, if and when Mr. Magi contacts you again, I need you to set up a meeting with him," states Howard.

"No way! I'm not doing that!" Katherine quickly barks. She stands and shoulders her large designer handbag. Her body language and facial expression leave no doubt that she is exiting and terminating this meeting.

"Mrs. West, please. We need your help. We feel John's life, and possibly your family's, may be in danger," offers Ross. She stands and gently but assertively puts her hand on Katherine's arm in an attempt to calm her down. This works, as Katherine takes a deep breath, and sits back down.

"As long as he is out there, and the wrong people are aware of his existence …" continues Ross.

"We believe it will be in the best interest of everyone involved if we have Mr. Magi in federal custody," interrupts Howard.

"Everyone involved? How the hell did I get involved? When did my innocent daughter get involved? Jerron only knows that I am a widow to an accountant who died 15 years ago. How do I drag him into this? We didn't hide blood money for any mobsters! This is John's mess, why should we have to be involved?" spews Katherine.

"I'm afraid that you, your husband, and your daughter are already involved," Howard replies bluntly. "Unfortunately, that's just how these people operate." His tone is ice cold.

Katherine buries her face into the palms of her hands. She is experiencing a mix of emotions—anger, fear, worry, hurt ... and buried somewhere in there is a touch of concern for John. She denies that emotion because it can possibly translate to still having feelings for the man she once couldn't picture her life without. Now that her life is perfect, and she is currently married to her version of "Mr. Wonderful"—she does not dare show concern for the former Mr. Wonderful, as John was known on the streets.

"Mrs. West, we just need you to play nice, and set up a meeting with Mr. Magi. We will give you a predetermined location. He never has to come anywhere near you or your home."

Katherine lifts her head from her hands and listens as Howard explains his suggestion.

"Once he shows up, our agents will take it from there. You never even have to be present."

Katherine's forehead creases as she thinks.

"If you can't help us out, we may have to resort to asking your daughter to help us set up a meeting," adds Howard.

Even Ross is surprised by Howard's threat.

"No! Listen, I do not want my daughter or my husband knowing anything about this! If I agree to help the FBI, I need to know that John goes back into hiding, and we never hear from him again," states Katherine adamantly.

Howard nods in agreement. Katherine takes a deep breath—physically, mentally, and emotionally. She then looks at agent Ross, making eye contact, forming a connection of trust.

"Where do you want me to tell him to meet?" asks Katherine nervously.

CHAPTER 11

At the Grumman Men's Federal Prison in Glendale, New York, a tall, middle-aged pale-skinned man picks up the blue pen to sign in at the visitation window. His signature is elegant and fluid, with its letters leaning to the right: Anthony Greenberg. Calmly, he returns the pen to the clipboard and lightly touches his clerical collar. He will sit and wait for as long as it takes to obtain a rare meeting with a particular inmate.

The wives, mothers, and children sitting around Anthony on hard plastic chairs are oblivious as to his true identity. He is the first cousin once removed of the late Salvatore "Sal" Mongelli Jr.—head of the Mongelli crime family—and he awaits a visit with his father, Richie Silvestri. Richie is serving time for a laundry list of convictions, although the most egregious is one for which he took a fall. After his cousin Sal's demise in the car chase with the FBI, Richie was framed for the revenge murders of three FBI agents. Richie's guilt was easy to believe; as children, he and Sal grew up in Brooklyn together, and their ties ran deep and strong.

Anthony Greenberg has eluded the FBI radar as a blood relative to Richie because his Jewish mother, Hannah Greenberg, refused to allow her children to take the name of a man who would not marry her. Hannah mysteriously disappeared without a trace when Anthony was young, and people have long suspected that Richie had her murdered for such a disrespectful act. Anthony only goes by Greenberg because when he was a child, his Mongelli relatives thought his Jewish last name would prove to be beneficial one day ... This is the time when that thinking pays off. Disguised as a clergyman, Anthony Greenberg-Silvestri visits his father without raising any suspicion.

Richie Silvestri enters the visitation room in which inmates can meet privately with clergy members of their particular faith, or religious beliefs. Richie is a large, Italian-American man, with a receding hairline, grey hair, and a borderline obese build. As he sits across the small table from his son, they barely greet one another. The awkwardness is due to the fact that Richie kept Anthony far from the family business—a business that took up most of his time, which meant very little time for father-son bonding. It wasn't until Anthony was an adult that he knew what his father did for a living, or even shared a meal with him. And in spite of that, and the fact that people suspect his father had his mother killed, Anthony is loyal to his father until the end.

"Tony, you look good, son," offers Richie as a greeting.

"Thanks, Pop. You too," replies Anthony.

"Don't lie, I know I look like crap," replies Richie.

Anthony looks down at the table. His lack of eye contact is a clear indication that he fears the man seated across from him, yet has love at the same time—sort of like an abused spouse. To the Silvestris, family loyalty is not just a polite suggestion passed down from one generation to the next. It is paramount.

"So, tell me something ... *Wonderful*," Richie continues.

"Nothing yet, I'm afraid," replies Anthony.

Richie clutches his chest as he produces a series of asthmatic coughs. He doesn't appear to be in good health. Although he is currently serving a life sentence, and knows that he will die behind bars, there is something he wants to obtain before his demise ... revenge for his cousin's death and the fall of the family empire—the empire that crumbled following John Magi's testimony.

"Are you OK, Dad, have you quit smoking?" asks a concerned Anthony.

"Don't worry about me. Just do your job and there will be a lot of money in it for you," replies Richie.

He is referring to over $3 billion in diamonds that only few even know were stolen.

Fifteen years ago, associates of the Mongelli organization pulled off a daring heist. By obtaining jobs with the cleaning company assigned to the World Trade Center, they broke into a hidden vault used to house diamonds and other rare gems for international transport. On the morning of the heist, just as they were making their entry into the vault, two airplanes hit the towers, committing the largest-ever terror strike on U.S. soil. Following the attack, the Metropolitan Transit Authority was given the order to shut down all subway trains in the downtown area. That stroke of luck allowed the thieves to use the underground tunnel leading to the subway system, and escape with over $3 billion worth of diamonds. After the collapse of the towers and other surrounding structures in the area, it was assumed that the jewels were lost in the devastation—buried in a tomb of the thousands who lost their lives that fateful day. For the days, weeks, even months following the September 11 attacks, as rescue crews searched for survivors, those responsible for the heist had the perfect man to hide all of that loot until they could spend it safely … a man trustworthy. That man was Mr. Wonderful himself—John Magi.

Richie Silvestri has no interest in the money—it is merely payment for the satisfaction of knowing that John Magi suffers from watching his family tortured and killed. His loyal son, Anthony, wants to grant his father this dying wish, but unfortunately for Anthony, a couple of dirty federal agents are also aware of the heist—information they gathered from the former mob accountant, John Magi. Fully aware of where the diamonds are hidden, these federal agents are set for life. The only thing standing in between them and early retirement is John Magi. They can't risk selling the diamonds only to later have Magi inform other agents of their existence. Therefore they must kill Magi, and make it look like a mob hit in retaliation for his testimony. With John Magi alive, these dirty agents run the risk of being exposed.

"Don't you worry, Pop, there is no crevice on this planet that John Magi can hide in. I will flush him out," promises Anthony.

"That's my boy," replies Richie.

"As soon as he sees his wife and daughter suffering, he will talk. Once he gives up the location of the diamonds, you will have your revenge. I will even use my phone to record his expression while I'm chopping up his little girl," states Anthony.

The proud father leans forward, kisses his son on each cheek and whispers in his ancestors' native tongue: "*Sei il polso di questa famiglia orgogliosa:*" *You are the pulse of this proud family.*

After uttering this phrase, Richie Silvestri stands and exits to return to his cell. Anthony is unsure of when his next visit will be, since he cannot visit often to raise suspicion as to his relation to his father. He does want it to be soon … as soon as he takes care of John Magi and honors his family. A determined Anthony Greenberg-Silvestri exits the room and makes his way to the visitors' exit.

•   •   •

Agent Michelle Ross sits in her office when her assistant knocks on her door to inform her of a visitor. The gentleman visitor is directly behind the assistant, and boldly invites himself into the office. The assistant exits to give Ross and her visitor some privacy, as it is apparent that they are familiar.

Ross doesn't realize that she has a huge smile on her face as she greets her visitor. The former underwear model, turned television sitcom actor is her ex-boyfriend, Ben Marshall. Ross hasn't seen Ben in quite some time, but when he called this morning during her run, she still felt something for the ridiculously good-looking man, who possesses more sex appeal than she could ever handle. As he steps toward her, he gently cups her elbow in his palm and pulls her slightly into him. The tiny hairs on the back or her neck rise, as does her blood pressure. He kisses her on her cheek and then politely backs away. Ross can feel her weight falling into him but manages to maintain her balance.

"Hey, so good to see you. You look amazing," offers the charming Ben.

"Hi, thanks ... what are you doing here?" Ross asks while silently willing the crimson to drain from her cheeks.

"Well, on the phone when I invited you out for a meal to celebrate, you said anytime ... so I figured now is anytime," replies Ben. He is holding eye contact.

"Wait, what? I can't ... I have a very important case ..." Ross utters.

Before she can complete her objection, Ben waves in two men carrying trays of catered food, and placing them on the table in Ross' office. Ben then tips them and closes the door behind them as they exit.

"Breakfast is served ... I know it's lunchtime," announces Ben with a playful bow.

"Wow, I must admit Ben, you've got style," replies Ross.

Ben pulls up a chair and invites Ross to sit. He then uncovers the trays to display a colorful assortment of quiches, croissants, fruit tarts, éclairs and more to sample from La Chatelaine, her favorite restaurant. Ross is impressed. Ben sits next to her, and they each reach for a glistening delicacy.

"So, you never said what the special occasion was," Ross says as she chews a delicious pastry.

"Well, the guest role I landed on the show ..." Ben begins.

"Yes, 'Pick of the Litter,'" responds Ross.

"Yup, well my character has been permanently added to the main cast," announces Ben proudly.

"That is wonderful, Ben. I'm so happy for you. You always stuck to your dream, and worked hard. Congratulations," offers Ross.

"I wanted to share this moment of success with you, because you believed in me when I was modeling and bartending part time," states Ben.

Ross smiles and continues to shove food into her mouth, swallowing the urge to embarrass herself and kiss her ex right in her office. Her attraction for him makes her feel vulnerable and that makes her uncomfortable. She likes to be in total control of her emotions at all times.

"So, what's it like being back in New York City now that you live out in Los Angeles?" asks Ross.

"Well, I guess I have to get used to the loud talkers, fast walkers, and rude drivers again ... since the show is moving production here," announces Ben with a huge smile.

Ross almost chokes on her food. She could hardly keep her hands off of Ben for the duration of this meal, how will she survive with him around regularly?

"Here, in New York ... really?" she questions as she quickly washes down her food with a chug of water.

"Yes, I'm back in the Big Rotten Apple," jokes Ben.

Ross laughs to be polite, but she has her concerns about Ben moving back to New York.

*　　　*　　　*

"I'm back in the city," says Jamie Magi as she speaks on the phone to Montez.

Jamie and Kyle are in his apartment packing a suitcase, as he plans on staying at her apartment for a while. With Kyle's injuries, Jamie feels that she can take care of him, and this can be a great time to test out living together. While Kyle packs a bag, Jamie adds items to a small box, collecting perishable food items from the fridge to bring to her place.

"I can't stay with my mom another night ... she cooks way too much. I'm afraid I'll get fat," jokes Jamie as she continues to speak on the phone.

The call is interrupted by an incoming call. The caller ID reads "Unknown" so Jamie doesn't answer.

"I don't know, it is from an unknown number ... yeah, we literally just got back in the city ... we're going to the game tonight," Jamie continues.

As she continues to chat with Montez, the unknown caller tries again, and again Jamie doesn't answer.

"Yeah, it says unknown number again ... no way ... probably some girl gave a wrong number to some weirdo, and just so happens to be my number ... yeah right, I should answer and pretend to be her gay lover," Jamie jokes.

As she laughs with her friend on the other end, the unknown caller tries again. Jamie looks at her phone and sees it is the same blocked phone number and refuses to answer. She has a good attitude about it as she continues to joke with Montez on the other line.

"Stop calling, dude! Get a clue, she gave you the wrong number, weirdo!"

* * *

"Come on, weirdo! If you're not going to buy anything, you can't use the phone," yells the owner of the Broadway Diner in Greenpoint, Brooklyn. Broadway is one of the oldest establishments in the borough, and even still has one of the original large, red phone booths with the folding glass door. John Magi is currently locked inside the booth using the phone. Due to the length of time John is spending in the booth, the irritated owner thinks he's dealing with a homeless man and threatens to call the police.

"The phone and bathrooms are for customers only. If you don't leave, I'm calling the cops," threatens the man.

John slams the receiver down in frustration. He violently slides the booth door open and aggressively stares the man down. The nervous old man wants no part of the angry and desperate stranger who is now in his face. The man swallows hard and steps back, allowing John to exit the booth. John continues to stare the man down as he moves toward the diner exit. The man breaks eye contact and heads back to the kitchen. John exits and walks down the block. He tries to think of his next move. He has no one to turn to, since all of his former friends are now his enemies, or dead. His only family is Jamie and Katherine, but not even he believes that connection exists anymore.

CHAPTER 12

The crowd erupts into a boisterous frenzy as the crack of a wooden bat propels the pitch from the visiting Red Sox hurler high into the night sky, and deep into the left-field seats. The Yankees slugger rounds the bases with his hands lifted above his head, as his teammates and hometown fans cheer the go-ahead run midway through the game. Among the elated New York fans seated behind the home dugout are agents Ross and Granderson. Enjoying the festive atmosphere, cold beers and stadium hotdogs, the coworkers share a toast to the temporary escape from work-related discussion. The ease, the comfort, the trusting friendship ... it is moments like these that Ross relishes sharing with her partner. They are also the reason she fights her physical attraction toward him, and avoids the risk of damaging the connection they currently have. There is no denying that had they not worked together, this professional partnership would have easily been a romantic relationship.

"How awesome is this? Yanks ... Sox ... here at the stadium," yells Granderson over the crowd noise and music blaring from the loud speakers.

"This is awesome! Thanks for inviting me," replies Ross.

The two tap beer-bottle necks in salute of the fun evening. Ross' phone vibrates in her pocket. She holds her phone up to see Ben Marshall's name on the caller ID. Granderson also sees the name. Ross sends the call to voicemail and returns her phone to her pocket to continue enjoying the game.

"Ben? That guy has some nerve, huh?" states Granderson in an attempt to start a conversation.

"Come on, Yanks! Let's break this wide open!" yells Ross toward the field in an attempt to avoid that conversation.

Granderson is not quite ready to let it go.

"It's bad enough he left to head out West in pursuit of an acting career, but then he had the nerve to cheat on you ... what a jerk," says Granderson.

Ross doesn't respond, but instead continues to watch the action on the field.

"I mean, I remember when you flew all the way out there on the redeye to surprise him, only to be devastated to learn that he was living with another woman," continues Granderson as he fuels the one-sided conversation.

Ross takes the bait.

"That was a different time, people make mistakes," she replies.

Granderson is mortified that she is defending her ex.

"You can't be serious! The guy broke your heart and you're defending him?" he spits.

"People change, Granderson," Ross says, keeping her eyes on the field. "That was a stressful period for us ... Him trying to break into the industry, and me focused on my career. Today at lunch, conversation was easy, and no hard feelings."

"Today at lunch? He's here in New York?" questions a surprised Granderson.

"Yeah, his show will be filming the next two seasons here," replies Ross. She doesn't want to continue the conversation, or offer any additional information.

Granderson is not doing a very good job of concealing his disappointment with the news of Ross' ex-boyfriend being back on the scene.

"Well, good for him. I guess he is going to try to get back together," states Granderson.

"Can we just enjoy the game? I don't want to talk about any expectations or motives. I'm focused on protecting John Magi and his family ... and right now, the runner in scoring position," replies Ross dismissively.

"Seems like Ben is the one in scoring position," mutters Granderson.

Ross hears him, but ignores the comment.

∗   ∗   ∗

Up in the cheaper seats, Jamie Magi and her boyfriend Kyle are enjoying the game as they share a large tub of popcorn. Both wearing matching jerseys and hats, they appear carefree as they join the chorus of other fan chanting: "Let's go, Yankees!"

Kyle occasionally winces in pain as he cheers with excitement—forgetting about his injured ribs and soreness. Other than getting a little beer spilled on them from a drunken fan in the row behind them, it is a perfect night for the young couple.

∗   ∗   ∗

The Yankees' game is on every screen at the Forty-Three Bar in Queens, however John Magi isn't watching. He sits in the corner alone, distracted from the other patrons who are completely engaged in the historic rivalry between the two teams playing. The bragging rights of the entire city ride on this series every season. The excitement in the place is electrifying with the home team ahead by two runs late in the game. However, John couldn't be further from the moment as he is lost in the muddled chaos that is his current reality. Not fully aware of any potential danger he or his family may be in, his next move becomes uncertain with each passing tick of the clock. Time is not on his side, and he can sense it. He desperately wants to reach out to his daughter and former wife, but doing so would jeopardize them, and himself. In this moment—in this bar, John Magi makes the difficult decision to leave his family to enjoy the lives they now have, since they appear to have completely gotten over losing him. He will, however, stick around and keep an eye out for his daughter ... this way he can finally feel like her father...the father he always wanted to be to her. The decision to stick around is motivated by his love for his little girl, and confirmed by the help--wanted poster on the wall. As long as they agree to pay him in cash, John will be the new dishwasher for Forty-Three Bar.

* * *

At the end of the Yankees/Red Sox game, Jerron West turns off the television in his living room. His wife, Katherine, who sits next to him on the couch, has fallen asleep. She was never much of a sports fan, but watches as a means of spending time with her husband. Jerron gets off of the couch quietly, as not to wake his sleeping wife. He then gently places a decorative throw over her to keep her warm. He steps back and stares at the beautiful woman he gets to share a home, a bed, and a life with. He looks at her with concern. Ever since the night at the hospital she has been a bit distant. He can sense she is keeping something from him. On top of that, add the suspicious call that freaked her out this morning, followed by her unexpected and secret trip into the city. Jerron can sense that his wife is keeping something from him, but is not sure what. It could be as extreme as an affair, or a sickness she is hiding ... or as simple as a surprise couple's vacation. So whether the mystery caller was a doctor with lab results, or a travel agent with the perfect travel package, Jerron is going to be keeping a closer eye on his wife.

* * *

As drunk Yankees fans roam the streets looking for open bars to continue celebrating the big win with a few more victory drinks, the buzz in the air doesn't reflect the tone of the two federal agents seated in the front seat of a dark sedan with government plates. Agents Howard and Evans are greatly concerned by the fact that they have failed to tie up the loose end that is John Magi. They are joined by a third agent, an Asian female named Sarah Wang, who discreetly enters the vehicle from the rear passenger door, and sits in the center of the back seat.

"So we're on schedule to move the last of the diamonds. The broker's point man tried to skim a little off the top, but he quickly changed his tune when I pressed the muzzle of my service weapon to his groin ... Actually, I think he may have enjoyed it," reports agent Wang coldly. "Who's ready to finally spend their cut of $3.6 billion?" she asks with bubbling energy.

She can tell by the lack of an enthusiastic response from her cohorts that something is not going according to plan. She leans forward and looks at the expressions of Howard and Evans.

"Um, what's going on ... is there something you guys aren't telling me?" she asks.

"Evans here botched the hit on Mr. Wonderful," announces a disgusted Howard.

Evans simply rolls his eyes and stares out of the passenger window.

"You big, stupid pile of wasted muscle! How could you mess that up?" questions Wang venomously.

Evans ignores her, but Howard seems both thrilled and peeved to elaborate.

"Well, Magi pulled a fast one by promising some schmuck a free one-way trip to Seattle, and a new identity. Big boy here didn't verify if the passenger that he picked up from the airport was Magi before emptying his clip into the poor guy," explains Howard.

"What? So where is Magi now?" asks Wang.

"It seems as though Magi planned on returning to his wife and daughter once he learned of Mongelli's death," replies Howard.

"Howard, you have to fix this!" Wang insists, rattled. "The plan was to kill the last of the Mongelli bosses, lure Magi out of protection, and then silence him once and for all ... then we could move the last of the diamonds. How can we move forward with the risk of him alerting the bureau of the heist, or informing any past associates that he turned over the diamonds to us?"

"Relax, Wang," states Howard.

"No, I won't relax!" Wang shouts a bit too loudly for the close quarters of the vehicle. "I said all along, why wait all these years when we could have just taken out Magi when we knew where he was?"

"Not while he was in FBI protective custody ... it would have easily come back as an inside hit," replies Howard without raising his voice to her level.

"Oh, so now he's out there talking to who the hell knows ... this stinks, and I don't like it one bit!" declares Wang.

"Chill out, Wang. John Magi will be taken care of, and Evans here will still make it look like a revenge mob hit. Mr. Wonderful will, in fact, contact his 'widow,' and when he does; she will set up a meeting and alert us. We're still on schedule ... just keep your end of the bargain and move those diamonds," says Howard confidently.

Agent Wang doesn't seem to share the same confidence as the rest of her team of dirty agents. She shakes her head and slides over on the back seat.

"You're in charge," she mutters before exiting the vehicle and slamming the door shut.

She storms off down the block and disappears around the corner. Now alone with Evans, Howard turns to the large agent and gives a stern order.

"This must end ASAP!"

•   •   •

"I will be there ASAP!" announces Ross into her phone.

She is smiling ear to ear as she ends her call. Granderson is not smiling, but rather looks annoyed as the two off-duty agents board the number four train from Yankee Stadium. The plan was to go out for dessert and a nightcap at the Forty-Three Bar after the game. As the slew of fans pile onto the train, Granderson and Ross are forced to stand in each other's personal space, which makes this particular conversation all the more awkward.

"Let me guess, you can't do dessert anymore?" questions Granderson.

"I'm sorry ... Ben left his script with the director's notes at my office today during lunch. He needs it for a table read in the morning. I told him I would meet him at the office," replies Ross apologetically.

The train rocks violently as it maneuvers along the elevated, outdoor track. This sudden movement causes Ross to fall into Granderson as she completely loses her balance. Granderson absorbs her weight and keeps her on her feet. As they stand eye-to-eye in close proximity, they both seem to be lost in the moment. Their lips almost touching ... their eyes locked in. Suddenly another sharp movement of the train pulls Ross away ... just enough to release her from the moment ... a moment in which she had temporarily relinquished her control and was willing to follow fate. But what was fate? Was it the first movement bringing her to her partner Granderson ... or perhaps the second one, pulling her away? One thing is certain: she is experiencing a sexual re-awakening. Not since her relationship with Ben—during the good times—has she felt this alive sexually. Could it be the fact that Ben is back in town? Or could it be the time spent with Granderson in a non-working capacity? Ross wrestles with this as she navigates her way through the complex combination of emotions.

The duration of the train ride is spent on awkward small talk about the game and the coming playoffs, until Ross reaches a stop where she must transfer to another train to go to the office. The two agents get crossed between a hug and a handshake as they prepare to part ways for the evening. The confusion creates a good chuckle between them before Ross exits the train and heads up the stairs to transfer. Granderson continues on the number four train on his way home.

•   •   •

In another train car, Jamie and Kyle ride to her apartment. The young, attractive couple stand chest to chest as they hold on to each other while the train rocks side to side. Jamie lays her head on Kyle's shoulder with her eyes closed. She is enjoying this happy feeling. Although he is injured, Jamie finds a level of safety in the strength of her man. His confidence makes up for any current physical limitations. In her eyes, he is her protector ... the closest thing she's felt to a strong man since she was a little girl and her dad would make her feel safe by his presence. Could this young man be *her* Mr. Wonderful?

Standing a few feet away, near the emergency exit door of the subway car, two eyes look intently at Jamie and Kyle. Wearing a light brown leather jacket and matching fedora, the man continues to stare at the couple as he shifts a toothpick from side to side in his mouth.

When Kyle and Jamie get off at their stop, so does the man. The well-dressed man walks several feet behind the couple as they emerge from the subway and walk along the sidewalk. With his hands in his jacket pockets, the man carefully keeps his eyes on the unsuspecting young lovers. His cognac-colored leather dress shoes stride confidently with each step Kyle and Jamie take. The couple stops at a crosswalk and takes the opportunity to enjoy a lengthy kiss. The man spits out his toothpick and reaches into his inside jacket pocket. He pulls out a box of cigarettes and removes one. He lights it and takes a long drag before blowing it out. He pretends to be checking his phone to avoid being discovered by the kissing couple. When the crosswalk signal changes, Kyle and Jamie continue walking toward her apartment building. The man also follows closely, but safely, behind. When they reach her apartment, Jamie opens the front door, and she and Kyle enter the lobby. The man stands across the street watching as the couple disappears behind the second door of the pre-war building.

The man is Anthony Greenberg-Silvestri. He blows smoke from his mouth and nose and drops the lit cigarette onto the sidewalk, then steps on it. He takes out his cell phone and makes a call as he walks away.

CHAPTER 13

As her alarm clock continues to flash silently, agent Michelle Ross remains in bed, staring up at the semi-dark ceiling in her bedroom as beams of morning light creep through the crevice between her window and curtains. The confused look on her face is mostly due to the presence of the nude man sleeping next to her. Ross replays the events of the night prior in her mind; one thing led to the next, culminating in the current predicament she now finds herself in. As her ex-boyfriend Ben, with his arm and leg still propped across her naked skin, continues to sleep, the woman who is usually in control of her emotions seems to be at a loss for defining what exactly she is experiencing. She is partially elated and still possessing the post--orgasm glow, after such a dry spell and lack of a man's touch. She is also partially disappointed in herself for allowing things to move so quickly—it's as if she didn't even make her ex work for the prize of her body. He's the man who broke her heart, yet less than 24 hours after his arrival back in New York, in a moment of passion, she made love to him ... several times. She is also feeling a sense of guilt, and this perplexes her most of all. Why is she experiencing this particular emotion? Why does she feel the need to keep last night's episode a secret from her work partner? She and Ben are two consenting adults who share a romantic history, and reconnected in the most intimate way, so why should she feel anything other than happiness?

Ben opens his eyes and sees Ross staring at him. His ego is caressed by the thought that his performance has left her so satisfied and completely in love that she watched him as he slept. He lets out a masculine chuckle from deep in his chiseled chest as he mounts her completely and begins to kiss her neck, shoulders and breasts. Her erect nipples and flushed face give away the fact that his exploring mouth turns her on. Ross finds her hands stroking Ben's hair as he buries his face forcefully into her assuming crotch. Her heels dig into the mattress and her toes curl as she throws her head to the side—burying her face into the pillow. The repetitious and relentless tongue of her lover, who seems to know her body better than she, sends waves of pleasure through her—forcing her to throw her head in the other direction. Her eyes are filled with pleasure as they open, but then fill with tears as a photo on her dresser comes into focus. As Ross stares at the photo of her and Granderson at last year's ugly sweater holiday party, she comes to the sad reality that although at the moment Ben has her body, another man actually has her heart. Her mind is no longer invested in the current pleasure that her body is experiencing, so she fakes an impressive orgasm ... not so much for the sake of Ben's ego, but to bring an end to a rather confusing exchange of emotions within herself.

* * *

Jamie Magi dismounts her boyfriend Kyle and crashes to the bed with her head on his chest. They are both sweaty and out of breath as they smile, their eyes filled with pleasure.

"I didn't hurt your ribs, did I?" asks a concerned Jamie.

"No ... that was awesome," pants Kyle.

After catching his breath, Kyle kisses Jamie and then gets up and walks to the bathroom. Jamie notices the time and remembers that she has to meet her friend Montez at their usual yoga class.

"Hey babe, will you be all right here alone for a bit this morning? I have my yoga class that I hate missing," yells Jamie to Kyle.

"Sure, just use me for my body and then run off with your yoga friends," replies Kyle jokingly.

He returns from the bathroom and lies on his back gingerly, next to Jamie.

"Aw, you're in a lot of pain ... let me call Montez and tell her I won't be able to come to class today," offers Jamie as she reaches for her cell phone on the nightstand.

"No, I will be fine. Go and do whatever you girls do in yoga, with those sexy pants," replies Kyle.

"OK, I promise I will be back as soon as class ends. I will rush home to take care of you," Jamie says with excitement.

She gets up and heads to the bathroom to freshen up and get dressed. She emerges from the bathroom topless and barefoot—wearing only her skintight, white yoga pants while brushing her teeth. Kyle marvels at the sight of his sexy girlfriend as he gazes at her bare back and firm, shapely buttocks.

"Wait a second ... are there any guys in this yoga class?" questions Kyle.

. . .

Katherine West wakes up on the couch and realizes that she fell asleep and spent the night in the living room. She peels away the cover, placed on her by her husband, and sits upright to see Jerron sitting in the kitchen working on his laptop.

"Good morning, sleepy head. I got a pot of coffee started," offers Jerron.

"Good morning. Thank you," replies Katherine.

She walks over to the kitchen and kisses her husband on his forehead and lovingly rubs his shoulders.

"Thanks for covering me. Did I miss the entire game?" she asks.

"I would say you missed most of the game. I didn't want to wake you or try to carry you upstairs," replies Jerron.

"I'm going to brush my teeth. What do you want for breakfast?" asks Katherine as she moves toward the stairs.

"How about I take you out to breakfast, so that I can tell you my surprise?" asks Jerron.

Katherine stops in her tracks. She is intrigued. She walks back toward her husband.

"Surprise? Now I'm curious," she replies with an anxious smile.

Jerron enters information into his laptop and then sits back in his chair.

"There ... all booked," he announces proudly.

"What's all booked? What have you done, Mr. West?" asks Katherine.

"Well, Mrs. West, your awesome husband just booked a family getaway weekend!" announces Jerron.

An impressed and excited Katherine leaps into her husband's lap and hugs his neck.

"That is so sweet, honey!" she replies.

"I figured we could use a nice mini escape ... Jamie can bring Kyle and we can just relax ... and I made sure there is no golfing, so no distractions," replies Jerron.

"My man! So where are we going?" questions an excited Katherine.

"I booked us a remote cabin upstate at Camp Taconic," he replies.

"Wow ... roughing it in the woods? This ought to be interesting," replies Katherine playfully, cupping his face in her hands and smoothing her thumbs across his cheeks.

"Well I wouldn't quite refer to Camp Taconic as roughing it. It is mostly where big executives plan company retreats and such," Jerron explains, smiling affectionately. "Nonetheless, it is miles away from the busy city."

Katherine is obviously excited and proud of her husband for taking the initiative to plan a getaway for them and also including Jamie and her boyfriend.

"I can't wait to tell Jamie," she states as she slides off his lap and runs upstairs.

When she reaches the top of the stairs, a touch of guilt pangs in her stomach. The secret she is keeping from her husband is weighing on her, dampening her happy state. She is worried that John may call the house again and Jerron will find out she is hiding this secret—not to mention her own daughter is also in the dark as to her father's existence. Can Katherine enjoy a weekend getaway with her new husband, while the secret of her former husband looms and poses a threat to the happy life she currently has? She not only feels anger toward John—*that* she can understand—but Katherine struggles with the other feelings that she cannot properly define as they relate to the man who once held her heart. Hearing his voice brought back a flood of emotions, and that scares her more than anything. Perhaps some time away with her husband and daughter is the perfect escape she needs right now, Katherine thinks. Perhaps she may even gain the courage to come clean to Jerron about the revelation of her "late" husband once John is back in FBI protection, and out of their lives again ... hopefully for good this time. One thing Katherine is certain of is the fact that she never wants to taint the precious memory Jamie has of her father ... it's best left in the fashion of a bad accident, and not a criminal abandoning his family, whom *he* put in jeopardy in the first place.

Katherine allows herself to ponder these thoughts but refuses to permit them to overshadow the joy she has in this moment. She is excited to call her daughter and give her the news of a fun weekend getaway.

.   .   .

John Magi signed up for a free trial membership at the Body Elements Gym in Sunnyside. Not for the equipment, classes, or the many good-looking fit women ... John is here simply to get a daily hot shower. After scoring some free clothes at the local church clothes drive, and a part-time job washing dishes at the Forty-Three Bar, he is staying under the radar and surviving on the streets of New York City.

Heartbroken by Katherine's lack of interest in even speaking with him, John's sole purpose now is to keep a watchful eye on his daughter as a guardian angel.

For 15 years John has lived two types of nightmares ... one was knowing that his beloved Katherine moved on and was making love to another man every night. Eventually he grew numb to that one. The other one however is one that he will never get over ... thoughts of former enemies harming his family—especially his little girl, Jamie.

As John runs on the treadmill at the gym, the thought of this overcomes him and he races faster and faster, speeding up the machine to match his inner intensity. It isn't long before he runs out of steam and jumps off of the speeding belt, placing his feet and weight onto the side rails. John hangs his head and pants heavily as sweat and tears drip down his face.

* * *

Jamie Magi is drenched in sweat as she and Montez exit their weekly hot yoga class. Each carrying her yoga mat and a bag with dry clothes to change into, the two young ladies enter the women's changing room at the yoga studio.

"Did you notice that weird guy? I think he watched the entire class from outside," states Montez to Jamie.

"No, I'm in love. I don't notice cute guys," replies Jamie jokingly.

"Um, I said weird, not cute, so busted!" replies Montez.

She peeks outside the door and sees the same guy just waiting outside the studio, then closes back the door of the changing room.

"These creeps like seeing women in wet yoga pants ... I mean the least he could do is take the class and sweat with the rest of us. Pervert," says Montez.

Jamie laughs and changes her clothes ... and the subject.

"So did you finish your profile for that dating site?" she asks.

Montez gives her a dirty look.

"I don't need help finding a man. A strong, confident black woman is too much for most men to handle anyway," replies Montez.

Jamie puts her hands up as an exaggerated sign of surrender. "I give up. I just think you're a beautiful, smart woman, and a great catch for some guy ... the right guy," she states.

"I think I will be all right ... thanks for the concern, though," replies Montez as she rolls her eyes playfully.

"I would say we've known each other for quite a while now, and you never talk about a guy or a hookup ... wait ... maybe it is the ladies you're into," jokes Jamie as she stands on a bench and pretends to do a strip tease.

A group of other women from their class enter the changing room when Jamie is in the middle of her erotic performance. They cheer her on and pretend to throw money at her. She is embarrassed, but plays along momentarily before getting off the bench.

Once they are changed into clean, dry clothes, Jamie and Montez exit the changing room. On their way toward the exit, they pass the same man, who is standing in the hallway outside of the yoga studio. Montez sees him and rolls her eyes. Jamie doesn't see him as her eyes are buried in her cell phone.

The man watches the two ladies and follows them as they exit and walk down the street. The man is Anthony Greenberg-Silvestri, and he has his eyes locked on Jamie. When the ladies walk around the corner, Montez looks back and sees the man approach the corner. He makes eye contact with Montez and then walks in the opposite direction. Montez looks at Jamie to see if she notices the guy that is potentially following them, but she is on the phone with her mother.

"Thanks Mom ... yeah, Kyle will love that. He always talks about going camping. This will be fun," says Jamie cheerfully into her cell phone.

Montez looks back to see the man walking away from them.

CHAPTER 14

Fifteen years ago, when FBI supervising agent Stewart Howard got word of a huge diamond heist pulled off by a group of local gangsters with ties to the Mongelli crime family, he devised a plan that required the aid of a handful of agents close to him ... agents he could trust ... agents that were as dirty as he. Per his confidential informant, the group of thieves learned of the secret vault housed below street level in the basement of one of the World Trade Center buildings in downtown Manhattan. Their risky plan and daring escape was made possible by the events now known as the worst terror attack on American soil. They had no idea that terrorists would crash those planes into the towers that day—creating the world's biggest diversion. This heist, with its score in the billions, would have been the greatest in the history of jewel heists, had it not been for one thing ... very few know it actually went down. For the record, the vault and all of its contents were destroyed—melted along with the tons of steel and concrete by the many gallons of burning jet fuel.

Those who are aware of this perfect heist include the captains and those high-up the chain of command in the Mongelli crime organization; agent Howard and his small team of trusted agents; and the Mongelli accountant, Mr. Wonderful—John Magi.

Howard's plan was to threaten Magi by convincing him that Salvatore Mongelli had put a hit out on him and that it would be in his best interest to turn over the diamonds to the FBI, to avoid prison and escape his imminent execution. In turn, the FBI would use his written statement and financial records to bring down the crime organization, and then fake his death and enter him into FBI special protection. However, Howard and his agents kept the diamonds … the diamonds that those up the ranks of the Mongelli family think John Magi has stashed away. Howard knew that eventually Magi would leave the protection of the FBI and then he would have Magi killed and make it look like a mob-retaliation hit.

Originally Howard had a team of five other dirty agents in on the scheme, three of whom he had set up and killed after sending them on a dangerous undercover assignment, then tipping off the thugs of their true law-enforcement identities. Richie Silvestri, who was later set up to take the fall and ultimately convicted in the murders of those agents, is out of the picture serving multiple life sentences … never to see the light of day again. Now with only agents Evans and Wang left to split the pot, the greedy and cunning Howard plans to tie up all loose ends … which may include terminating the last two dirty agents once Magi is silenced once and for all.

Unaware that Richie Silvestri's boy, Anthony, has any knowledge of the hidden stash, Howard believes that he is the only dog in the race to get John Magi.

As agent Howard sits in his office, he plots ways to rid himself of both Evans and Wang … not only to keep the money all for himself, but to ensure that no one ever gets wind of the diamonds or his involvement in the murder of fellow agents. He knows that there is talk of a dirty agent in the division who tipped someone on the outside about John Magi's flight information. He needs to point the right person in the direction of Evans and Wang. Once they are killed and later suspected as the moles, Howard will be off scot-free, rich, and on a beach in Trinidad. All he needs is an honest agent who plays by the rules and trusts him completely. He has the perfect agent in mind.

•   •   •

Agent Michelle Ross sits in her office when she gets a visit from the man she has been avoiding all morning. Granderson knocks on the door and enters.

"Hey, haven't seen you at the briefing this morning," he states.

Ross pretends to be busy working and too consumed in her work to even look up. She feels that he will be able to see the sex she had with Ben written on her face. She also tries to say as little as possible, thinking he will hear guilt in her voice. She's not sure why she feels compelled to suddenly avoid sharing her personal relationship with her partner and friend, but she does just that.

"Fell behind in some paperwork, trying to catch up," she replies vaguely.

Granderson closes the office door behind him, giving them privacy. Clearly he is interested in hearing what happened after the game last night, when Ross bailed on him to meet her ex.

"So did you make it home OK last night? I texted you but you never responded," Granderson continues as he tries to read Ross' strange body language.

Before Ross can respond, supervisor Howard enters the office without knocking. He is with tech specialist agent Ling.

"Agent Ross, I need to have a word with you," announces Howard sternly.

He looks at Granderson and dismisses him by using only a cold look. Granderson totally gets the message.

"OK, so I will catch up with you later," declares Granderson to Ross.

Granderson exits but tries to make eye contact with Ross on his way out. She completely avoids it. Howard closes the door and then approaches Ross' desk.

"Yes, what it is?" questions Ross.

Howard gestures for agent Ling to take a seat. Once Ling is seated, Howard begins to address them both.

"Ross, I am officially taking you off of the Magi protection case completely. I will personally oversee that operation now that I have an important assignment for you … I guess it is related in a way. I have gotten a tip from a source, one that must remain secret for their safety ... this source has led me to believe that we have one—possibly two—rouge agents within our division," states Howard.

"I knew it! An agent must have tipped off someone on the outside about John Magi's flight to Seattle," states a perked-up Ross.

"Well, it appears your suspicions may be correct. I am asking Ling to put a tracker on the agency-provided phones of agents Chad Evans and Sarah Wang," announces Howard.

Ross and Ling appear shocked to hear this news.

"But sir, can we legally do that without an order from a federal judge?" questions Ross.

"No need for a court ruling, Ross ... to track an agent's personal phone, yes ... not an agency-provided phone. That we can do with the order of a supervising agent, so I'm ordering it," replies Howard.

Ross and Ling get the hidden message in that response: Howard is the boss—don't question him about this.

"Ross, I trust you, and I know that you are a good agent," Howard continues. "Ling will report all his findings to you and you alone. This must remain within this room ... not sure who else we can trust, so keep this close to your vest. Not even your partner can know about this."

Agent Ling smiles and feels a sense of value. He is honored to be a part of a top-secret, internal mission.

"Yes, sir. You can count on me," declares Ross.

"Yes, you can count on us," echoes Ling, clarifying that he, too, is involved.

"Very well then. I will leave you two to do your thing," states Howard before he exits.

Once Ross and Ling are alone, Ross adds an additional task to her newly appointed tech-genius partner.

"Ling, I need you to get me the text history from a civilian cell phone," announces Ross.

"I don't think I can do that without a court order," replies Ling.

Ross touches Ling's hand and looks into his eyes seductively.

"So, you can't do me a wee little favor?" states Ross flirtatiously.

Ling rolls his eyes and pulls his hand away.

"Girl, you are so not my type. Now, your hunky partner, Grand-erson ... Mercy."

Ross is shocked to discover that Ling is gay.

"Oh, I'm sorry ... I had no idea you were gay," offers Ross, stumbling slightly over her words.

"No worries, I have strict, traditional Asian parents ... I hide it well," Ling replies.

There is a moment of awkward silence.

"What is it, man trouble?" questions Ling.

Ross takes a deep breath and considers her present company.

"Just between us, I sort of hooked up with my ex last night. He is back in town and I want to know that I can trust him before he further complicates my life," confesses Ross quickly, before she can regret talking about it.

"Oh, I feel like we're girlfriends now. No problem. I will look into his text history ... you know, low key," Ling replies with a smile and a wave of his hand.

"Thanks so much ... here is his number," replies Ross. She writes Ben's cell phone number on a sticky note and hands it to agent Ling. "OK, now let's talk about Evans and Wang," she states as she shifts back into business mode.

*   *   *

John Magi is the new dish washer at the Forty-Three Bar in Queens. He has just finished his first shift and is waiting at the back employee entrance with some other kitchen employees. Most, if not all, of these employees are paid daily in cash, off the books ... this is how the owners are able to keep cheap workers, who are otherwise ineligible to work legally. This is also how John likes it. He can work, and stay off the grid.

After he is paid a small sum of cash, the grateful John takes the subway to his daughter Jamie's neighborhood. There he stands at the corner, in eye-line of her apartment building, as if he is on patrol.

Hoping for a glance of his princess, if and when she comes and goes. He wants to keep an eye on her from a distance, but he understands he must also overcome his strong desire to speak with her. He is resolved in the fact that it is best that she thinks he died in that accident many years ago, yet his instincts tell him that she needs the protection of her father. In fact, those are the exact words that were uttered to him by the freakish psychic he encountered outside of the bus station when he arrived back in New York City.

John recalls the moment he stepped out of the New York Port Authority bus station near Times Square. As he stepped out onto the busy sidewalk, the hustle and bustle of New Yorkers and tourists alike zipped by him. Looking like a tourist himself, John felt a tug on the leg of his pants. Seated on a milk crate, with a hand-written sign next to her, was an old lady. He noticed her face and clothes were extremely dirty, as well her long, crooked fingernails. She looked up at him, but her eyes were empty, as if they were unable to receive light. Initially John thought she was simply a homeless beggar, in search of spare change, but the words she spoke to him let him know that she was much more than that. After mumbling a phrase in a foreign language, she clearly spoke these words: *"Your daughter will need your eyes."*

The woman then smiled, revealing yellow-stained teeth with a gap in the middle of the top row. John felt chills race down his spine as he quickly pulled his leg away from the strange woman. The words she spoke to him went through him like a bolt of lightning. How did she know he had a daughter? Was she some sort of witch … clairvoyant … seer? Whatever she, or *it* was, the psychic message confirmed John's mission. He kept his eyes on the creepy woman as he walked away—bumping into other pedestrians as he blended into the passing crowd.

Every time John recalls the memory of that interaction, his skin gets covered in goose bumps. He is not discrediting whatever supernatural forces are at work, however he is determined to keep his eyes open and available for if and when his Jamie needs him.

CHAPTER 15

Agent Michelle Ross has made it through the rest of the day avoiding agent Granderson. Now as she exits her office and heads toward the elevator he finally catches up with her.

"Hey, seems like I haven't been able to catch you since your private meeting with the boss," states Granderson as he walks quickly to match Ross' pace.

"Yeah I know ... it's been a crazy day," she replies.

The elevator door opens and the car is empty. Ross was hoping for someone else to be present to assist in avoiding personal, non-work-related conversation. She even stalls and briefly holds the doors open in case someone else is also going down ... no such luck. The doors close, giving the longtime partners all the privacy in the world.

"So, I'm sure you heard Howard has taken us off the Magi case," states Ross in an attempt to keep things strictly business.

"Yes, I know. I understand you and Ling are working together on a new top-secret assignment," replies Granderson as he fishes for any additional information.

"Well, it is only temporary ... you and I are still partners," she replies, looking straight ahead at the elevator doors.

"Oh, no doubt. I just hope you don't get bored hanging out with a geek all day," jokes Granderson.

Ross chuckles and then endures the awkward silence hoping the elevator will stop and for someone else to join them ... preferably a group of people. She tries looking at her cell phone—pretending to check emails ... anything to distract him from asking her about last night. Granderson politely and patiently waits, as not to disturb her apparent work. After the elevator dings and the doors slide open, revealing the lobby, she finally puts her phone away and begins to walk quickly toward the large exit doors. Granderson, however, keeps up with her.

"So now that I won't see you as much, since you will be on assignment with Ling, maybe we can go grab a quick bite to eat?" he suggests.

"When ... now?" questions Ross as she makes her spinning exit through the large glass revolving door.

As she gets out to the street it is as if she is seeing a ghost ... she didn't expect to see Ben standing in front of the building on the sidewalk ... and he is holding a large arrangement of long-stemmed red roses. She displays an awkward smile of shock. Granderson spins through the revolving door behind her and is still in mid-sentence.

"Yeah now, we can go to Forty-Three Bar since you canceled on me last night," he announces before looking ahead to see Ben with open arms walking toward them.

"Hey, beautiful," states Ben as he moves in and kisses Ross on the lips.

Ross instinctively reciprocates the affection, but feels weird knowing that Granderson is standing almost shoulder to shoulder next to her. She avoids any sort of eye contact with Granderson as she hesitantly greets Ben.

"Hey ... you. What a surprise," she states with a forced smile.

"These are for you," declares Ben as he offers her the pretty roses.

"Oh, thank you ... but what's the occasion?" she asks before wincing as she realizes that his response to that question could prove rather revealing.

"Um, not in front of your coworker," replies Ben with a wink and a head nod toward Granderson.

Granderson takes offense to the fact that she didn't introduce him, and that Ben reduced him to a mere coworker.

"Excuse me, I'm agent Granderson—her partner and close friend," declares Granderson sternly as he extends his hand.

Ross can feel testosterone-fueled tension building, but doesn't know how to defuse it. Ben senses Granderson's attempt to assert his dominance through intimidation, and he resents it.

"Ah, nice to meet you. I'm Ben … also her partner and close friend," states Ben boldly as he offers his hand to Granderson.

The two men shake hands firmly, as each makes a statement, and feels an intrusion on the part of the other.

"OK … Ben, what are you doing here? I thought you had table reads until late," interjects Ross in an attempt to break up the awkward exchange as she physically pries apart the hands of the two men.

"Well we got done early so I figured I would come and take my lady out for a surprise romantic dinner," replies Ben. "And maybe a sexy horse and carriage ride in the park afterward," he adds while looking directly at Granderson.

Granderson shakes his head and chuckles under his breath. Ross is quite embarrassed.

"Well, it's been a really long day and I don't know if I'm up for anything too fancy," replies Ross.

"I'm sorry I kept you up all night, but I promise to get you to bed early tonight," replies Ben as more of a jab at Granderson.

Ross is humiliated by Ben bringing up the intimate inference from last night, and responds angrily without even thinking.

"Excuse me, but can we not discuss any details of our private moments in front of my coworker?" she barks. She doesn't want to see how this conversation may culminate if these two men continue to foolishly compete with each other like peacocks flaunting their plumage.

Granderson is clearly offended by Ross' reference of him as merely a coworker. His jaw muscle makes a twitching movement as he instinctively crosses his arms across his chest. This is definitely not how Ross wanted him to find out about her hookup with Ben.

Ben, on the other hand, bears a smirk but apologizes.

"I'm sorry. I should not have said that," he offers.

"Granderson, I'm sorry you had to hear that," states Ross as she turns and makes eye contact with her partner.

"Hey, no worries. We're all adults here," Granderson replies. He doesn't look at her, instead focusing on the cars aggressively maneuvering past them on the street. She sees his eyes are clouded with hurt and that he feels betrayed. "I should be getting home anyway, so you two love birds have a good night."

Ross watches Granderson walk away and she can feel the emotional sting that he must be experiencing. Her body almost instinctively turns to go after him, but she gets a tug from Ben.

"I got us tentative reservations at Minnie Huang's. Let's hurry before they give our table away," announces Ben as he pulls her into the street while hailing a cab.

Ross looks back in Granderson's direction but he is no longer in sight. Suddenly Ross has lost her appetite. A taxi pulls up and stops. Ben opens the rear passenger door.

"Sorry, Ben, but I was just assigned a new case by my supervisor and I really just want to go home, take a hot bath and get in bed," Ross states.

"That sounds like a great way to spend the evening ... Come on, let's go," he replies.

"No, I meant alone. I'm tired and just want to be alone," she clarifies.

She leans in and kisses him on the cheek and then she gets into the cab. She gives the driver her address and then turns back to Ben.

"Maybe another night. Thank you for the beautiful roses," she states with a smile.

She closes the door and the cab drives off, leaving Ben standing with a puzzled look on his face.

•   •   •

John Magi has a puzzled look on his face as he watches activity out-side of Jamie's apartment building. Since he has been loitering on the four corners of this intersection for the past couple of hours, this is the first time he is seeing anything out of the ordinary tonight. John looks on discreetly as Jamie's boyfriend abruptly exits her apart-ment building and quickly limps to the corner directly across from where John is standing. There, Kyle meets with a young woman, and they both appear to not want to be seen together. John watches the brief, yet seemingly significant interaction between Kyle and the young lady.

.   .   .

Kyle looks nervous as he approaches Montez.

"Hurry up, she just got in the shower," states Kyle.

"OK, here. Make sure she thinks it's all your idea," replies Montez as she hands him a small jewelry box.

"I can't believe she told you that I have never surprised her be-fore," Kyle says as he hides the small box in his sock.

"Just make sure it remains a surprise—do NOT mention my name, and wait until you get up to the camp to give it to her. Now hurry up before she notices that you're gone," suggests Montez.

"I got this," replies Kyle before he quickly limps back to Jamie's building and then disappears behind the second lobby door.

Montez walks in the opposite direction and out of sight.

.   .   .

As John sits on the sidewalk, propped against the corner building, he is completely disturbed by the meeting that he just witnessed. He was unable to hear any verbal exchange, but he knows that Jamie's boyfriend appeared very suspicious and downright sneaky as he met with another attractive female. He also saw the young woman give Kyle something that he hid in his sock. Was this something as sim-ple as a local campus pot dealer giving two college kids their usual dime bag? Or was the meeting something much more sinister? In order to get more information, John needs to know more about the mystery girl who slipped something to Kyle. John decides to abandon his post outside Jamie's apartment building, and follow the young woman.

•   •   •

As John begins to stand to his feet, a pair of designer leather shoes steps in front of him. Suddenly a man standing over him—well within the perimeter of his personal space—approaches aggressively. The man is Anthony Greenberg-Silvestri.

"Mr. Wonderful, in the flesh!" states Anthony in a sinister tone.

The thug reaches down and applies a stun gun right onto John's collarbone ... rendering him incapacitated.

•   •   •

Every time the phone rings, Katherine West becomes a ball of nerves and emotions. Every time she thinks that she is prepared to play along with the FBI's plan to set up a meeting with John, she completely forgets her rehearsed lines and doubts that she can carry on even the briefest conversation with him. Her anger toward him is the easiest of emotions to describe and name. The rest just stir up further confusion. She hopes the FBI can catch up to him without her assistance, and she can avoid any contact with him, but if he does decide to reach out again, she would like it to be tonight ... before she leaves in the morning to spend a camping weekend with her new husband and daughter. That way she does not have to bear the very uncomfortable conversation with Jerron or Jamie at all.

As Katherine completes the final packing of food and snacks for the weekend trip, she has the cordless phone next to her. The last thing she wants to ruin her family weekend is her "late husband" calling and having her current husband answer.

She jumps and grabs the cordless home phone when she hears the ringing ... however it is actually her cell phone that has an incoming call. Her daughter Jamie shows up on the caller ID.

•   •   •

The reason for Jamie's excitement exceeds the expectations of a fun--filled weekend of camping. She calls her mother with her voice filled with glee.

"Mom, guess what? I think Kyle is going to propose to me this weekend!" Jamie gushes with excitement.

She looks to make sure Kyle is still out on the couch watching television, and she attempts to contain her exuberance and keep her voice at a minimum while sharing the news.

"Well no, he hasn't said anything yet … I think he wants to do it up by Taconic Mountain, overlooking the lake. It's very scenic there, and he mentioned taking a romantic hike," she continues.

She periodically checks on Kyle's whereabouts as she quietly shares with her mother.

"Well no, but when I got out of the shower, I heard him moving around so I peeked out the bathroom door and I saw him hide a small jewelry box in his weekend bag … No, I am not going to look at it, Mom! I want to be surprised and in that special moment, at the peak of the mountain, I want to see my engagement ring for the first time," she continues with a huge grin.

She listens as her mom shares in her excitement.

"I think you're right … he must want to get your blessing, and Jerron's, too. Old fashioned, and I like it. I am so relieved that you are happy for me, and not telling me that we're too young," she continues.

.   .   .

Katherine wipes a couple of tears from her eyes as she sits at the kitchen table chatting with her daughter. These are tears of joy as she shares a touching moment between mother and daughter. She also recalls her youth as well.

"I am happy for you, dear … and no, I will never tell you that you're too young or not ready … your father and I were younger than you kids when we got married. Besides, getting engaged before college graduation and entering the business world is common. I am proud of Kyle for stepping up and claiming what he wants for his future," she declares.

*　　　*　　　*

Jamie does an excited happy-dance in her mirror, and then realizes that she needs a manicure ... a realization that takes her excitement level up a notch, yet she tries to keep her voice down.

"Oh, crap! I was planning on roughing it this weekend ... I can't get engaged with camping hands! I need to do my nails ... my first photo of the ring on my finger must be social-media ready! Mom, I have to go! Don't say anything, not even to Jerron ... and when Kyle asks for your blessing, act surprised, OK? See you in the morning. Love you, too," Jamie rattles off into her phone.

After hanging up with her mom, Jamie peeks out in the living room once more. She takes a moment and stares at Kyle as he watches television. Then she returns to her bedroom mirror where she takes a few cracks at practicing her "surprised" face.

CHAPTER 16

After agent Michelle Ross completes her morning workout, she normally goes to her favorite coffee spot to get her favorite specialty drink before heading home to shower and get dressed for work. Her weekend routine is a bit different as she skips her running and goes to kickboxing class, spin class, and then maybe a weight-training session. Then she goes to her favorite coffee spot to get her favorite specialty drink. This morning, however, she is bypassing her workouts altogether and going directly to her favorite coffee spot ... to get her favorite specialty drink, and meet with a certain FBI tech genius.

Ross is already seated and enjoying her cinnamon dolce latte when agent Ling walks into the busy café that is packed with weekend hobby writers and hipsters. Ross waves him over to a small table in the corner and pulls out a chair that she held for him. She has also taken the liberty of ordering three lattes—assuming he would enjoy it as much as she does.

As Ling takes a seat across from Ross he greets her and immediately removes his tablet from his khaki-colored canvas shoulder bag.

"Hey, boss lady ... sorry to be late but I had to download the messages off my server," states Ling.

Sensing by his tone that he may be stalling, Ross slides one of the beverages toward Ling with her left hand, while snatching his tablet with her right. Ling winces and then quickly holds the drink up to his face, anticipating her reaction to the text messages to and from Ben's phone.

Ross has no visible reaction at all … and that makes Ling all the more anxious.

"So, that lying piece of scum! When was he going to tell me that he is having a baby with the girl he was living with in California?" mumbles Ross nonchalantly out loud.

Ling's eyes are opened wide as he is not sure if she expects a response from him, or if it was merely rhetorical babble. Either way, her calmness is unnerving. Ross continues to read the series of text messages but her facial expression doesn't change at all.

"Hmmm, he tells her that he will be staying with a cast buddy named Michael … I guess people in California pronounce *Michelle* as *Michael,*" she says while looking at Ling.

Ling forces a fake smile and chugs a sip from his drink. The awkwardness is wreaking havoc on his introverted personality. His eyes open even wider when she looks at the front door and then at the time on her phone.

"Ah, right on time. Excuse me," states Ross as she stands up from the table.

Ling is not sure what Ross is doing, but her unnaturally calm demeanor concerns him, given the circumstances. She picks up the third latte and carries it as she calmly walks to the front door and then exits the café. Lings turns to watch and can see out through the large glass windows as Ben stands with his arms open, expecting a warm embrace. However, he gets a face full of warm liquid instead, followed by an earful from a pissed-off Ross. Ling covers his mouth in disbelief and then quickly turns back around and sits up in his chair as if he did not just witness that scene. As Ben stands drenched and confused as to how his secret came out, Ross calmly walks back into the café and takes her seat across from Ling.

"So, I take it you invited your ex here … but how did you know I would find such dirt on him?" asks a timid Ling.

"I didn't know what you would find. Regardless, that was a break-up drink. I figured either way he would be sharing a drink or wearing a drink," replies Ross.

"Remind me never to tick you off," jokes Ling in an attempt to break the tension.

Ross smiles and then holds up her cup to toast. Ling holds his cup up as well.

"Here's to avoiding another HUGE mistake!" cheers Ross.

"How huge are we talking, girl?" jokes Ling like a mischievous teenage girl.

"Ugh, don't be gross!" replies Ross.

Ling laughs uncontrollably, in turn causing Ross to laugh as well.

"OK, now let's talk about running background on Evans and Wang," she states, getting back to business mode.

.   .   .

Jamie Magi barely slept a wink last night as the excitement of the weekend's events kept her awake. She has already planned her entire wedding in her head—the venue, the color scheme, the bridal party … all she needed was the groom, and he is just waking up next to her.

As Kyle opens his eyes, Jamie is dressed and in full makeup already.

"Good morning, sleepy head … how are you feeling?" she greets with a kiss on his forehead.

Kyle is a bit surprised to see her already up and dressed.

"Good morning. Wow, someone's excited to go camping," he replies.

"Oh yes! This will be an epic weekend! I can feel it. I can't wait to spend it with you … my rock … my jewel," she replies.

Jamie's love-struck gaze and terminology creep him out a bit, and he automatically thinks she knows about the surprise gift he stashed away.

"You know, babe, my life really sparkles by having you in it," she continues.

Kyle's suspicion grows deeper as she continues to act weird. He looks directly over to his weekend bag to see if the pocket where he hid the box is opened. It is as he left it, but when he looks back at Jamie, she has a huge anticipatory smile. He can't take the pressure.

"You know what? I have a surprise for you," he states.

"What? For me?" replies Jamie with an exaggerated fake shocked expression.

"Yes, let me get it for you," he replies.

As Kyle gets up and moves toward his bag, Jamie freaks out.

"Wait ... right now?" she replies.

"Yeah," he replies as he reaches for his bag.

"You mean right here?" Jamie replies

Kyle places his bag on the foot of the bed.

"Not up on Taconic Mountain overlooking the lake?" she continues.

Kyle unzips the pocket of the bag.

"Before talking to my mom ... before brushing your teeth?" she states, almost irritated.

Kyle looks at her as if she has two heads.

"What?" he asks as he takes the box out and hides it behind his back.

"OK, so I guess you are injured so you can't get down on one knee," she mumbles under her breath.

This is not her ideal scenario, or at least the way she envisioned all through the night. But she knows that she is in love with him, and is prepared to say yes either way. She smiles and accepts this as the moment she will never forget ... the story she will tell their children.

"Sorry, I don't mean to interrupt you. Go ahead, babe," she states with a loving smile.

Kyle continues to hold the small box behind his back.

"I know that I may not often do sweet things...surprise you and show you how much you mean to me, but I want to make you a promise starting today," he states.

Jamie's eyes light up and she pretends to be surprised when Kyle reveals the little red box and offers it to her.

"Aw, babe?" she replies as she takes the box in her hand. "Do you want to record this or take a photo with your phone or something?" she asks.

"No, just open it, silly," he replies.

Jamie opens the box with a premeditated expression. She maintains the expression, which turns to a genuine surprised look. Kyle has a gigantic smile as he awaits her response.

"Wow! A beautiful pair of earrings," she states, forcing a smile.

.   .   .

Katherine turns off the lights in the garage and punches in the code to arm the home security alarm system. She then briskly walks out of the garage, which closes behind her. She gets into the front passenger seat of their sport utility vehicle where Jerron is waiting for her with the engine running. They pull out of the driveway and head to the nearby Long Island Rail Road Station where Jamie and Kyle are waiting.

"Don't tell her I said anything ... and for crying out loud, try to act surprised," says Katherine to her husband.

Jerron only smiles, which makes Katherine uneasy. She punches his arm.

"I'm serious! She would never forgive me if she knew I told you," she continues.

Her phone rings and she answers it on the first ring.

"Honey, we are on our way ... I know, we are running a little late," says Katherine into her phone.

"It's all your mom's fault—she tried on six different outfits!" yells Jerron.

Katherine rolls her eyes at him.

"We are just passing the gas station now ... should be there in less than ten minutes ... see you in a bit," she continues before ending the call.

"It's all your mom's fault … she tried on six different outfits," Katherine repeats mockingly. "Well, excuse me for wanting to look perfect for my husband," she continues playfully.

·   ·   ·

John Magi has been handcuffed and shackled in the back of this cargo van all night. He presumes that his captors must have drugged him, because he is loopy and keeps slipping in and out of consciousness. He can tell that it is daylight by the beams of sunlight creeping in through some crevices and cracks in the rusty steel floor. In his semi-sedated state, he cannot be sure how long the van has been travelling since he first felt movement this morning. Two things he does know: this is not the method of the FBI, and he is in serious danger.

John tries speaking to yell for help, but he is far too weak to utter a sound. He barely musters up enough strength to lift his head to see a collection of chains and other rusty metal tools that are known methods of torture used by mobsters. John simply drops his head and buries his face against the van floor. Things look grim, and he accepts that his past has finally caught up with him. He has spent the last 15 years questioning every life decision he has ever made, and now in this moment, he deeply regrets them all. He guessed this is exactly how it would all end for him … begging for his life in the back of a rusty old vehicle.

·   ·   ·

Kyle and Jamie load their bags into the back of the vehicle and then close the trunk. Katherine steps out and walks to the back of the van to greet them.

"Hey, you two. So … all ready for a memorable weekend?" asks Katherine.

Her tone and demeanor are completely obvious and transparent. Jamie rolls her eyes and waves her hand across her throat to indicate to her mother of the "false alarm." Katherine is completely confused. Jamie realizes that her mother did not get her subtle hint, so she adjusts her hair behind her ears to reveal the new earrings.

"Hey, Mom, look at the pretty earrings Kyle gave me," states Jamie as she walks past Katherine and enters the vehicle through the rear passenger door.

Kyle maintains a goofy smile and gets into the vehicle through the rear driver's side door.

"Ah ... what a nice surprise," Katherine replies as she realizes that Kyle's surprise was not an engagement ring.

Katherine gets back into the vehicle in the front passenger side, closes the door and buckles her seatbelt. She keeps her eyes straight ahead, but can feel Jerron staring at her.

"Not a word, mister ... not a word," states Katherine while keeping her head and eyes straight ahead.

Jerron puts the vehicle in gear, and drives toward the highway.

"How about some music?" asks Katherine as she presses the car stereo's on button.

The radio comes on blasting:

We'll forever be in love, so there ain't no need to rush.
But one day I won't be able to ask you loud enough.
I'll say, "Will you marry me?"
I swear that I will mean it.
I'll say, "Will you marry me?"
Ooooh whoa, oooh oh.

Jamie shakes her head and rolls her eyes.

"OK, wake me when we stop for brunch," states Jamie with sass.

She covers her head with her jacket and buries her head in Kyle's lap. Katherine and Jerron try to contain their laughter at the awkwardness. This is going to be an interesting trip.

.   .   .

After travelling several miles along the New York State highway, Jerron, Katherine, Jamie and Kyle stop to have brunch, and then pull into a gas station to fill up before entering the mountainous highway up to Camp Taconic. After fueling up, the SUV pulls back onto the highway ... behind them, a black cargo van pulls out and follows. The SUV enters the Taconic Highway, and so does the black cargo van.

The cargo van follows behind at a close distance—maintaining a steady pace to match the SUV.

The driver of the black cargo van is Anthony Greenberg-- Silvestri ... his unwilling passenger ... John "Mr. Wonderful" Magi.

CHAPTER 17

After agents Ross and Ling wrap up their briefing and note-sharing meeting in the café, they both exit and go their separate ways. Ross is not heading home, but to visit her long-time partner, Granderson.

When Ross arrives at agent Granderson's Chelsea apartment, he is turning the key to his front door and balancing a large bag of freshly washed laundry and a couple of bags of groceries. Ross sees him struggling, steps in and tugs the laundry bag away to allow him a free hand to unlock and open his front door. Granderson seems quite surprised to see her, but welcomes the extra pair of hands.

Granderson turns the key, pushes the door and steps in, holding the door open as an invitation for Ross to enter his apartment. Still not having said a word to one another, the two partners walk through the entryway and down the short hallway to the kitchen. Granderson places the grocery bags on the kitchen counter and takes the laundry bag from Ross.

"Thanks, coworker," offers Granderson in a semi-rude tone.

"You're welcome ... friend," Ross replies with emphasis.

Granderson ignores her attempt to talk about the elephant in the room and carries the laundry into his bedroom. While alone in the kitchen, Ross notices a photo of her and Granderson from an office holiday party posted on his refrigerator. She walks closer to examine it, and finds herself smiling as she recalls the fun time they had that evening. There is also another group photo taken at that same party in which she and Granderson are standing together and she is kissing him on the cheek. She chuckles at that memory. She then removes a gallon of milk and a carton of eggs from one of the grocery bags and places them in the refrigerator.

"So, what brings you by a coworker's home on a Saturday morning?" asks Granderson sarcastically as he re-enters the kitchen.

Ross turns around and faces him.

"Look, I'm sorry about last night ... Ben was a prick ... IS a prick. I didn't mean what I said, or rather it didn't come out right ... you know you are more to me than just a coworker," she says.

"Ross, you don't have to sugarcoat things. I was just looking out for you. Your romantic relationship is none of my business. I just don't want things to be awkward between us," he replies.

"I don't want things to be awkward between us either, that's why I try so hard to fight ..." Ross pauses and decides to change the subject. "I see you bought breakfast items, how about I make us a nice brunch?" she says as she turns back to open the refrigerator door.

Granderson steps to the refrigerator and pushes the door back closed. Ross turns and is now eyeball to eyeball with him. Her natural instinct is to step back away to regain her personal space, but her back is up against the refrigerator door.

"That's why you try so hard to fight what?" asks Granderson as he moves in even closer to her.

She inhales quickly with almost a gasp as his physical closeness sends her brain into emotional overload. She turns her head away to the side and politely slides to her right, stepping away. Granderson leans his weight on to the refrigerator and continues to face it. Now behind him and slowly stepping away and out of the kitchen, Ross turns back around and addresses her attractive partner from a safe distance.

"I don't want to get all weird, I just wanted to come here to make sure things were not left unresolved before we go into the office on Monday," she states.

Granderson turns around to face her, and now leans his back up against the refrigerator. He drags his hand from his forehead down along his face in frustration, before looking directly at her.

"I'd say things between us have been unresolved for a while now ... ever since San Diego," he replies.

"San Diego was a mistake ... what ALMOST happened in San Diego was a mistake," she replies. Her face is flush as she thinks back to the evening the two of them almost took their work partnership to a more personal one.

"Can you look me in the eye and say that you haven't thought about that night? Because I can't stop thinking about it," admits Granderson as he lifts his back off of the refrigerator and stands upright.

"What?" Ross replies nervously, avoiding direct eye contact.

"Can you look me in the eye and say that you haven't thought about it?" he restates slowly as he steps a little closer to her.

His presence seems to push her backward, as her back is now up against the kitchen counter. He steps closely in and grabs her by her waist. Ross is now looking him eye to eye as he lifts her up and sits her onto the counter, and steps in closely.

"I don't think this is a good idea," she whispers before swallowing a ball of built-up emotion.

Respectfully, a rejected Granderson steps away from the counter. Before he can define his feeling as embarrassment and humiliation, Ross leaps off the counter and into his arms. As the surprised Granderson catches her and secures her body weight, he receives her mouth onto his. The passionate kiss, which feels long overdue to both partners, pauses momentarily as Ross pulls her T--shirt over her head and drops it to the floor. She seems perfectly free and comfortable.

As they continue to kiss passionately, Granderson lifts her and carries her out of the kitchen and into his bedroom. He continues to kiss her as he gently lays her down sideways onto his bed. Still planted on the floor, he stands to remove his shirt and unbutton his jeans. Looking up at him with lusty eyes and heavy breathing, Ross kicks off her sneakers, and then lifts her butt up off the bed to slide her yoga pants and panties down to her ankles. After stepping out of his jeans, Granderson pulls Ross' pants and underwear off the rest of the way, past her feet.

By digging her heels into the bed, Ross shifts her body toward the center of the queen-size bed, and receives Granderson's upper body weight as he mounts the bed on his knees. They continue to kiss on the lips and each other's neck, but Ross seems to need no further foreplay ... it appears that these two have been engaging in foreplay since that night in San Diego.

Ross reaches down and wraps her hand around Granderson's impressive manhood. He moans as her soft, warm hand strokes his pulsating erection. Granderson reaches underneath her and un-hooks her bra, exposing her perky breasts and erect nipples. As his mouth explores them, she gasps and fidgets her entire body. The per-fect combination of his tongue and teeth pushes her into a level of ecstasy that she has never experienced. She finds it difficult to keep her eyes open as his fingers caress her groin—occasionally entering inside of her soft, welcoming moistness.

Ross can feel an internal eruption building with every mo-ment—every wet kiss—every gentle nibble—every strong stroke of his manly hands. She finds her own hand rapidly building speed as she rubs his stiff, throbbing flesh. They both moan as they continue to manually pleasure each other. Not wanting him to climax before she can experience him inside of her, she guides the tip of his erec-tion directly to her wet entryway and pulls his torso close to her chest. With her heels against the back of his thighs, she invites him deep into her as she moans with delight. Ross throws her head from side to side and bites her bottom lip as her body adjusts to Grander-son's penetrating length and girth—stretching her beyond comfort, yet yielding thrilling gratification. Her fingernails press into his muscular back as her legs begin to quiver uncontrollably. Her rapid breathing matches the pace of his deep, powerful and consistent thrusts. Her eyes roll to the back of her head, and her mouth opens wide, but she cannot produce any sound as her body erupts from an internal explosion of pleasure.

As she catches her breath and finally produces a verbal indication of orgasm, Granderson quickly pulls out of her and falls on top of her convulsing body. As they both struggle to regain normal breathing patterns, she can feel his thick, warm flowing semen oozing onto her belly and running along her ribs.

Even after they both somewhat regain normal breathing, neither speaks a word. Instead they hold onto each other and bask in an incredible moment that they want to stretch out for as long as possible.

After several minutes of complete stillness, Granderson rises off of Ross. The dried-up, sticky mess between their abdomens causes them to chuckle awkwardly. As they can no longer avoid eye contact, the two partners who have just taken their work relationship into the realm of professionally inappropriate gaze at one another for a moment. Then suddenly—without speaking a single word—as if to mutually indicate that they have no regrets, they slowly kiss and keep their bodies intertwined. Right here ... right now ... is exactly where Ross and Granderson want to be. No concern about work, or office protocol ... alone in this perfect moment ... is all that matters.

CHAPTER 18

The SUV rolls along the winding backwoods dirt road, kicking up a plume of light dust as it navigates around the serene crystal water of Camp Taconic—a perfect getaway of sweeping acres, 200 miles from the city. For the past couple of hours the group of weekend campers has been travelling up the New York State highways, parkways, and interstates. Within minutes, they will arrive at their rental cabin.

When they pull up to their home for the weekend, all are pleased to finally be out of the car, and impressed by the scenic view that their rental property provides of the vast lake. Everyone pauses to breathe in the fresh air—unpolluted by overcrowded roads like in the city—as well as to take in the stunningly breathtaking view.

After the four cabin guests unload the SUV and carry their bags inside, a black cargo van drives up slowly and parks off to the side of the road, where thick brush conceals it. The van driver, Anthony Silvestri, turns the engine off and then turns to the back and addresses his captive passenger.

"Well, Mr. Wonderful, looks like we are finally here," he announces with a monotone demeanor.

John Magi is still experiencing the effects of being heavily sedated. He struggles to lift his head or even open his eyes.

"Don't worry, the sedative should wear off soon enough ... just in time for the big family reunion," Anthony states as he looks at his watch.

The driver's side of the hidden cargo van is flush against the think brush, so Anthony uses the front passenger door to exit the van. He then slides the side cargo door open just enough to retrieve a metal spade-like shovel with a long, wooden handle. He slides the door closed and walks back to the front passenger door. He reaches into the glove box and pulls out a silver 38-caliber revolver. After checking the cylinder to confirm that the weapon is fully loaded, he tucks it in the small of his back, and then looks to the cargo area and addresses his captive once more.

"Be right back ... got to get the family plot started," he announces coldly.

He closes the front passenger door, and then casually hoists the shovel over his right shoulder as he walks down the path to the trees at the back of the cabin. He whistles as he walks.

.   •̣   •

Inside the spacious, three-bedroom cabin, Katherine stores groceries and snacks away in the pantry, while Jamie fills a kettle with water to make a cup of tea. While Kyle starts a fire in the large, stone fireplace in the living room, Jerron goes out back to gather more firewood.

"So, no engagement ring?" asks Katherine quietly to Jamie now that they are alone.

"No, I guess I jumped to conclusions. Never make assumptions, and you won't have unrealistic expectations ... lesson learned," Jamie replies.

"Well, they are really nice earrings, honey," Katherine replies.

"I do like them. He has great taste in jewelry," Jamie replies as she checks her earrings out, using the shiny kettle as a mirror.

"So when the time comes to get the ring, at least you know it will be lovely," Katherine says with a smile.

"Yeah, it better be," replies Jamie.

After sharing a brief laugh, the tone shifts.

"Mom, how did you know that dad was 'the one'?" Jamie asks.

This question takes Katherine by surprise and off guard. She was trying to use this weekend getaway to escape any talk of John, yet here she is—less than 20 minutes of arriving, and John, and their past, is already coming up.

"Well ... honey, when you are with the right man, you just know it. There is no timeframe or written guideline to tell you when it is right. Your heart is the only indicator you need," replies Katherine.

"So many couples think it's right and just end up getting divorced after things get rough. I don't want to become another statistic," Jamie replies.

Katherine looks at her daughter with admiration at how she has grown into a young woman that reminds her so much of herself. She almost feels guilty for keeping the news of John's existence a secret ... but strongly believes that it is better that she not know.

"I'm sure you and dad would still be together if he were still alive," states Jamie.

That statement stings Katherine as she has considered that theory for years ... When Jerron was courting her aggressively, she wasn't ready to move on right away. Even after she married Jerron, Katherine cannot honestly say that she hasn't thought about the *what ifs*.

Before Katherine can find the proper response, the kettle whistles as the water on the stove comes to a boil. Kyle enters the kitchen and breaks up the mother-daughter conversation.

"Well, me ladies, we have fire," declares Kyle in a horrible attempt at an Irish accent.

*   *   *

At agent Granderson's apartment, agent Michelle Ross is stepping out of the shower. She wraps a towel around herself and uses a second one to wrap her wet hair. She possesses a certain glow that is specific to sexual gratification. As she stands gazing at her smiling reflection in the bathroom mirror, Granderson enters the bathroom with a towel around his naked body. He steps behind her and wraps his arms around her, with his forearms planted at the base of her breasts. Ross folds her arms onto his, and rests her head back onto his shoulder as he sensually kisses her neck. She lets her weight fall back into him as she allows herself to completely relax in his touch. She can feel his growing excitement pressing firmly against her ample rump. She wiggles her hips gently—acknowledging the presence of his continuously swelling organ. He nibbles her ear as her grinding intensifies his passion, and increases his desire for her well-sculpted femininity. His heart races as she tilts her pelvis forward slightly to create a gap between their bodies, in which she can reach her hand back, pull his towel free, and grab a handful of his thickening shaft. She repeatedly squeezes him in her hand while making her way from the tip to the base, and eventually cupping his testicles, massaging them as her back squeezes his full erection against his abdomen. He tugs at her towel until it falls to the bathroom floor. He then turns her around, lifts her up and sets her onto the bathroom sink. She pulls him toward her and opens her legs—welcoming him inside her slippery pink love. He enters her slowly and solidly until his pelvic bone meets hers. The hot and lusty duo makes love repeatedly, as if making up for lost time. It is as if they are the only two people on the planet, and nothing else matters. Even several missed calls from agent Ling to Ross' phone go unreturned. Granderson and Ross are completely lost in each other's presence.

.   .   .

Agent Ling has been trying to reach agent Ross on her cell phone, but with no luck. After their meeting at the café, Ross suggested that Ling should check all of Salvatore Mongelli's known associates and see if he can trace any of them to having contact with agents Evans and Wang. During his probing, he discovered something very vital and needs to get in touch with Ross. Although Howard instructed Ling to report only to Ross, with such time-sensitive information, Ling makes the decision to reach out directly to Howard.

Agent Ling is on the phone with supervising agent Howard.

"What is so urgent that you are calling me on a Saturday afternoon, Ling? And didn't I tell you to report to agent Ross?" questions Howard with irritation.

"I apologize, sir, but this cannot wait, and I can't seem to be able to reach agent Ross," replies a flustered Ling.

"I take it this has to do with Evans or Wang?" inquires Howard.

"Yes ... well, no, sir ... not exactly," replies Ling.

"You're trying my patience, Ling," replies Howard.

"Sorry, I was initially running background on agent Evans and agent Wang," announces Ling.

"OK, and?" questions Howard.

"Well, as Ross suggested at our briefing this morning, I cross referenced all known Mongelli associates to see if there had been any contact between them and the suspect agents, to see which one of them tipped off the person or persons responsible for the attempted assassination of John Magi. There was no connection there, but I did come across something crazy," Ling explains.

This has piqued Howard's interest, as he is curious to know if Ling's discovery, whatever it may be, has any bearing on his personal plans or vested financial interests.

"I'm listening," announces Howard inquisitively.

"Well, Sal Mongelli has a cousin named Richie Silvestri, who is serving consecutive life sentences for several convictions, including the executions of three federal agents. I ran deep background on Richie and it turns out he is NOT the last of the Mongelli bloodline," declares Ling.

Howard is puzzled. He is beginning to come to the realization that perhaps there is more to tying up his "loose ends" than simply killing John Magi.

"Go on," replies Howard.

"Richie had a girlfriend ... a Jewish girl named Hannah Greenberg. It is believed that Richie had Hannah murdered because she refused to let their offspring take the last name of a man who would not marry her ... and the Mongelli family had a thing against mixing Italian blood with any other groups. So the Greenberg name has not been on the FBI's radar for all these years. One in particular who has visited Silvestri recently...Anthony Greenberg," announces Ling.

Howard is pacing and growing nervous. He is trying to think of his next move. If there is a Mongelli relative out there, it is a good chance that they also know about the diamond heist. Howard has already thrown his accomplices, Evans and Wang, to the slaughter by setting up their agency phones to link them to the attempted murder of Magi and make them appear as mob-bought moles. He must utilize them one final time before Ross and Ling discover the planted data evidence in their phones. He needs to locate John Magi and silence him before Mongelli's boy tracks him down first. Word of the transfer of the diamonds from Magi to Howard must be buried with Magi once and for all. Time is not on Howard's side.

"So one of our agents tipped off Silvestri's kid for the hit on Magi ... Good work, Ling. See you Monday. Bye," Howard quickly rattles off before abruptly hanging up.

Ling thinks that Howard is still on the line and tries to finish reporting his discovery.

"That's not all. Silvestri had two sons with Hannah Greenberg ... twins, Tony and Jerry ... Anthony and JERRON," Announces Ling with a big emphasis.

He pauses, expecting a spectacular response from supervisor Howard. The silence on the other end of the call puzzles Ling. He initially thinks that Howard doesn't realize the depth of his findings.

"John Magi's wife is married to one of Richie Silvestri's sons!" Ling announces proudly—expecting praise.

There is still no response from Howard.

"Hello ... Sir?" says Ling into the phone before pulling it away to see that the call has been ended.

CHAPTER 19

As agents Michelle Ross and Steve Granderson share a bottle of red wine and snacks in bed, they avoid any talk of what effect the events of the day may have on their professional working relationship. Ross is wearing nothing but one of Granderson's long, white T-shirts, and he is lounging in his boxers and tank top.

As the duo sip from their glasses, and exchange sexually charged banter while feeding one another bite-sized morsels, the doorbell rings aggressively, followed by rapid, continuous knocking at the front door.

Not expecting company, or wanting anyone to know that he has crossed the line with his law-enforcement partner, Granderson gets out of bed and closes the bedroom door before answering the front door.

When he opens the front door to see who is knocking so aggressively, he finds agent Ling at the door with a frantic look on his face. Ling's face quickly shifts from panic to passion as he takes a gander at Granderson's muscular shoulders and chiseled biceps.

"Sweet Boy George and Madonna!" states Ling as he fans himself.

Granderson is clearly confused to see Ling at his home.

"Ling? What are you doing here?" questions Granderson.

Granderson closes the door just enough so he can fit his body in the jamb, while making certain Ling cannot see inside of his apartment ... or more specifically, his current company. After a quick glance down at Granderson's boxer shorts, Ling regains his composure and gets down to the reason for his unexpected visit.

"Sorry to bother you on your day off and drop by unannounced, but I've been trying to reach agent Ross. She is not answering her phone, so I went to her apartment, but she doesn't seem to be home," Ling states quickly before pausing.

Ling's abrupt pause and furrowed brow suggest that he is drawing a conclusion in his mind. He shifts his head and neck in an attempt to see behind the much taller Granderson. Granderson picks up on this and shifts his body in unison as he mirrors Ling.

Ross, who had been checking her voicemails left by Ling on her phone, bolts out of the bedroom with her phone in hand, and pushes her way in between Granderson and the doorjamb.

"Is this for real?" she questions in a panic.

Smiling as he looks at the two agents standing side by side, scantily clad in the doorway, Ling rudely invites himself into the apartment—walking in between Granderson and Ross.

"Talk about rebounding quickly," he mumbles.

Granderson looks at Ling in disbelief as the suddenly flamboyant man confidently makes his way into the apartment. Ross is looking at her messages on her phone as she walks in with Ling. Granderson shakes his head as he is completely out of the loop.

Ross and Granderson stand side by side in the hallway in front of his half-opened bedroom door, as Ling gets them up to speed.

"What the heck, Ling? Why didn't you contact me ASAP? This is major!" says Ross while still reading the many texts and emails sent by Ling.

"Um, I *tried* to contact you … but it seems like you may have been … tied up all afternoon," replies Ling as he shifts his head and neck in an attempt to look inside of the bedroom.

Granderson quickly shuts the bedroom door behind him.

"We have to alert supervisor Howard," states Ross as she begins to dial his number in her phone.

"I already did. I couldn't reach you, and I felt it was urgent, so I called Howard and told him everything," replies Ling.

"Can somebody please tell *me* what's going on?" interjects Granderson.

"Sal Mongelli's cousin is Richie Silvestri," replies Ross as she abandons her call to Howard.

"The guy is serving multiple life sentences … why is he a threat?" replies Granderson.

"Not him … his sons," replies Ross.

Ross rushes into the bedroom to get dressed. Granderson is still confused as he looks at Ling for further elaboration. Ling is proud to have more knowledge than the experienced field agent … for once.

"Jerron West … is really Jerry Silvestri," announces Ling.

Ling takes another full-body gander at Granderson. Granderson is visibly uncomfortable by the adoration, so he joins Ross in the bedroom to get dressed as well—closing the door behind him. A smiling and mischievous Ling steps up to the bedroom door and presses his ear against it.

"I'll just wait out here," he announces.

.   .   .

In the woods of Camp Taconic, twin brothers Anthony and Jerron share a long-overdue hug. The brothers have been on a secret assignment for their father, Richie Silvestri. For several years, the two siblings have avoided being seen together as they strived to maintain their secret blood relation to the infamous mob boss, Salvatore Mongelli, whom they knew as Uncle Sal. Today is a special family reunion. With Anthony's hair color and significant weight difference, the two men don't look at all like twins. However, their undying support of their father, Richie, is identical in both passion and commitment. Another commonality these two brothers share is their greed and desire of great wealth … hence their intense agenda.

Shortly after John Magi's alleged death, Sal Mongelli devised a plan to obtain information as to the whereabouts of the stashed diamonds. Suspecting that Magi's death may have been faked by the feds to protect him, Jerron would go under an alias and woo the newly grieving widow. Since Magi was such a devoted family man, Mongelli figured that news of a new man in his wife's life would quickly draw him out of hiding. And if the death of Magi was real, then Jerron could gain the trust of the widow, and discover where the diamonds were. When Sal Mongelli died in the car chase with the FBI and Richie Silvestri took the fall for the revenge killings of three federal agents, the plan shifted from recovery to revenge. Although the Silvestri brothers are seeking revenge for their family honor, there is no doubt that they are not just interested in settling a score … but very motivated by obtaining the big score … to the tune of $3 billion.

After winning over Katherine's heart and getting her to marry him, Jerron slowly discovered that she had no knowledge of the heist or where Magi hid the diamonds. Jerron knew that he was in it for the long haul, and would one day get to this moment, when he and his brother would outsmart the FBI and finally claim the reward Sal, the head of their family empire, died over.

As the two men embrace, they both declare a phrase in the native tongue of their Italian ancestors: *"Per la famiglia, per homor."* For family, for honor.

*   *   *

Granderson drives his navy sedan along the West Side Highway. Ross is in the front passenger seat, and Ling is in the driver's side rear. They exit the highway uptown and pull up to a brownstone home in the upper west side of Manhattan.

"I'm confused. Didn't Howard take us off of the Magi case? Why am I now working on a Saturday?" questions Granderson.

Ross ignores Granderson's complaining as she is focused on the house and the woman quickly exiting out of the second-floor entrance and running down the front stoop. The woman enters the car on the passenger side, and sits in the back seat behind Ross. The woman is Montez Bloom … aka special agent Monica Bloomfield.

Ross makes the introduction.

"Gentlemen, this is special agent Monica Bloomfield. She's been working undercover assigned to Jamie Magi," announces Ross.

Granderson is surprised to learn that Ross kept this from him.

"Bloomfield, agents Ling and Granderson," continues Ross.

Ross can tell by Granderson's look that he has lots of questions about the secret agent.

"Not even Howard knows about her assignment. A couple of years ago, during a surveillance detail, I discovered a federal vehicle following Jamie Magi. I enlisted agent Bloomfield directly out of Quantico in Langley, as I suspected there was a mole in our New York office," states Ross.

Bloomfield takes a tablet out of her shoulder bag. It is a later model than Ling's, with more features. This threatens him.

"Um, excuse me ... I thought I was the tech agent on this team?" states Ling to Ross.

Picking up on the tension in the back seat, Bloomfield strategically disarms Ling.

"Oh, I love those shoes ... and the paisley socks ... nice touch," Bloomfield offers, smiling and gesturing to Ling's feet.

"Thanks, girl," replies a flattered Ling. "I like her ... I could work with her," he states to Ross.

Bloomfield gives Ling a high-five before beginning to update Ross.

"So, once I learned that the family was heading upstate to camp, I figured we needed to keep tabs on her whereabouts in case Magi reached out. I was able to get Jamie's boyfriend to give her the earrings. One is a GPS tracking device, and the other has the capability to pick up audio, as long it remains charged," states Bloomfield.

Ling is impressed.

"So can you get a read on their exact position?" questions Ross.

"Not at the moment. We have to head up to Camp Taconic, where she said Jerron was taking the family. Once we are within a certain range, I should be able to get a signal," Bloomfield replies.

"OK, so let's go camping," Granderson replies.

"We have to hurry. I told the boyfriend not to give her the earrings until they got up to camp, because the jewelry case was the charger. I got a reading that the battery is already halfway drained, and if she left the case at home, then once we lose the signal, that's it, we lose her," reports Bloomfield.

"Buckle up and hang on," announces Granderson as he puts the car in drive and pulls off.

As the sedan reaches the highway entrance there is traffic backed up for miles. Ross buries her face in her hands out of frustration.

CHAPTER 20

John Magi's ankles are shackled together, and his hands are cuffed behind him. He is slightly coherent as he is hoisted over the shoulder of Anthony Greenberg-Silvestri. Anthony follows his brother Jerron from the cargo van to the back entrance of the rented cabin.

When they reach the cabin, and go up the five wooden steps up to the back porch, Jerron opens the door leading into the kitchen. No one is in the kitchen. Anthony enters behind his brother and drops the bound John onto the wood floor. John grunts and grimaces as his body slams painfully to the ground. Anthony adds to the agony by delivering a well-placed kick to John's abdomen.

Jerron stoops down to John and gets in his face.

"Now, Mr. Wonderful, we can do this the easy way, or the hard way ... Where are the diamonds?" he asks coldly.

"What? I don't have any diamonds," replies John weakly, trying to catch his breath as he rocks side-to-side—still recovering from the blow to his torso.

Jerron stands and delivers another painful kick to John's stomach. John folds his body and coughs as he tries to breathe. Realizing that hurting John won't break him, the twins resort to different measures.

"OK, the hard way it is," declares Jerron. "Honey?" he yells.

"I'm up here. The kids went out for a walk!" replies Katherine, yelling from the second floor.

"No! Leave her out of this!" John pleads weakly as he struggles to catch his breath.

Jerron stoops down once again and gets in John's face.

"You know, when I was banging your wife all these years, the truth is I had to imagine I was doing your daughter just to get it up," he states with a smirk.

This clearly enrages John. He squirms and wiggles in an attempt to counter attack. Jerron quickly tries to stand, but John is able to sweep his legs and trip Jerron, who falls onto his back—almost hitting his head on the steel kitchen island countertop.

"That was stupid. We're going to kill your whore wife, and rape your sexy daughter and make you watch!" declares an infuriated Jerron as he tries to get back to his feet.

At that moment, Katherine enters the kitchen.

"Who are you talking to…?" She questions before seeing the strange man standing over her hog-tied former husband. She freezes in horror and confusion.

John manages to kick Jerron with his feet and keep him from standing. He yells frantically to Katherine.

"Katherine, run!"

Katherine looks at the stranger – Anthony, as he pulls the shiny revolver from behind his back. She turns and runs toward the front of the cabin. As Anthony prepares to give chase, John uses his legs to push off of the kitchen island, and propels his body toward Anthony's feet—tripping him and causing him to fall and drop the weapon. When the weapon hits the ground with the hammer cocked, the impact causes it to fire a single shot. Katherine screams in fright and diverts from her path to the front door to run upstairs, clutching the banister like a lifeline.

Not at all fearing for his own safety, John just hopes that Katherine can run to a nearby cabin and get help. Katherine locks herself in a bathroom upstairs. Her hands are shaking in fear. She realizes she left her phone downstairs so she cannot call for help, even if she was able to get a cellular signal out this deep in the woods. She is trapped!

Downstairs in the kitchen, Jerron gets to his feet and unleashes a barrage of violent kicks to the shackled John until he himself is winded. He stops to catch his breath and yells to Anthony.

"Tony, go get that bitch!" he orders.

Jerron's face turns from rage and anger to shock and concern as he looks over to his brother's lifeless body. Thick, dark-red blood slowly forms a pool beneath him as he lies face down.

Jerron falls to his knees and crawls over to his brother. While kneeling over Anthony, he turns him over to his back and reveals a single bullet wound in his neck, with blood pouring out of it. Jerron pulls his twin brother up to him and weeps, crying out. His brother's lifeless body, obviously beyond medical aid, is heavy and slips from his hands.

John tries to move, but the beating he just received from Jerron renders him unable to budge.

Jerron turns his emotions back toward John. Grabbing the gun from off the floor, he walks over to John and stands over him with the revolver pointed directly at him. His face is that of a crazed person, dark and filled with fury.

"You bastard! My brother is dead! This is for my family!" he declares as he readies himself to fire the weapon.

John closes his eyes and prepares himself to meet his death. Jerron contemplates pulling the trigger, but stops. In a moment of lucidity, he realizes that killing John at this point would defeat the purpose of their entire plan. His brother's death would be in vain. He is determined to get what rightfully belongs to his family … by any means necessary.

"Where are my Uncle Sal's diamonds?" asks Jerron bluntly, his eyes filled with rage.

"I don't have any diamonds. I don't know where they are," replies a wounded John.

Jerron is frustrated, and almost squeezes the trigger.

"I bet wifey could make you talk," Jerron states.

He turns and runs upstairs, and his heavy footsteps travel from room to room. He thrusts open closets, and looks under the beds.

He then walks to the bathroom door and turns the doorknob. It is locked. He violently kicks the door open and sees that the bathroom window is wide open, a single sun-bleached curtain flapping in the incoming breeze.

"Damn it," he huffs, walking quickly over to the window. He can see the roof of the front porch is directly outside the window. Jerron turns and quickly runs back downstairs.

A shaky exhale can barely be heard coming from the bathroom linen closet. Katherine was too afraid to even breathe as she hid. She tries to think of what to do next, but she is far too frightened to even move.

As Jerron reaches the bottom of the stairs he checks to confirm that John is still helpless on the kitchen floor, then he tucks the revolver into his waistband and conceals it with his shirt before going outdoors. When he opens the front door, Jamie and Kyle are returning from their walk.

"Looks like it's going to rain," states Kyle.

The young couple walks past Jerron and enters the cabin. Neither Jamie nor Kyle notice the blood stains on Jerron's knees.

Jerron quickly realizes that he will not need Katherine after all, and that Jamie will be enough to get John to talk. He bears a diabolical grin before looking around out front and then shutting the door.

* * *

"Shut the front door!" declares agent Ling.

He and agent Bloomfield continue to geek out as they swap stories and favorite tech gadgets in the back seat of Granderson's sedan. In the front seat, Ross is on the phone with her supervisor, agent Howard.

"This can be a hostage situation, we're not sure. All we know is that Jerron planned the weekend so we can assume it is well thought out and that he selected a very remote location," she states into her phone.

"Hostage situation?" squawks Ling as he becomes anxious overhearing Ross.

Ross continues to speak with Howard on the phone.

"I think we should call in back up ... it's just me, two field agents, and a tech specialist," she continues.

"Hey, I resent that," interjects Ling.

"Will do, sir. OK," continues Ross before ending her phone call.

"Hey, so you said hostage situation ... Shouldn't I get a gun?" questions Ling.

Ross doesn't feel his question even warrants a response. Instead she relays orders from Howard to the others in the vehicle.

"Howard wants to keep this close to the vest, seeing that we don't know which dirty agents have any mob ties. It looks like it's just us," she states.

"So shouldn't I get a gun?" Lings asks again.

"When we get up to the lake and within range of Jamie Magi, we will be able to better determine what exactly we're dealing with here," continues Ross...ignoring Ling's building excitement.

"For all we know, there could be a dozen of Mongelli's relatives ... heavily armed," interjects Granderson.

"So shouldn't I get a gun?" repeats Ling with more emphasis.

"Howard is going to meet us there. Then once Bloomfield can get us an audio transmission, we can figure out our next move," states Ross.

"*So shouldn't I get a gun?*" repeats Ling, practically shouting.

The other three agents reply together in chorus: "No!"

A stunned Ling reacts with a flamboyant facial expression and then turns and looks Bloomfield up and down.

"And I was actually starting to like you!" he states.

He then rolls his eyes and then turns his attention to his tablet.

*   *   *

When agent Howard gets off the phone with Ross, he turns to agent Evans, who is sitting in the driver's seat of an unmarked federal vehicle.

"They're going to meet us at Taconic Lake. Let's hurry," he states coldly.

He then turns to the back seat and addresses agent Wang.

"Notify your broker ... we need to move the rest of the diamonds tonight!"

Wang gets her phone in her hand and begins making some calls.

"As soon as we confirm Magi is present, we take the entire family out," states Howard to Evans.

Wang hears this and stops dialing her phone.

"What about Ross and her team?" she interjects.

"Well, I suspect they will be killed along with the Magis by the Silvestri brothers, before we arrive to take down the Silvestris and save the day," replies Howard bluntly.

CHAPTER 21

It was as if she was staring at a ghost. As Katherine remains huddled in the bathroom linen closet, she recalls in her mind what it felt like seeing John alive—in the flesh. She isn't sure exactly what frightened her more, the strange man coming after her with a gun, or the sight of her "late" husband. As John warned her of the danger downstairs, in the confusion she didn't realize why Jerron was threatening to harm her. As she looked through the creases in the closet door and saw him holding a gun and looking for her, she realized she doesn't know what is real anymore, or whom she can trust.

Several questions and uncertainties race through her thoughts to the beat of her rapid pulse: Who is the strange man in the kitchen? What is John's involvement, and why after all these years has he decided to resurface? Most of all, why is Jerron out to harm her?

Katherine hears the voices of Jamie and Kyle entering the cabin downstairs, and a new fear begins to set in ... fear that her daughter has just walked into a death trap. With increased urgency, Katherine must figure out a way to get help for herself as well as her daughter and Kyle.

·   ·   ·

It is as if she is staring at a ghost. Jamie freezes in shock as she looks at her dead father ... only he is not dead, but shackled on the kitchen floor. She doesn't even notice the dead man, bleeding out of his neck, lying just a few feet away. Jamie is frozen in her tracks, as she cannot take her eyes off of John. He has aged a bit since she last saw him many years ago, but a little girl never forgets the eyes of her father.

Kyle, on the other hand, notices the body of Anthony on the floor and reacts immediately.

"Oh my God!" he screams as he backs up away from the body.

Jerron delivers a brutal right hook into Kyle's injured ribs. The surprise blow drops him to the ground. This action snaps Jamie out of her daze as she kneels down to assist her wounded boyfriend.

"Kyle?" she cries as she falls to her knees.

"Don't you lay a finger on her," John weakly cautions Jerron.

Jamie's attention quickly and instinctively turns back in the direction of John, as she hears her father's voice for the first time in 15 years. The voice she will never forget. The voice that she vividly recalls cheering her on when she began to pedal her first bike. The voice that read her bedtime stories and tucked her in at night as a child … and the voice that she dreamt about for several years after the accident.

John and Jamie lock eyes and hold contact for a moment. His eyes are filled with helplessness—hers are filled with fear and confusion. As they break eye contact, Jamie turns her head around to see a revolver pointed directly in her face … a revolver held by her stepfather.

"Jerron … what are doing?" questions a terrified Jamie.

"No! Please!" cries a helpless John.

Jamie's frightened eyes move back and forth between her father and stepfather.

Jerron suddenly buckles at the knees, as Kyle has mustered all of his strength into a tackle. But Kyle is far too weak from his injuries to do any significant damage. Jerron delivers a knee to Kyle's face, causing blood to gush from his nose. Kyle falls onto his back holding his bloody nose. Jamie tries to stop the bleeding by pressing her shirt against his nose and tilting his head back in her lap.

Katherine hears the scuffle from upstairs in the linen closet. She can't bear the thought of Jerron hurting Jamie. Abandoning her sense of self-preservation, as any mother would to save her daughter, she exits the bathroom and runs down the stairs. When she sees Kyle's blood on Jamie's shirt and Jerron pointing a gun at them, she panics, fearing the worst.

"Oh my God, Jerron, what have you done?" she cries. She rushes him but her strength is no match to the hostile and irrational man who is now also seeking revenge for the death of his twin brother.

Jerron uses one arm to fling Katherine down to the floor next to Jamie and Kyle. Jamie cries out and grasps her mother. They search each other's eyes for a glimmer of understanding but only find confusion mirrored between them.

Jerron points the gun at the three of them as he addresses John, who remains shackled in the kitchen.

"Where are the diamonds, John?" he questions with anger--filled eyes.

"I told you, I don't know where the diamonds are. I turned them over to the feds," explains John.

"Liar!" Jerron shouts, fueling his own rage like a spark to gasoline.

He steps over to Katherine and grabs a fistful of her hair. He pulls her up to her knees and points the gun onto her temple. Katherine closes her eyes and screams out loud.

"Why?" cries Katherine.

"No, Jerron!" screams Jamie.

Jerron's eyes indicate that he would not hesitate to pull the trigger. John looks into them through his haze of pain, through his restraint, and knows he must do something. Katherine sobs pleadingly.

"OK ... stop! Don't hurt her," John yells. "I know where the diamonds are. They're buried in a basement in Brooklyn."

Jerron smiles and releases Katherine's hair, causing her to fall to the floor. Jamie hugs her mother as they both weep.

"Well, John, I'm listening," states Jerron with an evil smirk.

•   •   •

"Can you hear anything?" asks agent Ross to agent Bloomfield.

"Nothing yet ... I am picking up a GPS signal on the earrings. Let's move further up the mountain to get closer in range and perhaps pick up some audio," replies Bloomfield.

Ross, Bloomfield, Ling, and Granderson load up into the sedan at the lake and continue to follow the signal up the mountain. They are followed directly by a car carrying agents Howard, Evans, and Wang. As the two cars coast up the winding mountain road, agent Ling works on his tablet. His facial expression indicates that he is looking at something troubling. He looks at Bloomfield to see if she can see his tablet's screen, but she is preoccupied with her own. He also looks at Ross and Granderson in the front seat, but it appears that no one is paying any attention to what he is doing. He turns his tablet face down and looks out the window. His furrowed brow suggests that he is in deep thought.

.   .   .

In the car behind them, Howard opens a gun case on his lap. In it are some handguns confiscated from mobsters during FBI raids. He confirms that they are loaded before handing one each to Evans and Wang.

"Now don't be sloppy. Do not use your service weapon on any agents or Magi and his family ... use these. Service weapons are strictly to be used to take down the Silvestri boys," orders Howard.

He then takes out one for himself and closes the case.

.   .   .

In the cabin living room, Jerron forces Jamie at gunpoint to fetch his fishing gear and tackle box from the den. He then orders Kyle and Katherine to sit on the floor with their backs touching. He instructs Jamie on exactly how to tie them together using rope and fishing line. Jamie weaves the ties around and between them, her face wet and raw from crying. She dares not whisper words of consolation to her mother and boyfriend nor they to her.

Once Kyle and Katherine are secured, Jerron sticks the gun into Jamie's back and forces her into the kitchen, where John is still on the floor.

"Now John, your baby girl is going to undo your cuffs and shackles … If you try anything stupid, I put a bullet in her skull. Are we clear?" Jerron clarifies.

"Yes, understood. Just be careful with that thing," John replies.

Jamie weeps as Jerron pushes her to the ground and throws her the keys to free her father.

"It's OK, sweetie, he won't hurt you," John states to comfort Jamie.

Her hands are trembling as she slowly unlocks the shackles that are binding her father's feet. A combination of the weapon in her back, and being this close to her "dead" father is sending her nerves into a tailspin. After freeing John's feet, her eyes meet his as she begins to unlock the handcuffs. She is so nervous that she drops the keys. Jerron moves the gun from her back and presses it behind her neck.

The feeling of the cold steel directly against her skin makes her even more nervous. She closes her eyes and cries.

"Daddy," she cries uncontrollably.

John is overtaken with emotion. Suddenly, in his eyes, Jamie is the little seven-year-old girl he remembers. A fearful child, pure and naïve to the world, seeking her daddy's consolation.

"It's OK, baby … everything is going to be all right. Just relax," John croons, his voice cracking as a tear streams out of his eye.

Jamie finds a peaceful place in her father's reassuring voice, and goes back to a time when he was her rock. She takes a deep, shaky breath and picks up the keys. She unlocks the handcuffs. John is free for the first time since last night and he has minimal feeling and movement of his hands. He repeatedly opens and closes them in an attempt to regain the circulation.

Jerron pulls Jamie by her hair and up to her feet. This violent action knocks one of her earrings loose. He grabs her tight to his body, while pressing the gun to her head. He pulls her away from John a few steps.

"OK, now we're going to go outside, we're going to get in the car, and you are going to take me to exactly where you buried the diamonds," Jerron demands.

He orders John to walk out the back door as he and Jamie follow behind. He then makes John get into the driver's seat of his SUV. He and Jamie get into the backseat, and he continues to hold the gun to her head.

"Don't be stupid, John. Just drive safely, don't try to alert the cops. When we get there, if there are no diamonds, I'm killing her while you watch, and then I'm killing you … slowly," threatens Jerron.

Jamie looks back at the cabin where her mother and boyfriend are tied up and helpless. She again begins to cry in silent, convulsing sobs, but dares not protest. John starts the engine and slowly pulls away. His only plan…is to wing it until he can come up with one.

CHAPTER 22

As Granderson pulls the sedan close to the cabin where Jamie's earring signal is coming from, they can see the lights on inside, and a black cargo van stashed off to the side. Granderson stops the car at a safe distance as to maintain the element of surprise. Evans pulls up behind them.

Granderson, Ross, and Bloomfield exit the car and walk back to the trailing vehicle to speak with Howard and the other agents. Ling is now alone in the back seat. He looks out of the rear window and can see the other agents engaging in conversation as Howard, Evans, and Wang exit their vehicle. Ling reaches over the front passenger seat and opens the glove compartment. He hopes that Granderson keeps a backup firearm in his car … he does. Ling quickly retrieves it, shoves it in the side of his waistband and then exits the vehicle. He holds his tablet against his side to help conceal the fact that he is carrying. He walks to the other vehicle to join the others.

"I'm getting a very strong signal from Jamie's earring coming from inside the cabin … but still no audio," reports Bloomfield.

"Keep trying, we really need to know what's going on in there," replies Ross.

"In the meantime, let's not alert them that we are here until we know exactly what we're dealing with," instructs Howard.

He splits up Ross and her team. He orders Granderson and Wang to go and quietly secure the cargo van. He wants Ross with him to sneak around to the back of the cabin, while Evans and Bloomfield prepare to enter from the side.

"Nerd, take over the audio device and alert us when you get a signal," he orders Ling rudely.

Ling is offended but follows orders. He transfers the audio surveillance link from Bloomfield's tablet and retreats back to his temporary mobile office ... the back seat of Granderson's sedan.

The other agents break into pairs as instructed by Howard. He has strategically set it up so that Ross and her team are in separate locations, and easier to take down in a coordinated ambush. His first mission is to eliminate Magi, his family, and the Silvestri boys ... for now; every agent is on his team ... for as long as he needs them.

Each agent has an earpiece with an attached microphone with which they can communicate without alerting the occupants inside the cabin.

Granderson and Wang get to the cargo van with guns drawn—prepared to meet resistance. Wang holds her weapon on the side door as a target as Granderson checks the front seat. The van appears empty. Upon checking the back of the van, they find rope, shovels, and other tools.

"All clear at the cargo van," Granderson reports quietly into the microphone.

Bloomfield sneaks around to the side of the cabin and ducks behind the trees—maintaining a close visual of the cabin. Evans is closely behind her.

When Howard and Ross get to the back of the cabin, they creep up slowly to the back porch. They quietly make their way up to the back window and duck down. Ross carefully peeks in and can see the kitchen. She can partially see Anthony Silvestri's legs lying on the floor, along with shackles near the body.

"Looks like we have a body in the kitchen," she reports to Howard and the others in her microphone.

Unaware of how many others may be injured, she decides to enter through the kitchen window that is slightly ajar. She quietly slides through the window and softly lands on the floor. She crawls slowly over to Anthony's body and checks for a pulse.

"I believe we have one deceased Silvestri," she reports quietly into her microphone.

Hearing Ross' voice in the kitchen, Katherine and Kyle yell for help.

"Hello? Help us, please!" shouts Katherine.

"Call the police!" yells Kyle.

Ross quickly runs with her gun drawn into the living room, where she finds them tied up and distraught.

"Mrs. West ... Kyle, are you injured?" she asks as she looks around to see if they are alone.

"It's Jerron, he has a gun and he took Jamie!" cries Katherine.

Ross calls in the other agents. Within seconds, all of the agents present pour into the cabin with guns drawn.

Granderson pulls out a pocketknife and begins to cut through the rope and fishing line to free Katherine and Kyle.

"Please, you have to hurry ... Jerron is crazy! He is going to hurt her!" pleads Katherine.

"How many men are there?" questions Howard.

"Two ... plus the dead guy in the kitchen," replies Kyle.

Howard thinks quickly: He will pin the murders of his agents on Anthony. He and his team will look like the heroes who shot Anthony while Jerron escaped, taking Jamie and Magi as hostages. He and his team will have to quickly track down the SUV and kill Jerron, Magi, and Jamie—blaming the death of the two hostages on Jerron—before they kill him in a blazing gun battle.

"It's John," Katherine says frantically. "Jerron and that man had him chained and demanded that he tell where some diamonds are or we would all be killed."

"Diamonds ... what diamonds?" inquires Ross.

That question makes Howard, Evans, and Wang tense. They shift uneasily. Evans is preparing to reach for his dirty firearm. How-ard makes eye contact with him and shakes him off.

"I have no idea. He kept asking about his Uncle Sal's diamonds," replies Katherine.

Granderson finally safely cuts Katherine and Kyle free. He and Ross help them get to their feet.

"Let's get them to a hospital to be checked out by a doctor," suggests Howard.

"No, I don't need a doctor. I need to rescue Jamie," Kyle insists.

"Relax son, we will take care of it," replies Howard.

"Did Jerron or John mention where they were going?" questions Ross.

"John promised he would take him to the place where he stashed the diamonds in Brooklyn," replies Katherine.

Howard is puzzled. He is well aware that the diamonds are not stashed away in Brooklyn ... unless John only turned over a portion of the diamonds ... in that case there is still a chance that John can provide proof that Howard is involved. If there are no diamonds, then Jerron will surely murder John and Jamie. Either way, Howard needs Jerron and John dead and unable to connect him to the diamonds. He contemplates his options.

Agent Bloomfield enters the room from the kitchen holding one of Jamie's earrings.

"She lost an earring! That's why we could only get a GPS signal. The one with audio is probably well out of range by now," she announces.

Kyle, who is still traumatized, recognizes the familiar face and is surprised to see his girlfriend's friend present.

"Montez? ... What are you doing here?" he asks.

"Hi, Kyle. I'm special agent Monica Bloomfield. Sorry we had to use you to give Jamie the tracking device ... but it was for her safety," she replies.

"Her safety? She is out there with a gun to her head ... I don't think she feels very safe right now," interjects a frustrated Katherine.

"Mrs. West, calm down," says Ross. Her voice is gentle but assertive. "We will do everything in our power to make sure she returns safely."

"Don't call me Mrs. West. I don't even know who that man is that I married," replies Katherine.

She is visibly shaken and upset. Kyle puts his arm around her as they sink into the crunchy leather couch to answer some questions that may assist in locating Jamie and John.

"We are going to notify the state police to be on the lookout for Jerron's SUV, but we don't want to create a situation that can result in a standoff or dangerous shootout with police," Granderson explains.

Katherine lets out the primal wail of a mother separated from her child. Kyle fights back his own tears and tightens his grip around her shoulders.

Ross proceeds cautiously. "In the meantime, we need to know a few details. What is Jamie wearing?" she asks.

.   .   .

Jamie's white T-shirt is still spotted with Kyle's blood. She sits nervously in the back seat with Jerron's gun held to her side. As John drives the SUV down the winding mountain road, he periodically makes eye contact with Jamie in the rearview mirror—occasionally checking on her.

"How are you holding up, kiddo?" asks John.

Jamie is too frightened to even speak.

"It's a long drive back to the city, so try to relax and make yourself comfortable," he adds.

"Shut the hell up, Magi!" Jerron spews. "Don't try to pretend like you're a good dad ... all of a sudden concerned about his little girl. You're nothing but a coward! You faked your death and went into hiding, leaving your precious little princess all alone. So do us all a favor and let's have a nice, quiet drive!"

Jamie's body is rigid with tension and every bump in the road startles her. John doesn't think she will survive the long drive without having a nervous breakdown. The crazed gunman seated next to her is growing increasingly unstable with every passing moment. John knows that there are no diamonds hidden in a Brooklyn basement.

He also knows that he cannot stall or drag this out much longer. He needs to get Jamie out of danger as soon as possible.

John sees a possible opportunity as the low-fuel light beeps and illuminates on the dashboard.

"Um, we're low on fuel. Perhaps we should stop at the station at the bottom of the mountain and fill up?" he suggests.

Jerron maneuvers his head to confirm that they are indeed low on gas. He is irritated further, as he didn't plan on things getting this far out of hand. He and Anthony planned on torturing the family up in the cabin and burying them all in woods. Now that things have changed drastically, and Jerron is working alone, he has no plan B and is making it up as he goes along. He has no choice but to stop for gas. Breaking down on the highway will only draw attention from state police.

"OK, we stop for gas, but you will get out and use my card to pay at the pump. Jamie and I will stay here, and if you try to run or alert someone, I put holes in her sexy little body," Jerron declares.

Jamie weeps and tears roll down her face. How could her step-father speak so coldly? It is as if he is a completely different person from the man who married her mom—she now sees he is not the man he pretended to be when he entered their lives a few years ago.

"Hey pumpkin, don't cry," John offers to his daughter. "Remember when you were a little girl and whenever we stopped for gas you would always cry until your mom or I went in to buy your favorite candy bar from that place? That place we would stop for gas by the park—remember that, sweetie?" He makes eye contact with her in the rearview mirror.

Jamie sees something in his eyes; not just a bottomless sadness. There is a father-daughter connection that Jerron can't detect. Having her father back with her, looking into his eyes, sends her childhood memories streaming back, and they are crystal clear. Jamie can vividly recall the name of the gas station by the park, because to keep her occupied while he was pumping gas, John would have her spell out the large blue-and-red sign—Quick Stop! Her favorite candy bar is easy to remember because it is still her favorite to this very day—Rocky Road Runner.

Jamie nods affirmatively while maintaining eye contact with John through the rearview mirror.

"That's my girl," John states.

When she sits forward and braces her head on the seat in front of her, Jerron assumes she is getting sick.

"Don't you dare throw up on my shoes," Jerron states.

John smiles, knowing that she is on the same page with him. Now that she is braced for a quick stop, he waits for the perfect opportunity.

Jamie says a silent prayer. She just hopes that her legs, near paralyzed with nervousness, will provide her the ability to run up the rocky mountain road and to safety.

John is waiting to reach the perfect bend in the road ... for just the right angle. He feels that this is their best chance. As the SUV hits a sharp left bend, he braces himself behind the steering wheel and slams down on the brakes. The sudden jerking motion not only pulls Jerron and the gun in the opposite direction from Jamie, but it propels him forward violently, allowing John to grab his shoulder.

Stunned by the sharp movement, Jerron is halfway in the front seat. As John holds him down, wedged in between the two front seats, Jamie pushes open her door and runs for the hills, willing her legs to pump over the wild terrain.

John holds Jerron down as long as possible, watching as Jamie hurls her body forward, creating distance between herself and the SUV. As Jerron begins to pull himself up, bracing himself against the seats, John slams on the gas, pitching Jerron backward. The tires squeal and Jerron's body thuds against the back seat. Holding his breath, John flings open the door and jumps out of the moving vehicle.

John hits the dirt road with a grunt and his body rolls several times. He raises his eyes in the direction of the SUV as it continues to travel downhill a few yards before running into a shallow ditch. It comes to a stop after crashing into a large rock. John hears the sound of splintering glass and can smell burnt rubber as the rock completely bends the front passenger wheel.

Jerron appears slightly dazed but able bodied as he slowly climbs out of the vehicle and looks around. His chest rises and falls deeply, and a smear of fresh blood glimmers on his chin, spreading from his quickly swelling bottom lip. John scrambles to his feet, ignoring the pain searing his limbs and ribcage, and runs up the rocky mountain road in the same direction as Jamie. John can hear two loud shots from Jerron's revolver cracking and echoing over the hills ... he just keeps pumping his arms and legs, running as fast and as hard as he can away from the gunfire.

CHAPTER 23

Both Katherine and Kyle refuse to go to the hospital to get checked out, despite the deep grooves in the arms and wrists where the monofilament fishing line dug into their skin. Their main concern is Jamie's safety. The two of them still sit side-by-side on the cabin's living room couch, surrounded by FBI agents in various stages of planning and investigating. Kyle has sweated through the back of his shirt, though not from heat, and the cabin smells of blood and perspiration. Neither Kyle nor Katherine has cellular service this far in the woods—most likely a part of the plan set by Jerron and Anthony to ensure the family couldn't call for help up in the mountain cabin. Agent Bloomfield uses a satellite phone to call Jamie's cell, but it goes directly to voicemail. They conjecture that perhaps she has not gotten to the bottom of the mountain as yet, and therefore hasn't gotten into cell range. However, Kyle realizes that she left her phone upstairs in a bedroom.

"I guess she didn't bring it on our walk since we couldn't get a signal anyway," concludes Kyle.

Ross suggests reaching out to Jerron's cell phone as well, however his phone also goes directly to voicemail. This gives them hope that he, John, and Jamie are perhaps still on the mountain.

"I think it's time we notify the state and park police to stop their vehicle before they make it to the highway," suggests Granderson.

Agent Howard, however, does not like that idea. He wants Jerron and Magi dead … not captured.

"I don't think that's a good idea at all," he objects.

Others in the room are puzzled as to why he would object to getting backup from nearby agencies. He can tell this is their thinking. They look at him with questioning expressions.

"We don't know how unstable Silvestri is, or what he is capable of … if he is surrounded, he may kill his hostages, and himself," explains Howard in defense of his position.

"Yes, but I respectfully disagree, sir," Ross interjects. "If we do nothing and allow him to get back to Brooklyn, who knows how much backup and reinforcements the Silvestri boys have waiting. I say we stop him while he is alone."

"I agree," adds Bloomfield.

Howard can see that he will not win this battle. He contemplates his next move carefully. He agrees that stopping Jerron and Magi before they make it back to the city, and before word gets out that he was given the stolen diamonds, would be in his best interest. He also realizes that if John—under duress—has already given Jerron information that the diamonds are in Howard's possession, catching them before they reach cellular range is crucial. After waiting 15 years to spend his money, the last thing Howard wants is to have to spend the rest of his life looking over his shoulder for any Mongelli relatives. Howard also knows that if the state police get involved and capture Jerron and Magi alive, they will potentially talk and ruin the well-devised plan.

"I'm going to make the call," announces Bloomfield as she begins to dial her satellite phone.

Howard has seen enough and feels that he is now out of options. He gives Evans and Wang the "get ready" sign as he calmly walks over to the kitchen. He draws his service weapon and stands over Anthony's body. He needs bullets from an FBI gun in the body. Howard stoically fires three shots down into the body, as the deafening gunshots startle Katherine and Kyle, and get the attention of the other stunned agents.

"Sir?" shouts Ross, as she is surprised to see him standing over the body.

On that cue, both Evans and Wang draw their "dirty" weapons. Evans aims his at Granderson, and Wang points hers at Bloomfield.

Everything seems to move in slow motion for agent Ross as she observes what is rapidly transpiring before her. As if time is standing still for a moment, she sees the weapons pointed at her team ... is this her life about to flash before her eyes? Is this what you experience right before you die? She has these thoughts as she realizes that she and her team are about to fall prey to a cold-blooded ambush. She doesn't hesitate as her instincts and training naturally kick in.

Ross dives with her arms extended and tackles Katherine and Kyle, knocking them behind the couch. Just as they hit the floor, two separate gunshots ring out, followed by a split second of eerie silence. From the floor, Ross quickly draws her firearm. She looks up to her left and sees Granderson still on his feet, starting to draw his firearm as Evans is down on the ground. She looks over to her left and sees Wang still holding her firearm, standing over a wounded Bloomfield. Both Granderson and Ross turn their guns onto Wang, who frantically points her weapon at Granderson. Ross immediately discharges two rounds from her firearm, striking Wang in the torso and dropping her to the ground.

Ross mentally drowns out the whimpering cries of the frightened Katherine and Kyle and quickly assesses the situation in the midst of the confusion. She can clearly see that Wang shot Bloomfield ... but who shot Evans before any of her team could react? She looks toward the front door and sees agent Ling still holding Granderson's backup piece in his shaking hands. He is clearly a nervous wreck and visibly upset as this is the first time he has used a firearm in the line of duty. Unlike the rush of shooting at a firing range, hitting a human target feels very much different.

Ross turns her attention to the kitchen, but the back door is open and the suddenly outnumbered Howard has taken off. She then turns her attention to the two civilians who are now huddled together on the floor next to her.

"Are either of you hit?" she asks.

They shake their heads without speaking, staring at her with wide, luminous eyes.

Granderson holds two fingers to Evans' and Wang's necks, finding a pulse on neither.

Agent Ross frantically tries to perform CPR on Bloomfield, kneeling over her and chanting "One, two, three," to the beat of the compressions.

She is too late. Bloomfield suffered a fatal shot to the side of her head. Blood spurts out of the wound with every futile beat. Ross exhales in defeat and lifts her hand, passing it over Bloomfield's eyelids to lower them.

The bullet traveled through the satellite phone ... rendering it useless.

Agent Ling is still in shock and standing in the doorway with the gun in his hands. He is trembling and crying. Ross and Granderson walk over to him. Granderson gently pries the weapon from his shaking hands as Ross calmly talks to him.

"Agent Ling, are you OK?" she asks.

Ling finally begins to blink his eyes and turn his attention from Evans' lifeless body to focus on Ross.

"You did good ... you saved Granderson's life," she states.

Ling looks over to the body of Bloomfield and his trembling increases. Ross can hear his teeth clattering together.

"Shhh ...there is nothing else you could have done to prevent what happened to her," affirms Ross as she gives him a consoling hug.

"I don't know how you got this gun or how you knew we were in trouble, but thanks, brother," offers Granderson as he also places his arm lovingly around Ling.

"How DID you know that we were in trouble?" asks Ross.

"Well, when I was at Granderson's apartment waiting for you two to get dressed ..." Ling states before pausing. After realizing that Katherine and Kyle could hear him, he quickly rephrases his statement. "While you two were getting ready, I went into the kitchen to get a drink of water. There was a photo on the refrigerator taken at a holiday party a few years back. In it, I noticed agent Evans was present. It didn't hit me until they pulled up here today. I recalled

Howard introducing Evans as being from the Seattle field office. So I ran an extensive background check and employment history of agent Evans. He was in the New York office, before being demoted ... the reason is unknown as the file is sealed."

Granderson and Ross listen intently as Ling goes on to explain how his suspicions led him to pull up data from his tablet.

"The night when Magi stole the kid's phone ..." Ling continues before Kyle interjects.

"What ... that guy? Jamie's dead father is who attacked me?" he questions.

"It's a long story," replies Katherine.

Kyle shakes his head in disbelief.

"Well, when we left the hospital, Howard ordered me to stay in the car, and give him my tablet to track the phone inside the bar," Ling continues. "I was bored and wanted in on the action, so I planned to set the audio up so that I could listen live to all the drama going on inside. However, I couldn't hear a thing. I must have set it to record instead. I never bothered listening to it, because they exited the bar disappointed and everything just seemed uneventful. I retrieved the audio just now while I was out in the car, and heard this ..." Ling explains before playing the recording from the night Howard and Evans sought out John Magi in the bar bathroom.

Ross and Granderson listen as the audio plays, and they hear the voice of Howard talking to Evans: "He lunged at you ... you had to shoot."

"I knew something wasn't right so I hacked Bloomfield's tablet ..." He pauses and looks at her body. "Sorry," he says toward her as he makes the sign of the cross. "So, I hacked into her tablet and engaged the camera. I had a bad feeling and figured I better get video footage. That's how I knew that things were about to go south, and in a hurry," he explains.

He shows them footage he recorded from Bloomfield's tablet: As she is holding the tablet at her side, the rear camera picks up Evans fidgeting with his gun ... only it is not a service-issued weapon. In the video, Evans clearly keeps purposely walking directly behind

Granderson. He looks suspicious and his body language suggests that he is preparing to attack Granderson. Due to the angle Bloomfield held her tablet, the camera does not pick up agent Wang, who is standing behind her.

Ross is shocked to realize that her boss—the man she looked up to and respected—could be capable of murdering other agents.

"I just don't understand. Why would he ... why would they attack us?" questions Ross.

Katherine, who knows all too well how one can be fooled, and not really know the person you trust most, interjects.

"FBI agents killing each other, and my daughter taken hostage by my husband ... or whoever that man is ... I think it's time we call 9-1-1," she states.

"Yes, we need to do that. Does ANYONE have a cellular signal?" asks Ross.

Ling and Granderson check their phones, but neither has a signal.

"Ling, can you hack into a cell tower or something?" she asks.

"I don't know if there are any within range," he replies.

"What about Howard? He is probably halfway down the mountain by now," interjects Granderson.

"Oh, I don't think he's gotten very far," states Ling as he holds up keys for both Granderson's and Evans' vehicles.

"Good work, Ling. He shouldn't get very far on foot. He no longer has the element of surprise on his side. We know he's the dirty agent that is willing to kill his brothers and sisters. Granderson, you and I will go out back and hunt that coward down," states Ross with a new determination.

She orders Katherine and Kyle to go upstairs and pull sheets off of the beds. After Ross, Ling, and Granderson collect all of the weapons from the deceased agents, they use the bed sheets to cover their bodies out of respect ... even Anthony's.

"Ling, give the keys to Evans' car to Katherine and Kyle. Katherine, you two drive to a nearby cabin ... I think we passed one a few miles down the mountain. Hopefully they have a landline that you can use to call 9-1-1," orders Ross.

Katherine and Kyle take the keys from Ling and get in Evans' sedan. Katherine is driving. She peels out quickly as they head down the rocky mountain road.

Ross orders Ling to use Granderson's car to head down to the main highway and try to pick up a signal on Jamie's earring audio tracker, so they can alert backup as to her exact location. He gets in Granderson's sedan and also navigates down the rocky mountain road.

Ross and Granderson look at each other and share a non-verbal agreement: this is for agent Bloomfield. They both have their weapons in hand as they head out the back door in pursuit of Howard ... who is considered armed, and extremely dangerous.

CHAPTER 24

Jamie is still running uphill at full speed when John finally catches up to her. She is exhausted and takes cover behind some bushes along the lake. She drops down on her stomach, and uses her elbows to hold her shoulders and head off the dirt. As she pants heavily, John slides to a stop next to her. He assumes the same planking position, and peers through the bushes for any sign of Jerron.

The sun is beginning to set and John is not sure if the darkness will act in their favor or be to Jerron's advantage. He doesn't want to take any chances. He wants to return to the cabin and get to Katherine.

"Come on Jamie, keep moving, it will be dark soon. We have to get back to your mother," John huffs.

"I can't go any further … you go, and then come back for me … I'll hide here," replies a scared and winded Jamie.

"Absolutely not. I am not leaving you alone," he replies.

"Oh no? Why not? Seemed pretty easy for you to leave when I was little," Jamie snaps back.

That stings John, but he knows that the comment is justified.

"Sweetheart, I am sorry I left. I have regretted that decision every moment for the past 15 years … I want you to understand that I didn't want to, but I had to … for you … for the sake of you and your mom," John explains.

Jamie puts her head down as she tries to catch her breath. She doesn't know how to respond to the ghost currently in her presence.

"I hope that one day you will allow me to explain my actions ... not justify them, but at least explain them to you now that you are mature enough to understand. Perhaps we can even start fresh," John continues.

"I'm glad that you're not dead, Dad," replies Jamie with a tearful half-smile.

"Now come on, let's go get your mom," John replies.

"And my boyfriend ... Oh my goodness, Kyle is the first boyfriend that you'll meet!" adds Jamie.

"I think I may have run into him on the street before," replies John quickly and vaguely. He hops to his feet and extends his hand to Jamie. She takes her father's hand and gets to her feet.

They run along the lake back up toward the cabin, not speaking, staying off the road and using the bushes and trees as cover. John had long envisioned the moment he would be holding his little girl's hand in a park by a beautiful lake ... but never in his wildest dreams could he have imagined that they would be hand-in-hand running for their lives from a deranged gunman.

John knows that Jerron's SUV is too damaged to drive, so he hopes that he and Jamie can make it back up to the cabin and free Katherine and Kyle before Jerron gets to them. John hates to even think what Jerron would do to Katherine in retaliation for his and Jamie's daring escape.

He is physically exhausted, dehydrated, and hungry, but he must ignore those feelings, and push his body up the rocky mountain road.

Agent Ling is driving Granderson's vehicle down the mountain. He speeds past the car driven by Katherine as she and Kyle slow down, coming to another rental cabin.

When Ling reaches the lake he periodically checks his phone to see when he is getting back into cell phone range. He reaches the point where the road splits in different directions at the foot of the one rocky mountain road, which takes visitors up to the top. Ling takes the road that leads back down to the highway. The agents took a different road on the way in, and that is how they managed to just miss Jerron's SUV heading down with John and Jamie. Ling notices that he is starting to get a muffled audio signal from Jamie's earring. He knows that he is close within range of her as he begins to hear static-muffled breathing. Ling spots the SUV disabled on the side of the road. It appears to have run up on to a large rock. The driver's door is still open and the two rear passenger doors as well. The signal from Jamie seems to be getting weaker.

Ling slows down and pulls close to the vehicle. It appears to be empty, but he stops to get out and make sure that no one is injured. He holds the tablet at eye level to see if the signal gets stronger.

The engine is still running as Ling slowly steps closer to the SUV. After confirming that it is, in fact, empty, he turns back to the vehicle he is driving. When he turns around he is startled to see the barrel of a revolver pointed in his face.

"Excuse me, but I need to use your car," declares Jerron as he cocks back the hammer on the revolver with his thumb.

Ling freezes in his tracks, drops the tablet, raises his hands in surrender, and closes his eyes. Jerron doesn't know that Ling is with the FBI. He assumes he is just a camp visitor that happened to stop to help another distressed motorist, but ended up in the wrong place at the wrong time.

Jerron quickly does the math in his head—one accidental shot from the gun killed his brother Anthony ... he later fired off two more rounds at John as he fled up the mountain. That only leaves him with three bullets remaining, and he is not about to waste any on this insignificant flamboyant Asian guy. He has plans for these three bullets, each with a name: Jamie, Katherine, and John.

"Turn around and kneel down! Keep your eyes closed!" Jerron barks, gesturing to the ground with his gun.

A terrified Ling concedes.

Ling kneels down on the ground with his hands on his head, facing the SUV. Behind him he can hear Jerron's footsteps retreating. He then hears Granderson's car door slam shut, and the sound of tires maneuvering atop the dirt and gravel road.

After Jerron completes the three-point turn and drives the sedan back up toward the cabin, Ling finally deems it safe to open his eyes. He is now stranded, and he needs to warn the others that Jerron is heading back their way. Ling assumes that Jerron has already done away with John and Jamie and that is why he is alone ... but he heard Jamie breathing through the audio transmission in her earring. As a non-field agent, he does not have a headset to even try to radio up to Ross and Granderson. He needs to get help. He checks his phone to see if he has any cellular service ... he does not. He picks up the tablet and notices that he is still receiving a very weak audio signal from Jamie. It appears that it is moving away from him—back up the mountain. He becomes hopeful that she is still alive. He decides to start trekking back up and following Jamie's signal.

.   .   .

When Katherine and Kyle pull up to the first rental cabin that they come to, they both exit the car quickly and frantically bang on the front door as well as the back door. No one seems to be there. Katherine looks through a side window and notices a hunting rifle mounted up on the wall above the fireplace mantle. She picks up a rock and smashes the window. Kyle begins to panic as glass shatters and falls to the ground. Katherine then uses the rock to clear any remaining shards from around the pane. She drops the rock, looks around and then at Kyle.

"Give me a boost through the window," she instructs.

"Oh my God! What? Now we're breaking and entering?" questions a nervous Kyle.

"Hurry up, Kyle!" demands Katherine.

Against his better judgment, Kyle interlocks his fingers and creates a step for Katherine. He then lifts her up as she climbs into the window.

"Now what?" he asks.

There is no response from Katherine, but he can hear her shuffling around inside the cabin. He continues to look around nervously as he waits outside for her.

"Nobody's home, and they don't have a landline, either," announces Katherine as she emerges from out the back door.

Kyle is surprised to see her brandishing a large hunting rifle.

"But I found something useful," she declares boldly.

Kyle is clearly not on board with this new plan of hers.

"What do you think you're doing with that thing?" he questions nervously.

"I am NOT putting my life in the hands of that group of agents. I can hardly even keep up with which ones are actually on our side," she replies as she walks confidently back to the car.

Kyle reluctantly follows behind. "Do you even know how to use that thing?" he asks.

She flips open the action and confirms that the rifle is loaded. She then flips it back like a seasoned professional.

"Jamie's dad and I used to go hunting and I've learned a thing or two," she replies.

Katherine walks over to the passenger side of the car and gets in with the rifle between her legs, pointed upwards.

"Well, hurry up! You're driving ... let's head down the mountain and contact the police!" she demands.

Kyle hurriedly gets behind the wheel and drives the sedan along the road down toward the lake.

*　　*　　*

Agents Ross and Granderson cautiously walk through the back woods area with guns drawn. They are in pursuit of their supervising agent who is responsible for masterminding the ambush that killed undercover agent Bloomfield. They know that he is capable of murdering fellow agents in cold blood, and if not for the quick-thinking actions of agent Ling, they, too, would have suffered a similar fate. They take no chances and proceed with absolute caution. Realizing that Howard is the dirty agent, Ross and Granderson try to figure out his motives, and if he has any more accomplices within the agency.

"According to the witnesses, the Silvestri brothers were seeking diamonds," states Granderson in a whisper as they continue walking through the trees.

"Magi hid a lot of dirty money for Sal Mongelli over the years. Do you suppose Richie Silvestri sent his sons to obtain some money that was stashed away?" replies Ross.

"Could be. Sounds like a big score if they went through all the trouble of getting Jerron to marry Katherine and waiting a decade and a half to come and collect," replies Granderson.

"There is definitely more that John Magi hasn't told the FBI ... unless he shared the information with a dirty agent," Ross concludes.

She and Granderson make eye contact as they share the same exact thought.

"Howard," states Granderson.

"That's why he ordered Evans to kill Magi on sight ... he doesn't want his dirty little secret to come back and bite him," Ross states.

Granderson sees something moving in the distance. They don't have a clear visual, but safely assume that it is Howard fleeing. Granderson points in the direction he saw movement and gives nonverbal signals to Ross, telling her to split up. They pursue Howard strategically in an attempt to cut him off and corner him.

CHAPTER 25

"It all just feels like a bad dream ... not real at all," Jamie says, breathing heavily, nearly gasping. "My stepfather marries my mom in hopes of getting something that my real father stole and stashed, who, by the way, I thought was killed in a car accident. Now step-dad wants to kill my mom, my now back-to-life dad, and me ... this is way too much for one day." She pauses, bracing her hands on her knees, grimacing at the ground beneath her feet.

She and John are continuing up toward the mountain as quickly as they can. They are both perspiring profusely and longing for a drink of water. John knows Jamie must have endless questions about the last 15 years. He tries to reconnect with her.

"First of all, I did not STEAL anything," John says. "Yes, I was an accountant for some very sketchy people, but I never personally stole anything."

Jamie gives him a doubtful sidelong glance.

"I swear! I would hide money for some bad people ... fake charities and non-profit organizations, and such," he explains.

Jamie stops to take a break. She is physically hurting from walking along the rocks and navigating through the think bushes. John urges her to keep pressing on, but she insists on a short rest. John gives in and they both sit on a large boulder. Jamie takes her shoes off and rubs her achy feet. John feels the need to continue ex-plaining his shady past.

"Look, kiddo, I am not saying that I was a perfect man ... far from it, but I loved my family. Your mother and you meant the world to me ... you still do," he confesses.

John tells Jamie how it all started for him. How he went from being a low-income seasonal tax accountant to working for one of the biggest crime bosses in New York and New Jersey.

One day when John was leaving his office, he witnessed his boss being roughed up by a couple of thugs. John naturally rushed to the aid of the older, frail gentleman he worked for. After John single-handedly beat up both of his boss' attackers, he chased them off with a hunting rifle that his boss kept mounted on his office wall. Although the gun wasn't loaded, the two thugs did not know that, so they fled back to their boss—who just so happened to be the notorious Salvatore Mongelli.

As thanks for his heroic bravery, and possibly saving his life, John's boss gave him the hunting rifle as a gift ... a rifle he used to take his wife hunting that very weekend. When John and Katherine returned from their hunting trip, John learned that his office was torched by arsonists and completely destroyed. His boss was never heard from again. The next day, John was approached by some men who overpowered him and forced him into a minivan. He was then driven to a secret location where he met with the man himself: Sal Mongelli. The crime boss was not only impressed with how John man-handled the pair of thugs who were sent to rough up the old man, but also by his excellent accounting skills and knowledgeable financial background. He offered John three options: Be tortured and killed; watch his wife tortured and killed; or work for him as an accountant. John took the job.

After John had been working for the Mongelli crime family for a couple of months, Katherine became pregnant with Jamie. Sal Mongelli treated John well, and made sure that his little girl would want for nothing. He thought about quitting and just running away with his family after Jamie was born, but he knew that his last day working for Mongelli would be his last day, period. John was a trusted and loyal employee, and was the best at making dirty money appear legit. Sal trusted him so much that when his men pulled off the biggest heist and hit the international diamond safe at the World Trade Center, he trusted John to liquidate the billions of dollars' worth of precious stones.

The heist was not only planned well, but the events that transpired on that Tuesday in September made the escape flawless, and destroyed the evidence that there even was a burglary at all.

However, John didn't know that an undercover federal agent, working under agent Howard's supervision, alerted him of the heist and Mongelli's plan to move the diamonds through local and international jewelers as well as shady brokers. Howard learned through the undercover agent that John was Mongelli's trusted man, solely in charge of moving the diamonds. Once Howard obtained this information, he killed his own undercover agent to keep the FBI office or other agents from learning of the heist. Howard figured that the only thing better than pulling off the perfect heist that no one knew about, was ripping off the criminals who pulled off the perfect heist that no one knew about.

Howard recruited a team of dirty agents—agents as dirty as he—whom he could trust to keep their mouths shut for a cut of the big score. It wouldn't be an immediate pay out, because it would take years to move that much in diamonds, but well worth the wait. The elapsed time would also allow Howard to eliminate his team one by one—keeping more for himself, and reducing the risk of anyone else ever learning about the biggest heist that never happened.

After recruiting his team, Howard approached John Magi with recorded audiotape obtained by his undercover agent letting him know that they had enough to send him away to prison for many years. He also leaked false information to Mongelli that John stashed the diamonds for himself and that he would testify against the entire organization. Now with a bounty on his head, John had nowhere else to turn except to Howard and the FBI for protection from Mongelli.

Howard then offered John full protection if he turned over the diamonds to his team. He would give an official witness statement, which excluded the diamond heist, in exchange for protection and a new life.

The only wrench in Howard's plan was the then-rookie agent Michelle Ross ... smart, untainted, and by the book. She was assigned to John Magi's special protection case. She and her partner Granderson helped stage the perfect accident in order to fake John's death, and then kept him hidden for 15 years.

All John Magi knows is that he was faced with the most difficult decision of his life.

"I was just moving money for them, and the next thing I knew, an FBI agent had me on tape and then the bosses wanted me killed, thinking that I wanted to keep all the money for myself," explains John. "Either the mobsters were going to kill me, or the FBI would make me rot in prison, in which case the mobsters would have come after you and your mother. The only solution was to make them think that I was already dead. They knew how much my family meant to me, so if I was gone without you, they would believe that I did, in fact, die, and was not off in witness protection. I love you and your mother, so leaving you was the only choice." Tears flood his eyes.

Jamie has tears rolling down her face. This is the first time she is hearing what John had to sacrifice to keep her and Katherine safe. She falls onto his chest and the father and daughter share a long-overdue embrace.

As they enjoy this special moment, they are startled by footsteps approaching them. They quickly stand to their feet and prepare to run. They look toward the sound of fast-moving footsteps.

"That was beautiful!" shouts agent Ling in between heavy breaths.

Using the audio signal from Jamie's earring, he was able to track them and overheard John's touching confession to his daughter. He is winded as he obviously ran to catch up to them during their rest.

"You must be John and Jamie Magi?" Ling continues.

John and Jamie are surprised that he knows their names. John balls up his fists and is ready to defend himself and his daughter.

"I'm FBI agent Patrick Ling," he quickly introduces himself and shows his ID to thwart the tension.

Jamie and John nearly collapse against each other with elation.

"Your loved ones are safe and heading to a cabin with a landline. They will be pleased to know that you both are safe as well," Ling states.

Jamie sobs loudly—out of joy and relief this time—the sound resonating harshly in her dry throat. "I was worried sick and so scared!" she bawls. Then, calmer; "Now we don't have to run all the way back up to the cabin."

"I don't have a car," Ling says apologetically. "I found you on foot. I followed the audio signal from your earring."

Jamie gives him a completely bewildered look. Instinctively, she reaches for her earrings, realizing for the first time that one is gone.

"Your earrings are tracking devices," Ling continues.

"Kyle gave me a tracking device? I ..."

"Not quite," Ling interrupts. "Your friend gave Kyle the earrings. He didn't even know. He just thought she was helping him pick out a nice surprise that was your style."

"My friend?"

"You know, your sassy sista' with good style," Ling waggles his head.

"Montez? Why would Montez do that?"

"You mean FBI special agent Monica Bloomfield," Ling explains.

"My friend Montez is an undercover FBI agent? That explains a lot," replies Jamie.

Ling bites his tongue, thinking of the fate of agent Bloomfield. John can see that Ling is not sharing everything.

"OK ... but? Katherine and the kid are safe, but?" presses John.

"But ... Jerron stole my car at gunpoint and is on his way back up to the cabin. I'm guessing to get two more hostages since you two escaped," Ling states anxiously.

"What?" cries Jamie frantically.

"Come on, let's go!" declares John as he begins running up the mountain.

Jamie follows him and so does agent Ling.

.   .   .

As Jerron peels up the rocky mountain road, he sees another vehicle approaching rapidly. Because of the narrowness of the single-lane road, cars must pull over and yield, allowing oncoming vehicles to pass. With the momentum pulling the downward vehicles, the climbing vehicles often surrender the right-of-way. Jerron, in all of his rage, refuses to stop. He revs his engine and increases his speed as if playing a game of chicken with the oncoming vehicle. He is on a mission and he expects the approaching driver to yield ... or else.

.   .   .

"Watch out for this lunatic!" warns Katherine as she rides in the sedan with Kyle in the driver's seat.

Kyle's eyes light up as he sees the headlights of another vehicle quickly approaching. It is dusk, and not fully dark, but he cannot see the face of the driver through the windshield to determine if he sees them or not. Not taking any chances, he quickly pulls over.

As he pulls over to his right to allow the approaching sedan to pass, through the dust kicked up by the tires, he and Katherine are stunned to see the profile of the passing driver. The driver does not notice them as he is focused on getting up the mountain in a hurry.

"That was Jerron!" announces Kyle as he continues to drive down the mountain.

"What are you doing?" asks Katherine as she looks back at the sedan speeding up toward the cabin.

"What do you think? I'm taking us down to notify the authorities," replies Kyle as he continues driving and checking the rearview mirror.

"No way! Jamie could be in the trunk of that car ... we have to go after him!" she demands.

"Mrs. West, I strongly suggest that we go to the authorities," Kyle replies nervously.

"Well, I'm the only authority in this car! So turn around and go after him!" demands Katherine as she readies her rife.

Kyle can see that Katherine is determined. He slows the car down and then makes the wide three-point turn in the narrow road. He reluctantly puts the car in drive, and heads back up the mountain … in pursuit of the man who wants to shoot them.

CHAPTER 26

Ross walks carefully through the woods with her service pistol ready in hand. The eerie stillness creates tremendous stress for the well-trained field agent as she hunts down the much more experienced and desperate supervisor Howard. Desperation, personal greed, and his cold-blooded nature along with his total disregard for human lives make him not only a crafty target, but also a very dangerous one. Ross knows that Howard will not hesitate to take her life, and that fact makes her heart race and her palms sweat. Her own heartbeat drowns out the sound of the nature surrounding her. With each step she can hear the deafening gunshots that took the lives of her fellow agents just moments ago replaying in her head. The evening breeze and smell of the nearby Taconic Lake are dull compared to the smell of gunpowder and human blood that penetrated her nose and lungs back in the cabin. There is no escaping the constant replay of the murderous scene she has just experienced, but she must block it out and focus on her encounter with the dirty agent she is pursuing down the back mountain woods.

Agent Granderson cuts off the back path to the lake in an attempt to corner Howard as he tries to escape on foot. He spots a beaming light cutting through the brush several yards ahead. He quickly moves in that direction, with his firearm cocked and locked straight ahead. He cannot radio directions to Ross in the event that Howard will also pick up his transmission. Granderson slows his pace when he gets within 40 yards of the light, yet continues to move stealthily toward it.

.   .   .

Agent Howard is running for his life. He showed his hand to a team of agents whom he himself has trained, but they survived his ambush, and are now hot on his trail. He is not going to prison after waiting all these years to cash in on his perfect plan ... he would rather die here in the woods first, and he is willing to take anyone and everyone with him. He hears movement nearby and decides to take off his flashlight and navigate by the remaining low late--evening light. He keeps moving quickly toward the lake.

.   .   .

Granderson notices the small beaming light ahead of him completely disappears. He assumes that his presence has been realized. Not taking any chances as to whether Howard has spotted him, he ducks down and holds his position as not to walk into a direct ambush. He watches for any movement up ahead.

.   .   .

As John, Jamie, and agent Ling continue to race up the mountain, Ling gets the full story from John about surrendering a truckload of diamonds to agent Howard and his partners. He also informs Ling of his full written statement given 15 years ago. Ling records the entire conversation to save as a permanent file to be used against Howard and his team of dirty agents.

.   .   .

Ross approaches the road that meets Taconic Lake before it splits. There she sees movement in the distance and stays low as she moves toward it. As she looks further ahead, she can see the beam of a flashlight facing upward and moving up the mountain.

.   .   .

Agent Howard sees a moving beam from agent Ling's flashlight and he freezes. He notices another male and a female travelling with Ling and initially assumes that it is Ross and Granderson moving quickly toward him. He ducks down into the bushes and peers through with his weapon aimed at the unsuspecting trio. Howard is determined not to be taken alive.

As the beam from Ling's flashlight gets closer, Howard can hear the voice of John Magi. He suddenly realizes that this group is not a threat to him and that he can keep moving down the mountain before the woods are completely pitch black. Although John Magi being alive is no longer his greatest threat, Howard wickedly decides to put a bullet in the man who has been a nuisance to him and his plan for riches.

Howard waits until the trio reaches within a few yards and then he squeezes the trigger of his 40-caliber handgun, sending four rounds in the direction of the three unsuspecting targets.

.   .   .

Granderson hears the shots ring out and runs in that direction with his gun ready. Ross also moves quickly in the direction of the flashlight beam.

.   .   .

The gunshots catch Ling by surprise, and he drops his flashlight to the ground and runs downhill for cover. The dropped flashlight spins, sending its bright beam moving in the form of a lighthouse. When it comes to a stop, the beam rests on the sprawled-out body of Jamie, as she lies motionless on the ground.

.   .   .

Jerron reaches the last cabin at the top of the mountain and brings the sedan to a screeching halt. He swings the driver-side door open and exits the vehicle. With the shiny revolver in hand he walks up to the front door of the cabin and violently kicks it open. He is enraged. When he looks inside the living room expecting to see

Katherine and Kyle still tied together, he is surprised to see three bodies covered in sheets and blood everywhere. He checks the bodies and doesn't recognize any of the deceased. He walks into the kitchen and sees his brother's body also covered. He is not sure what happened here, but he realizes that his and Anthony's perfect plan is not so perfect after all.

*   *   *

As they approach the cabin, Katherine instructs Kyle to turn the headlights off and not to pull up too close. Kyle stops the car and turns the engine off.

Katherine quietly exits the car and carefully shuts the door halfway.

"Wait here," she orders.

With rifle in hand, she moves like a tactical swat team member toward the sedan driven by Jerron. She leads with the rifle, as she makes sure no one is in the car. She then quietly reaches into the vehicle, near the bottom of the driver's side, and pops open the trunk. After confirming that Jamie is not stuffed in the trunk, she carefully walks backward, with the rifle pointed straight ahead, as she moves back to Kyle.

"Listen, if I don't come back out of that cabin in three minutes, I want you to haul ass down that mountain, and do not stop until you get to a police station ... do you understand?" she clarifies.

Kyle is visibly nervous, and afraid for her. However he can see the determination of a mother protecting her family. He nods in agreement. Katherine takes a deep breath and slowly moves toward the cabin.

As she gets to the half-opened front door, she can see one of the bodies partially uncovered. Using the end of the rifle, she slowly and quietly eases the door open wider. Just as she clears the doorway, she is startled by Jerron as he walks out of the kitchen. He is carrying his brother's body over his shoulder and is about to make his exit out to the car. He sees her and flings Anthony's body behind him to the floor, quickly reaching into his waistband and retrieving his weapon.

Katherine has her rifle locked onto him.

"Honey, I'm home!" she announces with a blend of sarcasm and anger.

Jerron raises his arm and aims his weapon at Katherine.

"I want a divorce, asshole!" she declares.

Two deep, deafening cracks ring out as she fires two shots from the rifle—both striking him in his upper torso and knocking him backwards and down to the ground. As Jerron lands on top of his brother's body he looks up at her, choking on his own blood.

"And I'm keeping the house!" she spits.

* * *

John crawls on his knees over to Jamie as she lies motionless on the dusty ground. In the midst of the excitement, his adrenaline doesn't allow him to immediately feel the burning pain in his shoulder where one of Howard's bullets pierced and exited his body. As his mind begins to register the intense pain, he himself collapses next to his injured daughter.

Agent Howard quickly makes his way over to John as he struggles to reach out his hand and grab Jamie. He recognizes the voice of the FBI agent whom he once trusted and offered his sworn statement—a statement that put away most members of the Mongelli crime family. The voice of agent Howard gets closer to where John lies.

"Mr. Wonderful ... you have caused me so much grief," Howard states through an enraged scowl as he walks toward John. "I should have done this 15 years ago." He lifts his weapon.

John is still reaching out for Jamie when Howard discharges a round from his pistol. The bullet strikes John in the back, causing him to fall flat. His hand lands on top of Jamie's hand.

"I love you, princess," John whispers as he looks at the closed eyes of his daughter. Blood runs across her face from her eyes as if she is crying blood. John's eyes close as Howard walks directly up to him and his now standing directly over him, looking down.

Howard aims his gun directly at John's head and prepares to fire at point-blank range.

As three piercing gunshots ring out, Howard falls to his knees in excruciating pain. The bullets from Ross' service weapon rip through the back of his knees. As Ross stands a few yards behind Howard, she orders Howard to drop the weapon he is still holding in his right hand.

"Agent Stewart Howard, you are under arrest for the murder of special agent Monica Bloomfield!" announces Ross.

She keeps her weapon fixed on him as she steps closer. Howard turns as he falls onto his butt. He is sitting up facing Ross as she carefully approaches.

"So what now...are you going to kill me, Ross?" questions Howard doubtfully. "I'm not going to prison!" he continues.

As Ross briefly takes her eyes off of Howard to observe the condition of John and Jamie, Howard quickly raises his weapon and points it at Ross. A fourth single shot rings out in the night air, as a bullet from agent Granderson's gun rips into Howard's shoulder, causing him to drop his weapon and fall flat onto his back.

Ross looks over at Granderson, who still has his weapon fixed on Howard. She is glad to see her partner, and thankful that he has her back. She flashes a smile and with a wink of her eyes she says, "Thanks ... partner."

CHAPTER 27

State and local law enforcement agencies, along with federal agents, swarm the woods near Taconic Lake. Sirens and lights from emergency vehicles fill the night sky as officials converge on the sprawling property. Agent Ling sits with other agents giving his eyewitness statement. Agent Howard is in extreme pain as he is rolled along on the rocky terrain, strapped to a stretcher. His left wrist is handcuffed to the metal rail of the stretcher as he is taken over to the back of a waiting ambulance.

John Magi is also strapped to a stretcher. He has an oxygen mask on his face as emergency medical technicians work quickly to get the critically wounded man into the back of an ambulance, hooked up to an IV, and off to a nearby hospital.

Jamie Magi is in bad shape as she is placed into a helicopter and airlifted to a nearby medical facility. Fortunately for her, the bullet that grazed her face was not a direct hit, as it first went through her father's shoulder before making contact with her. Unfortunately for her, the force knocked her back, causing her to smash her head onto a sharp rock. Doctors will have to hurry and try to stop the swelling around her brain before she suffers irreversible and permanent brain damage.

A distraught Katherine rides in the helicopter with her daughter. Kyle looks on nervously as the chopper blades turn rapidly, kicking up dust and wind, as it takes off and away. He will join Katherine at the hospital after giving his statement to the two police officers questioning him.

The medical examiner's van is parked in front of the cabin up on the mountain as investigators begin carrying bodies from the cabin, and loading them into the van.

Agents Ross and Granderson are separated as they give independent statements to FBI officials. Crime scene technicians process all of the vehicles and rooms in the cabin, and collect evidence. All weapons are collected. They will be taken to a lab where they will be tested and analyzed to give a detailed account of exactly what happened here on this mountain.

*   *   *

When the helicopter carrying Jamie lands on the roof of the Sprainbrook Medical Center, she is immediately taken into surgery, where doctors will work frantically to save her.

While she is in the operating room, agents from state and federal agencies arrive with Kyle, who waits in the family waiting area, as Katherine is taken to a private room to give her statement and eyewitness account to law enforcement officials.

Katherine goes into deep detail about the last few years of her life: how she married Jerron, who went by the name of West, and never suspected he had any ties to the Mongelli crime family. She denies having any knowledge of stashed diamonds or cash taken during a heist a decade and a half earlier. She signs her statement, which includes how she shot Jerron Silvestri in self-defense. After giving her very detailed statement, Katherine joins Kyle as they await word on Jamie, who has been in emergency surgery for over two hours.

*   *   *

Agent Ross arrives at the hospital and enters the waiting area to meet with Katherine and Kyle. Katherine gives her a hug of thanks and praises her and her team for keeping them alive. Both Kyle and Katherine express their deep gratitude.

"I can't take all the credit. It was the bravery of special agent Bloomfield, who befriended Jamie and was smart enough to get Kyle to give her those earrings," Ross explains. "Without her, we never would have been able to track you down before the Silvestri brothers murdered you all. She is the real hero here … rest her soul."

There is a brief moment of silence, as if the three of them are paying respect to their fallen hero. Ross is visibly choked up.

"Bloomfield was not only a great agent, but since coming to New York she has grown to be more like a little sister to me," states Ross as she fights back tears.

She changes the subject from Bloomfield to Jamie.

"How is she … any word from the doctors?" inquires Ross.

"Nothing yet … she didn't look well when they brought her in," replies a worried Katherine.

Granderson enters the waiting area and walks over to where the trio is standing.

"Mrs. West …" he greets before being cut off by Katherine.

"Just Katherine is fine," she interrupts.

"Yes, well, Katherine, I am sorry about the ordeal that you and your family are going through. My thoughts and prayers are with you all," he states genuinely.

"Thank you for that, and thank you for protecting us and keeping us alive … Now we just wait for Jamie and John to pull through," Katherine states, holding her hands in a prayer-like clasp with white knuckles. She surprises herself as she realizes that she is not just concerned for her daughter, but for John as well.

"How is John?" Katherine asks.

"He is in critical but stable condition. Unfortunately, we can't question him or get a statement, as he is not responsive," replies Granderson.

He then turns to Ross and the reason for his intrusion.

"Speaking of statements, director Solomon is here. He wants to talk," he announces to Ross.

Ross' face indicates that a visit from director Solomon is a big deal.

"Excuse me, folks. I will be back to check on Jamie," she states before walking purposefully out of the room.

Granderson walks behind her, but then stops and turns back to Katherine.

"John is down in ICU. Apparently the bullet that struck Jamie was altered by first going through his shoulder. It is quite possible that had she been hit directly, things would be much worse. I think that is something he would like to know … and it should come from someone he really cares about," he states.

Kyle begins to walk as if volunteering to go visit John. After taking four steps, he notices the puzzling scowl he is getting from Granderson, and realizes that he meant Katherine.

"Oh that's right, you meant he should hear it from his widow," blurts Kyle as his own statement confuses him.

Granderson exits behind Ross, leaving Katherine and Kyle alone.

"Kyle, if there is any news from the doctor have them page me down at the ICU. I will be back soon," announces Katherine.

"Will do," replies Kyle.

Katherine takes an exaggerated deep breath and then exits the room and walks toward the elevators.

·　　·　　·

FBI Director Edward Solomon is a seasoned man with a full head of grey hair, clean-shaven face, and thick eyebrows. He stands a strapping six foot, four inches tall, and carries a medium build. He has never personally met agent Michelle Ross, but she knows everything about him. She is honored to stand in his presence as his highly esteemed reputation precedes him. Director Solomon is sitting in the hospital conference room when Ross enters. Upon her entry, he stands and approaches her. His intimidating stature matches his leadership, confidence and serious demeanor.

"Director Solomon, I'm agent Michelle Ross," she announces as she extends her hand.

"Agent Ross," replies Solomon as he shakes her hand and then gestures for her to take a seat.

When she takes a seat, she realizes that she is at the head of the long conference table, and there are several other high-ranking FBI officials also present.

"Agent Ross, first off, let me start by stating that you and your team have done a phenomenal job here, and prevented further loss of life," declares Solomon.

"Thank you, sir," replies Ross. She is unsure how to read the stoic faces of the others seated around the table, as well Solomon's dry tone.

"The details are starting to come together, and there are still more questions than answers," Solomon continues. "We are not yet able to interview John Magi, and agent Ling's recording of Mr. Magi's account is rather troubling. Naturally we have to conduct an extensive internal investigation within the entire New York field office. I intend to clean house, and unfortunately you and your partner will have to undergo some scrutiny, as I'm sure you are aware, agent Howard claims that there are several others who knew about the World Trade Center heist."

"Sir, I can assure you that I had no knowledge of it prior to this evening," replies a stunned Ross.

"I'm sure then that our investigation will reflect that … I do hope that this is the case. You have a bright future with the bureau; I would hate for you to throw that away to cover for anyone on your team," states Solomon sternly.

Ross surveys the faces around the table. Each mirrors the tone of the director. She remains speechless as she sits paralyzed by the allegation—or hint thereof.

"Howard didn't offer much else before requesting a lawyer," Solomon concludes. He signals to an agent standing by the door. That agent then opens the door and summons agent Granderson, who walks in with a nervous look on his face. The mood is that of a group of hungry lions, and Ross and Granderson are two sheep.

"Agent Granderson and agent Ross, I need you both to surrender your weapons," Solomon declares as two agents step behind the party in question.

Ross and Granderson look at each other, as they are shocked and confused as to what is happening.

"Are we being detained, sir?" Ross inquires.

"No, not at this time. You will both be assigned to desk duty until my investigation is complete, after which you will either return to the field, or join agent Howard in federal prison." Solomon speaks without the slightest adjustment to his emotionless facial expression.

Ross and Granderson turn their weapons over to the agents standing behind them. The two agents then step away and Solomon is satisfied.

"I will also be needing your passports surrendered within the next 24 hours," he adds.

Granderson is angry, and storms out of the room without uttering a word. Ross is visibly upset, as her job is not merely what she does ... but who she is. She drops her head in disappointment as she turns and walks of out the conference room.

*　　　*　　　*

Down in the ICU, after being directed to the room where John is being kept, Katherine walks down the hall and stops when she reaches room 17-A. She slowly pushes the glass door open and walks into the brightly lit room, which swells with the resounding beeping and hissing of the various machines and hospital equipment. As she steps past a light-blue curtain, she gets her first glimpse of John. She is immediately transported back in time—15 years earlier when she eulogized her then-husband. John lies motionless and unconscious with a breathing tube taped to his mouth. On the table next to his bed, a tablet belonging to agent Ling is propped up with a note written on a small piece of paper. On the note, there are only two words: *Play me.*

Katherine turns and looks back at the door. Through the glass door she sees agent Ling smiling and waving. He then gives her a "thumbs-up" sign and walks away. Katherine steps over to the motion-activated tablet. When she picks it up, the screen illuminates and powers on. On the 12-inch screen she sees a play button icon with the text: *Mr. Wonderful—John Magi's story.*

Katherine presses the play button and listens as the voice of her one-time husband reverberates through the speakers. Through the sounds of the air, lake, and woods, John shares with his daughter the events that led to him getting caught up with Salvatore Mongelli, and the heart-wrenching decision that he had to make to spare her and the woman he loved since the day he met her.

As the recording of audio from Jamie's earring continues to play, Katherine experiences a flood of emotions as she recalls and relives several of the events John mentions ... the good, like John taking her hunting; the bad, like John's office being burned down in a deliberate act of arson; and the ugly, like having to watch the love of his life weep at his own funeral. Tears roll uncontrollably from Katherine's eyes as she hears John talk about how much it hurt to have to sit by and do nothing as she gave her heart to another man and remarried.

Perhaps the most moving part of what John finally got to share with his daughter is how he never, for one single moment, stopped thinking about or loving them.

As the recording ends, Katherine wipes tears from her face. She grabs John's hand and for the first time in over a decade, she is touching her first love. That realization overtakes her and she drops her head lightly onto his abdomen and sobs intensely.

CHAPTER 28

The sun begins to rise, and the Sprainbrook Hospital staff shift changes. There are still a lot of police and media presence around. Several reporters try in vain to harass hospital employees as they exit the main entrance, and walk to their vehicles in the staff parking lot. Everyone is seeking answers to the bloodshed involving federal officers on the Taconic Mountain. In an effort to protect the identities of the deceased until their next of kin can be notified and properly identify the bodies, FBI Director Edward Solomon holds a brief press conference outside the hospital lobby. His agenda also includes protecting the names and identities of the three surviving agents as well as the civilian survivors. As he stands in front of the lobby doors, reporters holding mini recorders and smart phones swarm the tall man with the powerful stature and stoic demeanor.

"Director Solomon, is it true that relatives of Salvatore Mongelli got into a raging gun battle with federal agents at the camp site?" yells one female reporter as she holds her recording device in Solomon's direction.

"How many mobsters are now in custody?" yells a male reporter.

Solomon simply raises his hand slightly. That brief gesture and pause commands the entire crowd gathered as they anxiously await a statement from the FBI director. As the agency's top cop, his presence here speaks volumes as to the magnitude of the events of last night.

"Let me start off by saying that we lost some good agents up there last night ... men and women that took an oath to protect and defend this great country. Unfortunately, sometimes that oath and bravery is met by the challenge of paying the ultimate sacrifice. Let's also remember that these aren't just robots with a federal badge ... but people, with families. So I trust that each of you will respect that fact and allow us to properly notify those families before you report and print your stories," announces Solomon.

There is a sudden outburst of questions and general clamor from the group of media professionals. Solomon doesn't directly address anyone in particular, but rather continues with his statement.

"As for exactly what took place at the camp site last night, some of our agents tracked a possible kidnapped victim from the city to the grounds of Camp Taconic. As they made contact with the victim or victims, they were met with resistance from the perpetrators involved. Our investigation is only in its infancy stage, but as details become available, our public relations coordinator will relay information to you as long as it doesn't hamper or compromise any ongoing investigation into this matter. Thank you," concludes Solomon as he walks to the parking lot.

The media personnel yell additional questions for clarity and more details. Director Solomon continues to walk away, surrounded by several agents and other law enforcement. Local police and armed hospital security herd the mob of reporters away from blocking the entrance to the hospital. Within minutes, the police position metal barriers to establish a perimeter and keep the media at bay, and from hindering hospital personnel, patients, and guests from obtaining access.

◦　　　◦　　　◦

Inside the lobby, observing the circus unfolding beyond the large tinted-glass doors, agents Ross, Granderson, and Ling are huddled together.

"So wait, you guys have no guns, and are assigned to desk duty? Hey, welcome to my world!" jokes Ling in an attempt to lighten the tension. "Trust me ... it beats being out there chasing mobsters and rogue agents, and getting shot at."

Granderson has a new respect for the little, flamboyant, geeky agent since he saved his life back at the cabin. Out of respect he smiles at Ling's comment, but in no way finds the situation even slightly amusing.

Ross is in no joking mood and is extremely frustrated.

"Solomon is right ... I mean, how well do we really know the agents we work with and what they're actually capable of when billions of dollars are at stake?" she blurts in a dry tone.

"What's that supposed to mean?" replies an offended Granderson. He senses the accusatory tone in her voice.

Ross doesn't respond. She shakes her head and turns away in the opposite direction of the front entrance.

"Where are you going, Ross?" asks Granderson.

Ross stops and turns back toward him and Ling.

"Well, I'm definitely not going out there to face those hounds," she replies, referring to the thirsty group of hostile media assembled out front.

She walks to the reception desk and asks for a side exit. Granderson and Ling follow her.

* * *

Sundays at the hospital are normally quiet with a small staff and a skeleton crew of doctors. Due to the shootings last night, there are more than the usual doctors on staff as several surgeons performed hours of surgery on Jamie Magi throughout the night.

They have successfully stopped the bleeding and swelling that was suffocating her brain. She is currently in a medically induced coma as doctors continue to monitor her progress. Thick white gauze pads cover her eyes that were heavily damaged by the bullet fragments that grazed John, and embedded into her corneas.

Katherine and Kyle stand outside of her recovery room getting the news from the chief surgeon. They are both elated to learn that she is expected to survive her injuries.

"The bad news is that we are not yet sure of any permanent brain damage or physical limitations she may experience. There is also a great possibility that she will never regain her vision. As time progresses, we will know more," the surgeon explains apologetically.

The news hits both Kyle and Katherine and they console each other in the hallway as the surgeon walks away.

*　　　*　　　*

At the men's federal prison in Glendale, Richie Silvestri is notified that he has visitors. The former street-thug smiles confidently as he is escorted to the private visitation room. Expecting to see his two sons, Anthony and Jerry, bringing him good news about killing Magi and his family and obtaining the diamonds, Silvestri is stunned to see two male federal agents seated across the table. His demeanor instantly reduces down from joy to grave concern.

"Have a seat, Richie," states one of the agents.

"What's this about?" questions a nervous Silvestri as he slowly and cautiously takes a seat.

"Let me guess, you were expecting the twins?" asks the other agent mockingly.

Richie is surprised to learn that the feds know about his sons. He is equally stunned and mortified to discover that both of his boys were killed last night. The news is enough to enrage him, but the cold-blooded mobster doesn't shed a single tear. Instead he turns his rage toward another man.

"And Magi?" he questions.

The agents don't offer information as to the status of Magi and his family. They do question Richie about the diamonds and the heist, but he naturally denies any knowledge of a heist or any diamonds.

"Come on, Richie, we tell you that your boys have been killed and the first thing you do is ask about John Magi. We already know about the diamonds," declares the first agent.

"What, did you put a hit on Magi and his family because of the diamonds?" asks the second agent.

Their questioning further fuels his rage. He slams his fists onto the metal table as he stands to his feet. The two agents also stand and prepare to defend themselves.

"Good day, gentlemen," Richie announces calmly as he exits back to his cell.

.   .   .

After his surgery, agent Howard wakes to find himself still cuffed to his hospital bed. He is groggy from the anesthesia, and cannot move his legs. He soon realizes that he is not alone. His old friend and lawyer Arthur Stavros walks over to his bedside.

Arthur is a Greek-American man in his early 60s. He is nearing retirement and taking on a very limited caseload. However, when he got the call from his old college friend, he came promptly to represent his legal rights and interests.

"Stewart, how are you feeling, buddy?" asks Stavros of his friend and client.

"Arthur, great to see you," replies Howard weakly.

"I came as soon as I could. The traffic out of Jersey was atrocious. Now, whatever statement you made, I will get it thrown off the record, since you were shot and under duress. You just get better, and let me do my thing … and whatever you do, do not talk to the media," states Stavros.

"Thank you. Just know that when I get out of this, there is a lot of money in it for you, pal," replies Howard.

"That's good, since I started billing you the moment I left my house on a Sunday," replies Stavros with a devilish grin that indicates he is as greedy, and perhaps as unscrupulous, as Howard.

The two old chums shake hands. As Stavros exits the room, he passes two state police officers guarding the room of the corrupt federal agent.

"What have I just signed up for?" mumbles Stavros as he makes his way to the elevator.

.   .   .

Katherine exits the elevator and walks down the hallway to room 17-A, which now has a police officer seated outside the door. She waves to the officer and then quietly enters the room and takes a seat on the edge of John's bed. He is still unconscious and breathing via the various machines that he is hooked up to. She holds his limp hand and then speaks to him as if she is certain that he can hear her every word.

"I forgive you for leaving me and Jamie all those years ago," she says quietly. "Now I understand why you had to make the choice you made. I can't imagine what it was like for you to live a secret life for all of those years, alone and away from your family."

Katherine pauses and rubs her thumb over the blue veins on the back of his hand. John remains motionless, his face placid.

"Jamie made it through surgery," she continues, her voice wavering. "The surgeon says they don't know yet if she has brain damage, or if she'll recover her sight. I am praying that you both pull through so that we can all be a family again."

Katherine leans in and kisses John gently on the forehead.

"I love you, John … thanks for coming back for us," she whispers.

As she stands to leave, she thinks she feels his hand squeeze hers. She keeps her hand in his for a moment to see if he indeed responded, but she doesn't get a reaction.

CHAPTER 29

Early Monday morning, agent Michelle Ross skips her daily run and heads straight to the office. She is meeting with agent Ling in his office. After spending the entire night going over the case, Ross is more determined than ever to find any dirt on Howard and all of the dirty agents that worked with him.

"OK, let's start with the ones we know for certain … Evans and Wang," states Ross.

Ling pulls up data on his computer, which is displayed on his large monitor.

"Well, after checking their phone records and cross-referencing all their similar contacts with Howard's, I didn't find much. All of the possible suspect agents have been killed in the line of duty," states Ling.

"Howard had to find a broker to unload the diamonds for cash … we need to find out whom he was dealing with over the years," replies Ross.

Agent Granderson knocks on the door and then enters quickly and shuts the door behind him. Before he can utter a word, Ross speaks up.

"Hey … look, I'm sorry for how I acted yesterday at the hospital. I guess the stress got to me. I have never doubted your honesty or loyalty. You are the best agent I know," she declares to Granderson.

Granderson smiles. Ling frowns as he loudly clears his throat.

"One of the best agents I know," she corrects herself for Ling's sake.

Ling smiles.

"Well, you're going to really think I'm great now," Granderson announces as he provides her with a file folder.

"What is this?" asks Ross as she opens the folder.

"Well, believe it or not, it is much easier to solve a diamond heist that we know actually existed. The trouble is, until this weekend, the FBI had no prior knowledge a heist even occurred," replies Granderson.

"You got your hands on a list of all of Sal Mongelli's crew that was killed or arrested in September 2001? Genius ... I could kiss you," replies Ross with excitement.

Ling loudly clears his throat again to remind them of his presence and that they are in his office.

"Yes, and when we cross reference that list, with the names of those unaccounted for ..." Granderson starts his thought and allows Ross to complete it.

"Frankie Sterlacci!" announces Ross gleefully.

"I was able to access Howard's case files. According to the log of one of Howard's undercover agents inside the Mongelli family, out of all of the men that went in to do the heist that morning, Sterlacci was the only one to not return. The men present reported a shootout with two armed guards in which Sterlacci was shot and left behind," announces Granderson.

This is very intriguing to Ross. She has Ling pull up digital records and files from that fateful day. They notice something.

"How many armed security guards did Mongelli's men say they got into a shootout with?" asks Ross.

"Two," replies Granderson as he checks the undercover agent's report.

"Well there were three armed security guards on duty that morning ... It says here that all three were killed in the collapse. All three of their weapons were accounted for, according to the security company. Not many autopsies were conducted from the victims on that day, as most were assumed to have died due to the fire or crumbling rubble," states Ross.

Ling searches for the identities of the guards on duty the morning of the heist.

"Let me pull up their information ... Dough Eichler, Nicholas Trama, and Ryan Quinlan," states Ling as he reads off of his monitor.

He is able to pull up last-known addresses and contact information. Ross notices that on agent Sarah Wang's phone, she listed a contact as "The Traumatizer aka Broker." She also referred to "My guy Nicholas" in a message to Howard. This brings Ross to a theory.

"OK, so let's just suppose that this Nicholas Trama is the Traumatizer, and he is somehow connected to this whole thing," suggests Ross.

"Yeah, but he's dead, remember?" replies Ling.

"Remember John Magi is 'dead' as well," replies Ross using air quotes.

"I say we also dig into Mongelli's guy, Frankie Sterlacci. If he made it out of the building alive, he knows about the heist, and therefore could be working with Howard," Granderson suggests.

As the trio brainstorm, they are interrupted by a knock on the door. The door opens and standing there is a very attractive woman. She is extremely fit, well proportioned, and well dressed in a skirt suit. She has long shapely legs and muscular calves that are further enhanced by her three-inch heels. She wears her thick blonde hair down and away from her face. She is FBI agent Amanda Huffman ... Howard's interim replacement as supervising agent ... and Granderson's ex-fiancée. She steps into the room confidently and begins to speak directly to Granderson.

"Ah, someone told me that I would find you down here," announces the beautiful agent.

Granderson is surprised to see her, and even more surprised when she walks up and gives him a hug. Knowing their history, he is uncomfortable with the affectionate greeting in Ross' presence.

"Amanda? What are you doing here?" asks Granderson as he politely tries to maintain arm's distance.

"Well, it's nice to see you too," replies Huffman as she pulls away.

Realizing who she is, and impressed with her good looks, Ross turns to Granderson.

"This is Amanda ... THE Amanda?" questions Ross.

Agent Huffman extends her hand to Ross as she formerly introduces herself.

"Supervising agent Huffman ... I will be taking over for agent Howard here," she announces.

Ross shakes her hand.

"Wait, so they transferred you here from Chicago?" asks Granderson.

"Yes, it was a last-minute decision. I got the call over the weekend from director Solomon. Due to Howard's influence here, they preferred to fill the position from outside this office," Huffman explains.

"Well, welcome back to New York. This is agent Michelle Ross, and this is agent Patrick Ling," Granderson announces as he introduces the rest of the team.

"Nice to meet you all. And very nice to see you again," states Huffman to Granderson.

Ross stares at the attractive agent who is clearly flirting with Granderson. Ling notices Ross' expression and smirks at the possible tension.

"I will be evaluating each of you as internal affairs conducts its investigation," continues Huffman.

"Looking forward to it," replies Ross with sarcasm.

"Grandy, I'm taking you to lunch later so we can catch up. Do you mind walking with me to my office?" asks Huffman.

"Sure, are you now in Howard's office?" asks Granderson as he and Huffman exit the room together.

Ross and Ling are now alone in his office.

"Grandy?" states Ross mockingly to Ling.

"Do I sense a little jealously?" questions Ling.

"Me, jealous of her? No ... just because the woman he almost married is now back in town ... oh and, yeah, she also happens to be my new boss ... I'm not jealous!" replies Ross.

Ling is not buying her response. He stares at her.

"What? Don't judge me. Just let me know what you find on Frankie Sterlacci and Nicholas Trama," states Ross before exiting Ling's office.

Ling smiles and makes an aggressive feline growl while clawing dramatically at the air.

.   .   .

At the Sprainbrook Medical Center near Taconic Lake, a team of nurses and medical personnel rush into room 17-A. Patient John Magi has flat-lined. The loud, steady beep resonates through the room and out into the hallway where Katherine is told to wait. She looks on frantically through the glass window of the door as the resident physician on duty works desperately to revive the unresponsive middle-aged man.

"No heartbeat, doctor!" announces one of the ICU trauma nurses.

"Come on Mr. Magi ... help us out and fight," states the doctor to his patient. He rubs defibrillator pads together and then yells, "clear!"

Katherine cannot bear to watch any longer. She turns her back to the wall adjacent to the door and leans against it. She covers her mouth to muffle her weeping as she slowly slides down to the floor where she sits, feeling hopeless.

Within minutes some of the nurses exit the room. None of them make eye contact with the tearful woman seated on the floor just outside the room, with her back against the wall. By their lackadaisical pace, Katherine can presume that there is no longer a rush to revive John. Either he is in the clear, or beyond assistance. As the doctor emerges from the room Katherine can tell by the grim look in his eyes that the news will not be favorable.

The doctor looks at Katherine still seated on the floor—her legs too exhausted to sustain the magnitude of this weekend's events. As the doctor shakes his head negatively, Katherine doesn't even attempt to stand. She buries her face in her hands before he can utter the dreaded phrase: "So sorry ... we did everything we could."

.   .   .

Upstairs in Jamie Magi's room, Kyle is asleep on a chair next to the window on the side of her bed. He is startled out of his slumber by the sound of Jamie's weak, frightened cry. He quickly jumps to his feet and steps over to her bedside. He gently caresses her hand and softly speaks to her.

"It's OK babe, I'm right here," he announces, before calling for help and alerting the staff that she is awake.

Jamie is on the verge of hysteria as she wakes up in severe pain and with the thick gauze covering her eyes. It takes Kyle and two nurses to restrain her. A third nurse rushes in and puts more pain-management drugs into her IV. Everyone in the room works on keeping her calm as they await the arrival of the doctor.

.   .   .

When Katherine gets word that her daughter has woken up, she rushes up to her room. She meets Kyle, who is pacing anxiously outside the door.

"Hey, what's going on ... can we go in?" asks Katherine anxiously.

"The doctor is in with her now. They made me wait out here. How is her dad?" replies Kyle.

The disappointment of the response to her question pales in comparison to the sting brought on by his question.

"I'm afraid John didn't make it. The machines are breathing for him, but basically he is no longer with us," she announces with her eyes down toward the floor.

Kyle gives her a supportive hug, which only creates a greater burst of emotions—causing her to shed a few tears. As they break apart from their embrace, Katherine dries her eyes with a ball of tissue she brought up with her.

"They said that I am listed as his next of kin ... and Jamie and I as his only living relatives. They are waiting on me to give the call to pull the plug. I want Jamie to say her goodbyes first," she continues.

"I'm so sorry for your loss, Mrs. ..." Kyle hesitates, as he doesn't want to offend Katherine by calling her by her married name, West ... so he takes the safest route. "Mrs. Katherine."

Kyle pauses as a nurse quickly walks toward them with another doctor behind her. They both pass Katherine and Kyle and head directly into Jamie's room and close the door behind them.

For the next several minutes, Katherine and Kyle stand in the hallway awaiting word of Jamie's status. When the door finally opens the two doctors emerge and meet with them out in the hallway.

The treating physician explains the status of Jamie's overall health, and then introduces the second doctor as the hospital's eye specialist, Dr. Kerry Donohue.

Doctor Donohue begins in a soft but firm voice. "The damage to Jamie's corneas is severe," she says. She pauses for a moment. Nurses in pastel scrubs and soft shoes pad silently around them like apparitions. The doctor looks back and forth between Kyle and Katherine.

"We will definitely run more tests, but both corneas have been so severely damaged, I don't expect her to regain her vision," she continues. "The trauma will leave Jamie permanently blind. She is not taking this well so she really needs your support right now. I'm sorry."

Kyle collapses to the floor with his head in his hands.

Katherine is overwhelmed and is not sure how she will even begin to tell Jamie more bad news ... that her father has died ... again.

CHAPTER 30

Agent Granderson enters his new boss' office. Although a decade
has passed since he and his former fiancée parted ways, she looks
exactly the same as the last time her saw her. Supervising agent Huffman walks in ahead of Granderson and sits on the edge of her desk
and crosses her legs. Things didn't work out between the couple
years ago when Huffman moved to Chicago to take a promotion.
She called off their engagement as she felt her fiancé would be sacri-
ficing his chances of moving up the ranks had he left the New York
field office. She has married and divorced since then and now that
she is back in New York City, she is blatantly flirting with her former beau. Knowing how much he always loved her long, shapely
legs, she positions herself in front of him to properly display one of
her best physical assets.

   Granderson sits in the chair in front of Huffman's desk, facing
her. She gently swings her foot back and forth, periodically "ac-
cidentally" grazing his shin with the tip of her shoe. Completely
oblivious to her subtle teasing, Granderson appears simply happy
just to see an old friend.

   "So ... Amanda Lynn Huffman ... How the heck have you
been? It's been what ... 10-11 years?" Granderson opens the pre--
work-talk dialogue.

   "Wow, has it really been that long? Well, you still look amazing," replies Huffman.

They both seem to be avoiding the subject of their past engagement and why it ended.

"It looks like you're almost settled in already," states Granderson as he observes the many personal items placed neatly on her desk and shelves.

Huffman is disappointed that he is not checking out her exhibited legs. She decides to up her game ... and her skirt. While pretending to partially turn her upper body in order to look back at her shelves, she shifts her weight to her right hip and with her left hand she cleverly slides her skirt up to mid-thigh before turning back to face Granderson. Now displaying more skin, she is hopeful that he will take notice and get ideas similar to her own ... ideas of rekindling the strong sexual energy they once shared. Granderson, however, seems oblivious and uninterested, and perhaps the reason for his indifference is knocking on Huffman's office door.

Agent Michelle Ross opens the office door and enters without an invitation. She is carrying a small office plant.

"Hi, sorry for the interruption but I just wanted to welcome the new boss and bring a gift for your office," announces Ross. She steps right up to the desk and hands the plant to Huffman. Immediately Ross notices the very obvious flirting conducted by her new boss ... and apparently her new competition. Huffman takes the plant with a confused look on her face. She then looks at Granderson and notices how he is checking out Ross' rear end. The new boss realizes instantly that winning back her former man will meet some resistance with his very attractive partner in the picture.

"Why, thank you ..." Huffman replies and pauses as if she doesn't recall Ross' name. This tactic employed by Huffman is to send a message to her competition reminding her of her insignificance.

Ross picks up on it by the glare in Huffman's eyes.

"It's Ross," she declares—also declaring war as she reads through Huffman's motives.

"I'm sure this will brighten up the room. Thank you," replies Huffman in a dismissive tone.

Everything in Ross is telling her to just exit the room, but being as stubborn as she is, she decides to stay.

"So look at the time … are you guys going to lunch?" states Ross as she pretends to look at her watch.

"Yes, we are going to the Thai place across the street, you should come with us," replies Granderson, much to the surprise of Huffman, who was hoping to spend alone time out of the office with her ex.

"Yes, you should totally join us," states Huffman as sincerely as she can.

"Are you sure? I wouldn't want to intrude," replies Ross as sincerely as she can.

"Nonsense. Lunch with an old friend and my best friend sounds perfect," replies Granderson.

Ross smiles as she looks at Huffman. She counts her first victory as Granderson referred to her as his best friend, and Huffman as merely an old friend. Huffman flashes a fake smile in return. It's game on, and challenge accepted. This should be a very interesting lunch.

*　　*　　*

Down in the tech lab, agent Ling makes a significant discovery. He is able to clone agent Sarah Wang's cell phone number and use it through his tablet. He received a text message from the contact she saved as "The Traumatizer aka Broker." The text message is simple, yet pivotal: *Bring the last of the ice to the stack s tonight 10 P.M. Found a buyer that can move them ASAP.*

Ling is not sure exactly where the stacks are. He assumes it is a usual meeting spot or code between Wang and the broker, therefore he cannot ask for an exact location as to tip him off and alert him that he is not actually communicating with Wang. Ling grabs his tablet and a file from his desk and races up to Ross' office.

*　　*　　*

MR. WONDERFUL • 193

As Ross, Granderson, and Huffman exit the elevator in the lobby of the federal building, Ling approaches them, frantic and out of breath. After just missing the trio upstairs as they got into the elevator heading to lunch, he had to take the stairs and race down to the lobby to catch them. Clearly what he has to present to Ross is very important ... if only he could get it out.

"Ling, are you OK, buddy?" asks Granderson.

Ling holds up one finger as he leans forward, gasping for air.

"We were just heading across the street for a bite, you coming?" Granderson continues.

Ling is still severely out of breath. He shakes his head negatively and hands the tablet to Ross. She looks at the text message displayed on the screen and is puzzled.

"What is this?" asks Ross.

Ling is finally able to get some words out of his mouth.

"The Traumatizer!" huffs Ling.

The trio looks around; searching each other's faces for a glimmer of understanding, then back at Ling in confusion.

Ling throws his head back in an exaggerated manner before making a second attempt to get out more words.

"The number Wang saved as 'The Traumatizer aka Broker'... I think it's Nicholas Trama," Ling states in between breaths.

"So clearly he thinks he's talking to Wang. He doesn't know that she was killed. This is epic, Ling!" replies Ross, allowing Ling to catch his breath further.

"Yes, whatever messages he texts to her number will be ported directly to my tablet," Ling states.

"Great, so can you respond as her also?" asks Granderson.

"Yes, but I don't want to risk tipping him off. Once he realizes that he is not communicating with Wang, we may never find him," replies Ling.

"Smart thinking. I wonder what he means by 'the stacks'?" questions Ross.

"I have no idea, and I am afraid that if it is a usual meeting place for him and Wang, and I ask for the location, it will tip him off," replies Ling.

Huffman feels out of the loop but chimes in with what will be a safer option for the agents.

"Well, why not respond and tell him you need him to meet somewhere close to our offices ... like the park? This way we can have ample manpower and surveillance to apprehend him," suggests Huffman.

"I think that will only spook him ... he probably knows that Wang is a federal agent, and he may feel it is a setup," replies Granderson.

Huffman's reaction is cool but she feels the sting of Granderson disagreeing with her. She feels even more out of place as the newbie on the team. Ross is in deep thought ... she has an idea.

"Ling, can you pull up the call log from Wang's phone on your tablet?" she asks.

"Sure, but I can only get a general region," he replies.

"That's fine ... did her phone ping off of any cell towers near eastern Pennsylvania in the past week or so?" she asks.

"Um ... yes, actually. As recent as last Tuesday," replies Ling.

"I know exactly where he wants to meet," announces Ross.

She remembers attending an annual music festival in the town of Bethlehem, Pennsylvania. The main stage was located at the old steel stacks, which were preserved after the mill shut down. All of the locals there refer to it as "the stacks".

"It is only 90 minutes from Manhattan on I-78. We need to hurry so we can get there and set up a perimeter before he shows up expecting to meet with Wang," states Ross.

Huffman is very impressed with Ross. She recognizes how much of a good agent she is, and from one female agent to another, she gives her a nod of respect.

"Well, what are you all waiting for? If you leave now you can beat the traffic," states Huffman.

"We're going to need back up, and at least two surveillance teams," suggests Ross.

Huffman takes out her cell phone and makes a call.

"This is supervisor Amanda Huffman at the New York field office. I need to speak with supervisor Landis," she says confidently into her phone.

Ross is very impressed with Huffman. She recognizes the power and agency connections that she has, and from one female agent to another, she gives her a nod of respect.

"You guys should hurry," Huffman instructs, still holding the phone to her ear. "Ross, you're in charge. I am providing you with all the support you need on the ground there in Pennsylvania. Report back when you have this guy in custody." Then into her phone, "Landis, I have a unit coming to your area to conduct a contact and apprehend."

Ross, Granderson, and Ling are still standing around. Huffman notices this and pulls the phone away from her ear.

"What ... why are you still here?" she asks.

"Solomon took our weapons and placed us on desk duty for the duration of his internal investigation," replies Ross.

"So technically we can only investigate from here and not go out in the field," Granderson adds.

Huffman shakes her head. She can't believe the amount of action taking place on her first day back in New York. She returns the phone to her ear.

"Correction, I am BRINGING a unit to your area," she continues as she quickly walks to the underground parking garage.

Ross, Granderson, and Ling are excited – hi-fiving each other as they follow Huffman.

CHAPTER 31

It isn't until late afternoon that Jamie Magi is permitted to have visitors in her hospital room. She miraculously pulled through surgery with the use of all of her motor skills, but is told that she will never regain her vision. She is still recovering emotionally from that devastating diagnosis, and her eyes are still covered with thick gauze pads to prevent any infection to her opened wounds.

Katherine and Kyle enter the room to find a nurse adjusting Jamie's intravenous drip dosage. The nurse announces their arrival before she politely exits to give the family their privacy.

"Ah, your family is here to see you, Jamie," announces the nurse.

Jamie moves her head around like a small animal trying to locate movement in a dark room.

"Mom?" cries Jamie in a frightened voice.

"Yes, I'm here, sweetie," replies Katherine as she quickly makes her way over to the bed and grabs Jamie's hand.

Jamie squeezes her mother's hand and cries out in a panic.

"Mom, they say I will never see again," she cries.

Kyle makes his way over to the bed. Tears are streaming down his face but he tries to remain strong for his girlfriend. He takes her other hand and holds it. Jamie jumps initially at his touch. She is obviously still very traumatized by the events from the past weekend.

"Kyle is here too, sweetie," announces Katherine.

"Hi, beautiful," says Kyle softly as he bends down and kisses the back of her hand.

Jamie is a wreck. She cries uncontrollably as she tries to digest the future she is now condemned to. Her mother and boyfriend try in vain to cheer her up, consciously using cheerful voices while speaking soothing words. Nothing seems to work as the focus of her new life sentence crushes the dreams she envisioned just a couple of days ago.

"Mom, where is Dad?" asks Jamie.

She cannot see her mother's face, but she senses a pause. Kyle looks at Katherine as he, too, can feel the apprehensive hesitation.

"Honey, your dad is downstairs ..." Katherine starts to reply before breaking down.

She covers her mouth and cries silently, but Jamie can feel her hand trembling as she weeps.

"Mom?" cries Jamie.

Kyle can see that Katherine is in no condition to break the news to her daughter ... news that she herself is still attempting to register. As Jamie grows increasingly upset by her mother's delayed response, Kyle begins to break the news himself.

"Babe, your father ..." he begins before Katherine signals for him to stop.

Jamie moves her head from the right to the left, as if watching a tennis match ... from the direction of her mother's voice, to the direction of Kyle's voice, and then back to her right as Katherine begins to speak.

"Sweetie, your dad didn't make it. He is breathing because of the machines, but he is gone ... I'm sorry," weeps Katherine.

She drops her head onto Jamie's until their foreheads touch. Kyle watches in anguish as his girlfriend experiences the death of her father for the second time in her life.

.   .   .

Agent Ross is in the back seat of agent Huffman's government--issued car as it rolls along Interstate 78 westbound when she gets a call from one of the police officers at the Sprainbrook Medical Center. Huffman is driving and Granderson is in the front passenger seat. Agent Ling is also in the back seat with Ross, and continues to monitor his tablet for any incoming messages from Nicholas Trama.

"Well, bad news ... we lost John Magi," announces Ross as she ends her phone call.

"No! We need his testimony to tie Howard to the diamonds," replies Granderson.

Ross is a little emotional. She, too, would like to have John alive to testify against Howard and help clear her and her team of any wrongdoing, but she also bonded with him after years of vowing to keep him and his family protected. She feels like a member of the family, as she practically watched Jamie Magi grow up.

"Now securing Mr. Trama is even more valuable as he is the only link connecting Howard and his crew to the diamonds and other cover ups," adds Ling.

Ross doesn't want to cry ... at least not in the presence of her new boss and coworkers. She stares out the window at the scenic mountain views as they pass a sign that reads: *Welcome to Pennsylvania.*

· · ·

Back at the Sprainbrook Medical Center, agent Howard is handcuffed to a wheelchair being pushed down the hallway, escorted by two state police officers and a federal agent. He has been cleared by doctors to be moved, and is being transferred to a hospital outside the King's County Jail. There he will continue treatment before he is transferred to the jail, once properly arraigned by a federal court judge. As he reaches the lobby, his old friend and now defense lawyer, Arthur Stavros, is there to meet him.

"May I have a word with my attorney?" asks Howard.

The nurse stops the wheelchair and Howard summons Stavros over with his finger. Being that they have no privacy, Stavros leans down close to Howard. Howard whispers something to his lawyer and slips him a note that he wrote on a hospital notepad. Stavros crumples the note in his hand, concealing it from the officers standing by. After their interaction, Stavros steps aside and the nurse continues to push the wheelchair toward a back entrance, away from the lurking media.

Out back, a medical transport van is waiting to take Howard to his next destination. He is loaded into the back of the van, strapped to a stretcher, and then handcuffed to it. The state police officers and the federal agent will escort him. They load up and secure the doors before driving away. A marked state police vehicle rides closely behind the van.

As the nurse reenters the hospital through the back entrance, she rolls the now-empty wheelchair past Arthur Stavros, who is standing in the lobby reading the note passed to him by his long-time friend and client. After reading the note he quickly walks to his car and drives out of the hospital parking lot.

*　　*　　*

Upstairs in Jamie's room, Katherine is on Jamie's bed sitting up next to her daughter, cradling her head against her abdomen. Jamie appears calm and napping as Kyle returns from the cafeteria with cups of hot coffee. He hands one to Katherine gently as not to wake Jamie. Katherine takes the coffee and sips quietly. Kyle sits in a chair near the window and looks on while sipping his coffee. Katherine's phone rings and it startles her and wakes Jamie. Kyle takes Katherine's spot on the bed next to Jamie, and cuddles her head while gently stroking her hair. Katherine exits the room and goes out to the hallway to take the phone call.

*　　*　　*

At the historic Hotel Bethlehem on Main Street, agent Ross and the New York field office team meet with the Lehigh Valley field agents to prep their very sensitive operation. Ross slips away from the group to make a courtesy call to John Magi's widow. The irony is that this call comes days after it was Ross who informed Katherine that John was alive, and that she never was a widow.

Ross feels like she failed to fulfill the promise she made to John ... to keep him alive and protected. She never imagined that the agency that was supposed to protect him would be the very thing that he would need protection from.

Katherine tells Ross that she was waiting for Jamie to see her father before pulling the plug. However, due to Jamie's condition, Katherine sees no point in prolonging the inevitable.

The revelation of Jamie's prognosis further upsets Ross, but she maintains a stern image for the sake of her team. After ending her call with Katherine, Ross rejoins the other agents. She is determined to capture Nicholas Trama and use his testimony to put Howard away for good.

The agents are going over a map of the steel stacks and the grounds surrounding the area when Ross rejoins them.

"So the second surveillance van should park here ... this will also give us a vantage point to observe any accompaniment that Trama may have," states Huffman.

She sees Ross return to the huddle.

"This is agent Ross' operation ... give her your full support as her team leads from van number one," she continues.

Granderson can see a look in Ross' eyes that he has never seen before in her. She is focused, determined, and hungry for this mission to get underway.

"I just got off the phone with John Magi's widow, Katherine. I learned that their daughter ... the little girl I've watched grow up from a seven-year-old with braces to the beautiful young college senior that she is ... well I learned that she is completely blind," Ross shares. The team is silent, absorbing this sad and shocking news. "One of the bullets that took the life of her father has also taken her vision. The pretty, sparkly diamonds that this whole mess is about ... well she will never look at a diamond, or anything pretty, again. I'm ashamed by the fact that it is one of our own that is responsible for this—that greed takes precedence over honor. I can't bring her father back, and I can't bring her eyesight back. But with your help tonight, I can get that family a step closer to justice. Not just Jamie Magi's family, also one from our own family, special agent Monica

Bloomfield. The man that we will be meeting tonight is the only living connection to agent Howard and the other dirty agents tied to all of this. If we get Trama, we get Howard. This is the reason I signed up for this job. Let's do this!" declares Ross as she leads the charge for a successful mission.

The agents from both jurisdictions are fired up and ready to give Ross all the support that is required. Huffman looks at Ross with admiration of her spirit, purpose, and passion. It is in this moment she realizes that she wants to recommend that Ross take over as permanent supervising agent once the internal investigation is complete. She looks in Granderson's direction and notices the look in his eyes as he looks over at Ross. Huffman also realizes that this is the same way he looked at her many years ago. This is a connection that she dare not disrupt.

"Hopefully you won't be needing these, but just in case," states Huffman as she offers handguns to Ross and Granderson.

*　*　*

When Katherine gets off of the phone with agent Ross, John's doctor approaches her in the hallway. He is sensitive to her grieving, but urges her to make a decision about her husband. They can keep him breathing on the machines but since John is a registered organ donor, he can save lives of other patients around the region. John is not going to return miraculously, so to delay pulling the plug is to delay helping someone else who has a chance to live.

Katherine is receptive and willing. She knows that John—Mr. Wonderful—would want to help as many people as he could. That is just the way he always was. Katherine also personally knows someone who John would especially wish to donate an organ to if he had a say in the matter.

"Doctor, can we discuss the possibility of an eye transplant?" Katherine asks.

CHAPTER 32

With both FBI surveillance vans keeping a watchful eye on the historic Bethlehem steel stacks underneath the Pennsylvania night sky, agents Ross and Granderson sit intimately close on a metal bench facing the old train tracks. Under the guise of two lovers seizing an opportunity to share kisses under the stars, the two partners embrace as they relay communication back to the vans parked in the distance via in-ear radios.

Their natural chemistry doesn't go unnoticed—especially by the New York field office interim supervisor, agent Amanda Huffman. She manages to conceal her awkward emotions from the rest of the team inside the van, and for the sake of this mission she maintains her professional leadership position.

"Not so convincing, you two ... my gosh you're distracting all the heterosexual agents among us," jokes agent Ling into a microphone.

The other agents in the van chuckle ... except agent Huffman.

"OK, let's act like grown-ups everyone, we have incoming," announces Huffman.

"Got him," replies Ross as she looks over Granderson's shoulder to see a Caucasian male walking in their direction.

Ross begins to kiss Granderson even more passionately in hopes that their public display of heavy affection doesn't tip off their subject. As the man continues to walk in their direction, agent Ling zooms his camera in for a tighter shot of the man's face, however he walks with his head down.

"Heads up, we've got another bogie approaching," announces an agent from the other surveillance van.

Granderson looks behind Ross' head and notices a Caucasian male approaching from the other direction.

"I've got eyes on number two," Granderson reports softly as Ross continues to kiss his cheek.

Ling tries to get a close visual of the second man but from his vantage point he can only see the back of the man's head. Both men seem suspicious as they approach the steel stacks cautiously and look around as if hoping to not be observed. These men are definitely up to something. Unsure of which is Trama, Ross softly radios in to the rest of the team.

"Stand down," she orders.

The team looks on as the first man passes by Ross and Granderson and walks over to the second man. They interact with one another and then one of the men gives the other a small brown paper bag. In exchange, the other gives him folded cash. As the two men begin to part ways, Ross gives the order to the team standing by.

"Move in! Move in!"

With that command, Ross and Granderson jump to their feet and draw their weapons.

"FBI, freeze!" yells Granderson as he points his weapon at the two startled men.

One man immediately drops to his knees with his hands raised. The other man turns and thinks about making a run for it. Within seconds, both teams of agents converge onto the area and surround the two men. The second man decides not to run and instead raises his hands.

As the agents quickly detain the two shady men, they discover that neither of them is Nicholas Trama... just two local lowlifes conducting a drug deal.

"Clearly, this area is used by the locals for illegal activity," states Huffman.

"Well it's poorly lit and obscure with a few ways in and out. No wonder Trama and Wang chose this place to do their transactions," replies Ross.

As the agents begin to escort the men away, Ling sees a man in the distance standing by the train tracks. The man notices the activity and turns back toward the dark tracks.

"Looks like we have a runner," announces Ling.

Ross and Granderson see the man running away and quickly follow him. The man runs along the tracks as fast as he can. He is clearly familiar with the area as he effortlessly navigates through the darkness. The two agents in pursuit have trouble keeping up even with their flashlights. The old, abandoned tracks that used to serve as the only means for cargo trains to get in and out of the steel factory have not been maintained and offer dangerous terrain.

The man disappears around a bend and then runs along the shallow river. He looks behind him occasionally to monitor those chasing him. As he reaches a low and narrow wooden bridge, he climbs up onto it and runs to a rusty old pickup truck that is parked at a 90-degree angle off the road at the edge of the bridge. He quickly opens the driver-side door and hops into the truck. He starts the engine and puts the gearshift into drive. He is about to pull off when he hears the voice of agent Ross.

"I wouldn't do that," declares Ross.

The man looks to his left and sees Ross' gun pointed directly at him through the opened window. He looks over her shoulder and can see Granderson walking up with his weapon drawn. The man throws his back against his seat with his hands up. His body language displays his admitted defeat. Ross carefully reaches into the truck window with her gun fixed on the suspect. She opens the door and orders him to turn the engine off. The man complies by putting the gearshift into park and turning the key.

"I'm agent Ross with the FBI. I'm going to need you to slowly exit the vehicle, sir," Ross announces.

"I knew this day would come ... too good to be true," he replies as he gets out of the vehicle with his hands raised.

"What's your name, sir?" she asks.

"Trama ... Nick Trama," he replies.

. . .

As Jamie Magi sleeps in her hospital bed, her boyfriend Kyle sleeps on the chair by the window. Down the hall, Katherine sits with a group of doctors—including the staff eye specialist, Dr. Kerry Donohue. They discuss the options as well as the risks of performing a risky eye transplant.

"So you're saying you will be able to use donor corneas?" asks Katherine.

"Well, I don't want to get your hopes up, but with a donor I think it is quite possible that we can fully restore Jamie's sight," replies Dr. Donohue.

A single tear rolls slowly down Katherine's cheek, as if it is the last one she has remaining after such an emotional weekend.

"Thank you," she offers to the doctors seated in the room.

"No promises, but there is a chance," replies Dr. Donohue.

"Well thank you for giving us a chance," adds Katherine.

"Now, as we discussed, because John is a donor, all medical bills for dialysis, artificial nutrition and hydration, cardiopulmonary resuscitation, and mechanical ventilation that is used to keep his organs vital for transplant will be covered in full by the hospital," states one doctor.

"Being that Jamie is an adult, ultimately the decision to go forward with the transplant is strictly hers. We can move ahead as soon as she signs the documents," adds Jamie's treating physician.

Katherine is thankful for the opportunity to be able to share some positive news with her daughter.

After consulting with the doctors, Katherine returns to Jamie's room. She walks quietly over to her bed and looks at her sleeping daughter with the gauze over her eyes. Katherine gently brushes some loose strands of hair from Jamie's face. She leans in and kisses her forehead softly, as not to wake her. Then she exits the room quietly.

. . .

Katherine makes her way into John's room. The sounds of the various machines seem louder with the stillness of the night. Katherine makes her way to John's bed and grabs his hand. She speaks to him as if she is certain that he can hear every word.

"Well, John, it looks like you will always be looking out for our daughter after all," she states in a whisper. "You will be helping so many people ... saving so many lives. You are giving the gift of life, John. That is truly selfless. Thank you for coming back to us. Thank you for saving me and Jamie from Jerron. We know that you always have been, and always will be, our guardian angel."

She kisses his face several times ...for the last time.

"Sleep in peace," she whispers.

. . .

Early in the morning back at the FBI New York office, agents Ross and Granderson are questioning Nicholas Trama in connection with the stolen diamonds. Because the federal statute of limitations has expired for the heist that took place 15 years ago, the agents will use this as leverage to get Trama to talk freely and candidly. Unlike agent Howard, who will face murder and conspiracy charges, they will try to get Trama on international smuggling charges and other federal crimes. For now, they just need his full, detailed story.

As they sit in a small room with a rectangular table in the center, Huffman and Ling observe and record from outside via hidden cameras and microphones.

"Mr. Trama, as I'm sure you are aware, the federal statute of limitations has expired, so you are not under arrest for theft," states Granderson.

"Really? So why am I here?" asks Trama.

"Well, you can spare yourself international criminal charges by cooperating with our investigation of corruption. How often did you meet with agent Sarah Wang?" replies Ross.

"Before I tell you anything, I want to work out a deal," states Trama.

"OK, what's your deal?" asks Granderson.

Trama swallows hard as he thinks about his family.

"My family thinks that I died that day in the tower with the others ... I will tell you whatever you want to know, but I need to know that they will never hear about this. I don't want to disgrace them and put them through this mess," states a semi-emotional Trama.

Ross and Granderson share a look and nod in agreement.

"We can't make any promises, but your family doesn't need to hear about this," replies Granderson.

"Well, where should I begin?" asks Trama.

"How about you start from the beginning? What happened that day?" replies Ross.

Trama is hesitant as he replays the day that forever changed his life, and landed him here in federal custody.

"Well it was a regular Tuesday ... just like any other Tuesday in New York," begins Trama.

CHAPTER 33

Fifteen years ago, Nicholas Trama completely hated his life. He dreaded waking up at four o'clock every morning to work the morning shift for a low paying, boring job … long shifts with lousy benefits, and little vacation time. The only silver lining in reporting to work each morning was the fact that for 12 hours he escaped the crappy little studio apartment that he shared with his annoying girlfriend, Tina. Nicholas felt smothered by her overbearing jealously, verbal abuse, and constant bickering. Tina would pick a fight over the simplest things. She would fuss about the way he chewed his food, made the bed, and one time she even complained about the way he breathed. It got to the point where he no longer felt comfortable being home.

One day Tina told Nicholas that she was pregnant and that he had to get a better-paying job or ask for additional overtime since she would have to leave her job as a nail technician, as the chemicals and fumes are not safe for an expecting mother. Although in his mind he questioned if the baby was even his—as Tina was known for spreading the love among the fellas in the neighborhood—he looked forward to working weekends and some extra shifts. All of the extra hours and additional workdays translated to more time away from the emasculating tongue-lashing and constant nagging he experienced daily at home.

What started out as just another boring Tuesday at work suddenly became a ticket to freedom and a whole new life.

When Nicholas reported to work every morning, he clocked in and reported to a supervisor, who signed off on his security firearm. At the end of each shift, the firearm was to be signed back out before each security officer left the building. That particular morning, after working a time-and-a-half shift that ended at three o'clock in the morning, Nicholas went to the bathroom and decided to lock the door, turn off the lights, and take a nap before starting the morning turnaround shift.

While sitting on the toilet and leaning against the wall, he was startled by the sounds of gunfire outside. Since he started working there, this was the first real action. By the yelling and various voices, he could tell that the vault was being burgled. His first instinct was to remain quiet and still in the dark employee bathroom. After all, for what they were paying him, he did not wish to put himself in danger. After a few moments of silence, he heard a loud bang—like a heavy explosion that rocked the entire building—followed by mass chaos as fire alarms rang out throughout the entire basement level. The sprinklers in the bathroom began to shower down on him. It was then he thought about the two other security guards on duty, and their safety. He decided to go out and assist them.

Nicholas readied his firearm and took a deep breath. As he placed his hand on the knob of the bathroom door, he could feel the intense heat. He quickly opened the door and was almost knocked back by the sudden burst of immense heat. At the time he didn't know that the burning jet fuel would reduce the entire building to rubble, but he knew that conditions were getting worse—in a hurry. The dark smoke began to fill the hallway leading to the vault. He dropped to his knees and crawled toward the vault where he saw the bloody bodies of the two other guards on the floor. There was also another body … most likely one of the would-be thieves … shot during the exchange of gunfire.

When Nicholas took out his cell phone to call 9-1-1, he saw that he had several text messages from Tina as well as others who knew that he worked at the World Trade Center. That is when he first realized that his building was the second to be hit by a plane in a strategic terrorist attack. This was also the moment that he realized that this could be his ticket to a brand-new life.

He looked over at the opened vault, and then over to the opening to the secret subway tunnel used to move the international treasures undetected underground. He was sure that the burglars escaped through the tunnel. He quickly entered the vault to find that it was almost completely empty. This was definitely the work of professionals with major connections. Not only did they know about the secret tunnel and the international trade vault, but they also knew that it would be full and ready for a pickup the very next day. The professionals pulled off a major heist…but they left a few diamonds behind in the skirmish with security.

Nicholas ran to the security desk, where his brown bag lunch still sat untouched. He dumped out the contents onto the desk and took the empty bag into the safe. He was sure that firefighters or police would be coming down to the basement soon, so he raced against the clock. He filled the bag with the remaining diamonds—some of which had fallen to the floor. He also grabbed some foreign bills … as many as he could fit into the bag. He then quickly exited the vault and closed the large iron door.

Nicholas was now choking on the thick smoke that was quickly filling the basement level of the building and sweating as the heat continued to rise in the room. He took his uniform off and undressed the dead thief. He put on the dead man's clothes and dressed him in his uniform. He carefully planted his wallet, phone, and gun on the dead man. He could tell that everything in the basement level would be destroyed soon and that he needed to make his escape immediately. He knew that he would not make it up through the lobby area as flames filled the stairwell. He decided to exit through the same tunnel as the burglars.

As he frantically made his escape, Nicholas took an exit to the regular subway tracks. There, he was able to carefully walk along the dark train tracks, avoiding the deadly third rail. With the thick smell of smoke still singed on his clothing, he noticed a rushing herd of large sewer rats also racing away from the tracks below the World Trade Center. Looking behind him, he could see a cloud of white dust filling the tunnel and moving rapidly. He continued to move quickly away from the approaching eerie plume.

With the cloud of smoke and dust behind him, and the light of the next subway station in front of him, Nicholas saw this moment as his rebirthing. As he traveled frantically with determination through the tunnel—or birth canal—he moved forward to the light ahead—his new life. The cloud—his former life, continued to pursue him relentlessly.

Reaching the subway station, he scrambled up from the tracks to the platform, and ran up the stairs to the street level. When he exited the subway, he looked like a homeless person, with dark ash on his face, wearing clothes two to three sizes too small, and holding a brown paper bag. As his eyes adjusted to the brightness of the street, he noticed several people covered in grey dust staring back, dazed, at what once was their place of employment. The building had now completely disappeared beyond the increasingly darkening air around them. There was widespread panic as a loud rumble shook the ground beneath him. People began to run for cover—ducking into stores and underneath cars as a second wave of thick smoke filled the streets. Nicholas ran as far away as he could.

Later that evening, through the chaos and devastation, the entire city was a mess. People that were stranded in the city were given free rides to wherever they needed. Nicholas took a ride to Pennsylvania where he used some of the cash he found in the pockets of the dead man's pants to rent a motel room.

With everyone thinking he died in the building with the other guards, he was now free to flee the country and start a whole new life. However, since he didn't have any form of ID, he couldn't get very far. That is when he asked around and reached out to a known international broker—someone who finds buyers for merchandise and won't ask where they came from. This broker was shady, and used a courier as a middleman, but Nicholas had no other options. Not only did the broker give him cash for the diamonds, but also for the value of the international bills he snatched from the vault.

Nicholas used the cash to live. He bought a small house in the Pocono Mountains, and a used pickup truck. Far from the extravagant life he envisioned, but free from the dull life he once knew. He later learned from social media updates that Tina had a son who was half Dominican—so Nicholas wasn't the father after all.

Once he ran low on cash, he reached out to the broker for work. Since the broker developed some trust in Nicholas, he was given a job as a contact—a middle-middleman of sorts. One of his clients was the dirty FBI agent, Sarah Wang. The irony of that was she wanted to move and trade the same diamonds taken in the heist when Nicholas was on duty years ago. Although he did not initially know that she was a federal agent, Nicholas knew that eventually things would catch up to him. He wanted out of the game, but the money was all cash and easy to come by.

After moving most of the diamonds between Wang and the broker, Nicholas had to set up one final pickup and delivery. Unfortunately for him, he ran into agent Ross and her team.

*　　　*　　　*

After giving his statement to Ross and Granderson, they have questions about the broker. However, Nicholas adamantly denies ever meeting the mysterious criminal or having any knowledge otherwise.

"I swear, we only communicated through a courier," declares Trama.

"Well, how did this courier reach out to you?" asks Ross.

"I receive a box in the mail containing a pre-paid cell phone. I am told who to meet and where. After I make a drop, I get an envelope with cash and instructions to destroy the pre-paid phone. They were pretty careful in case I got pinched by police, I wouldn't be able to flip on them," he replies.

"But agent Wang had a number saved for you. What number is that?" asks Granderson.

"That is my actual cell phone. It's a month-to-month plan I use, so I use a nickname and not my real name," replies Trama.

Agents Huffman and Ling are listening to Nicholas Trama's incredible story from an adjacent room, and are now joined by director Solomon and his team conducting the internal investigation.

Solomon has more questions for Trama and wants to press him further for information about the broker.

"Have them ask him about the final drop from agent Wang," orders Solomon to Ling.

Agent Ling then relays the message from his tablet to Ross' phone.

When Ross' phone vibrates on the table, she reads the message from Ling.

"Mr. Trama, this final pickup and drop from agent Wang, when were you to meet with the broker, or this courier?" she asks.

"I don't know. I would usually be contacted within 24 hours on the pre-paid phone with further instructions," he replies.

In the other room, Solomon turns to Ling.

"Do we have that pre-paid phone in our possession?" he asks.

"Yes sir, we do," replies Ling.

"Well, let's give the man back his phone," Solomon orders.

Solomon instructs Ross and Granderson to terminate the interview with Trama. They plan to await a call from the broker's courier, and then have Trama play along while they monitor it.

"Hopefully the broker doesn't already know that we have one of his guys in custody," states Solomon.

Within a couple of hours, Ling gets an alert on his tablet and connects to an incoming call to Trama's pre-paid phone. The agents listen in as Trama answers the phone.

Ross and Granderson are sitting in the room with Trama as his phone rings.

"Now don't you even think about tipping them off. Let them believe that you successfully got the pickup from Wang and are ready to move forward," instructs Ross to Trama.

Trama reluctantly agrees and then answers the phone.

"Hello?" states Trama into the phone.

A distorted voice is heard on the other end of the conversation, as the caller uses a filter as a vocal disguise.

"Tell your FBI buddies that their guys are the real criminals," announces the caller before hanging up.

Clearly the courier was watching Trama and witnessed the sting operation.

"It appears that they know Trama is in custody, sir," announces Ling.

"Oh, you think?" sarcastically replies an annoyed Solomon.

Solomon storms out of the room and his team follows him. Ross and Granderson leave Trama alone in the interview room and join Huffman and Ling in the other room as they discuss their next possible move.

CHAPTER 34

Director Solomon leads a team of FBI agents, who are accompanied by a major crimes unit from the New York Police Department, as they conduct a raid on agent Sarah Wang's lower east-side apartment. When they arrive, they discover that the lock on the door was recently tampered with, and remains unlocked. The scraped paint along the jamb near the deadbolt is a clear indication that someone pried the door open. Upon making entry into the apartment, they are surprised to find the entire place has been completely ransacked.

"Whoever was here thoroughly searched the place. Not sure if they found what they were looking for," reports one female agent to director Solomon.

"No doubt they came for the same thing we're looking for," replies Solomon.

He is frustrated to yet again be one step behind.

"If agent Wang stashed the diamonds here, I think it's safe to say that someone has already recovered them," states the female agent.

"Well, I want every video camera within a seven-block radius to check for footage of whoever got here before we did ... and have every piece of furniture, every item of clothing, and every appliance taken to the lab and searched over. And rip up this entire carpet," orders Solomon.

At his command, the entire team scrambles and gets to work.

*   *   *

"I don't think she hid the diamonds in her apartment," whispers Arthur Stavros to his friend and client Stewart Howard.

Stavros is visiting Howard, who has been released from the hospital and booked into the Kings County Jail. As the attorney and client meet in a private room, they sit across from one another at a small round metal table. Stavros is in a plastic chair, and Howard is shackled at the waist to a wheelchair.

"Are you sure?" Howard asks in a soft voice.

"I had my guys go through the entire place with a fine-tooth comb. I can assure you, they are not in her apartment," replies Stavros.

Howard clenches his lips and fists tightly. He looks off to the side as he ponders any other options.

"Perhaps she was planning to double cross you ... maybe hid them in a storage or safety deposit box, in case you double-crossed her first ... or worse, your friends at the FBI already got them before my guys did," suggests Stavros.

Howard is racking his brain as he tries to figure out what to do next. He has no way of contacting Wang's broker, as that was how he played it safe ... not have contact with the broker directly, as not to be later implicated.

"Those diamonds are not only my way to pay you for representing me, but if the FBI finds them in Wang's apartment, they will link everything back to me. We need to find those diamonds!" declares a frustrated Howard.

Stavros shakes his head and stands up. He grabs his briefcase and places his fedora on his head.

"Not 'we,' Stewart ... you. This is way out of control. You're on your own, pal," he announces as he walks away.

Howard is stunned that his old friend is abandoning him.

"Arthur ... get back here, you coward!" yells Howard.

He turns violently toward Stavros and tips his wheelchair over, falling to the ground. He looks up to see his old friend stroll casually away—his fancy dress shoes clicking down the long corridor.

"Arthur, you bastard!" yells Howard toward Stavros' back.

Two correctional officers rush into the room to assist Howard back into his wheelchair. He attempts to fight them off as he continues to scream obscenities at Stavros.

•　　•　　•

During a memorial service for fallen agent Monica Bloomfield, Ross, Granderson, and Ling sit together. The mood is somber, yet there is also a feeling of pride in honoring a young agent who loved what she did. Before director Solomon takes the podium to give a speech, he gives a medal of honor and a folded flag to Bloomfield's parents, who are seated in the front row.

"I heard Huffman gave Solomon her recommendation to permanently fill Howard's position," whispers Granderson to Ross.

Ross smiles but doesn't offer much else.

"So ... are you going to take the position?" he presses.

"I'm not sure. I think I will finally take that much-needed vacation," she replies.

•　　•　　•

At the Sprainbrook Medical Center, Jamie Magi has made it through a seemingly successful transplant surgery and the doctor is cutting the bandages from her eyes. Jamie is sitting upright in her bed.

"Now, Jamie, for some time you may be very sensitive to sunlight. This is completely normal. It will take time to adjust," warns Dr. Donohue.

She orders the nurse to close the blinds in the room. As she removes the bandages, Jamie squints as she opens her eyes. She is staring into a round handheld mirror. With the exception of a little post-surgery swelling, she looks like her normal self. She is all smiles as she lowers the mirror and sees the faces of her mother, Katherine, and boyfriend, Kyle.

"I can see!" she gleefully declares.

She hugs her mother, her boyfriend, and her doctor. She is truly overwhelmed with joy and grateful to her father and donor.

•　　•　　•

After an intense FBI internal and criminal investigation, former agent Stewart Howard pleads guilty to multiple charges dating back many years. He is subsequently sentenced to 99 years in the Grumman Men's Federal Prison.

Now with a permanent limp, he walks with the assistance of a metal orthopedic cane. Upon arriving at the prison, rumors have spread quickly among the inmates that he is the dirty former agent solely responsible for framing several key players in the Mongelli crime family.

Having many days that he regrets, Howard has a flashback of one day in particular.

A dark-colored sedan violently rear ends Sal Mongelli's silver sports car, causing him to lose control and crash into a large tree off to the side of the road. A male driver exits the dark sedan and calmly walks toward the wreckage. When he reaches the door of the mangled sports car, Sal looks out the window, over toward the man. Sal is in obvious pain and bloody from the impact of the deployed airbag. He tries to reach beneath his seat for his weapon, but his legs are pinned by the steering wheel. Realizing that he is helpless, and not expecting mercy from this man, he resorts to maintaining his dignity and tough-guy reputation.

After retrieving a cigar and lighter that is clipped to the visor, he lights the cigar and blows smoke out the window at the man.

"See you in hell, pig ... You and your whore mother!" he spits hatefully in a heavy New York City accent.

The man standing outside the car is FBI agent Stewart Howard. He calmly reaches in through the driver's window of the sports car to grab Sal, who, due to his injuries, puts up a weak, futile struggle. Howard grabs Sal's head and quickly and violently twists it—snapping his neck and killing him instantly.

Howard then reaches into the jacket pocket of the deceased and takes out a sterling silver flask by using a white handkerchief. He pours the liquid contents from the flask onto Sal's face and shirt and uses the handkerchief to wipe the flask clean of his fingerprints, then drops the empty flask onto Sal's lap. Next he uses the lighter to ignite the mob boss' clothes – setting off an immediate blaze.

After looking around to make sure no other vehicles are around to witness his actions, Howard retreats back to his vehicle to call in the accident.

Howard recalls that day as if it were just this morning.

During shower time, Howard strips naked and leans his cane up against the tile wall. He runs the shower and feels it with his hand to test the water temperature. Once it is warm enough, he steps underneath the showerhead. Standing in the shower with his head down as the water beats against his back, he looks down as the water trickles down the drain between his feet. He closes his eyes as he lathers his head with shampoo. After rinsing, he reopens his eyes and notices a small, wallet-size photo of two young men. He recognizes the young men in the photo as Anthony and Jerron Silvestri.

Howard quickly turns off the water and steps out of the shower. He reaches for his cane, but it is no longer there. Suddenly several men step around the corner and block his exit. The leader of the group is Richie Silvestri—the man Howard framed for the murder of three FBI agents.

"So, I hear you're the prick that has my family's diamonds," states Silvestri in a calm voice.

"Help! Guards!" screams a terrified Howard.

The men in the group chuckle as they move even closer toward him.

"No one in here is going to help you … dirty pig!" replies Silvestri as he spits in Howard's face.

Howard backs up against the wall and cowers with his head tucked behind his arms. As a barrage of blows rains down on the disgraced former federal agent, his blood trickles across the moldy shower floor and spirals into the drain.

*   *   *

Katherine realized that she could no longer live in the home she once shared with Jerron. She decided to sell the house and do something that she and John talked about doing from the day they got married:

she uses the money from the house to buy a boat. As a tribute, and in honor of John, she names the boat *Mr. Wonderful* in his memory.

.   .   .

It was also one of John's wishes to grow old and retire to a life out by the ocean. So Katherine, Jamie, and Kyle take the *S.S. Mr. Wonderful* out to the deep and hold a small funeral service for John Michael Magi. Jamie says a few words before ceremoniously releasing her father's ashes off the back of the boat. They each throw white rose petals out as well. As the ashes and petals float and mix with the waves, tears roll from behind Jamie's thick sunglasses. This is the second time John's eyes have cried at his own funeral.

.   .   .

On the white sand beach in Tobago, agents Ross and Granderson sit under a cabana in their bathing suits. Although they look comfortable and completely relaxed, they are not actually on vacation, but working undercover.

After video cameras picked up footage of the men who ransacked Wang's apartment, they traced them back to Arthur Stavros. They learned that once Stavros found the diamonds, he played his buddy Howard and kept the findings for himself. After conducting surveillance on him, they followed him here to the Caribbean, where he is meeting with Wang's mysterious and illusive broker. Ross and Granderson hope to bring down Stavros and the big broker in one shot.

Agent Ling is watching from a hotel balcony and communicating through in-ear transmitters to Ross, Granderson, and three other undercover agents on the premises.

"OK, we have activity ... I have eyes on Stavros. He is sitting by the pool," reports Ling.

"Any sign of the broker?" questions Ross.

"That's a negative," replies Ling.

"Nobody makes a move until we have the broker in sight. He's the big fish here," orders Ross.

Ling watches as an attractive woman brings a drink in a pineapple over to Stavros.

"The old guy has still got it. He's chatting up the waitress," reports Ling.

*   *   *

As the pretty woman hands Stavros a drink, she introduces herself as his contact. She has dark eyes and long, black hair. She smiles with feminine confidence, as she appears to know how to make men feel at ease. Her name is Jessica Mongelli—the daughter of Salvatore Mongelli—aka The Broker. Behind her uncle's back, she has been secretly trading the diamonds that she believes belong to her father … and he would undoubtedly want her to have the money. She has made it her life's mission to retrieve every last jewel. Using inside knowledge from her father's conversations she overheard, she learned about the one mobster, Frankie Sterlacci, who was killed during the shootout with security guards during the Trade Center heist. Like the rest of the Mongelli family, she initially assumed that John Magi double-crossed her father and possibly faked his death, in which case he would seek out a broker to move the diamonds overseas. She put her feelers out and got a hit when Nicholas Trama first looked to move some of the stolen diamonds. She later discovered that the dirty agents had the rest of the big jackpot. With her contacts overseas, she has managed to move all of the diamonds, and is attempting to collect the last of them before disappearing for good.

"I left the diamonds wrapped in the towel, as we discussed," states Stavros.

He sips the drink and tries to play cool in the presence of such an attractive woman.

"Yes, but it appears that you are a bit short. According to Ms. Wang, there should be at least three times that amount. You wouldn't be trying to stiff me, would you?" replies the young woman in a flirtatious manner.

*   *   *

Ling watches on. He has no audio, but her body language does not seem suspicious. She stands at the table appearing to be polite as an old guy hits on her.

"Boy, this gal knows how to earn her tips," states Ling into his microphone.

*   *   *

"I swear, that is all that was there at the apartment," replies Stavros.

Jessica smiles. She doesn't trust or believe him. She turns to walk away.

"Hey, what about my money?" he asks.

She stops and politely responds with a smile.

"There's a secret message written inside the bottom of your drink. You will clearly see it once your drink is empty," she states.

She walks away and Stavros quickly guzzles his drink and then looks in to the bottom ... he sees no message, but his vision becomes blurry. He tries to stand to go after the woman, but he collapses to the ground.

*   *   *

"Man down! I repeat, man down!" reports Ling into the microphone.

He gathers his things and runs down to the pool. Ross and Granderson grab their badges weapons hidden inside a beach bag and rush toward the pool. When they get there, they meet Ling and the other three agents. Granderson checks Stavros for a pulse but he has none. Foam oozes from his mouth, and they know immediately that he was poisoned. They search the area but the mystery woman is nowhere in sight.

*   *   *

Upon learning her identity, locating the dastardly cunning daughter of the late crime boss proves to be quite the challenge ... however one that agent Michelle Ross is up for. If need be, she will devote the rest of her career to bringing full closure to this very complex, and continuously evolving case.

●　　●　　●

When the young newlywed couple, Dwayne and Natalie, move into the apartment once owned by agent Sarah Wang, they love everything about it … except for the bathroom. Being do-it-yourselfers, they decide to knock down the wall, and extend the shower through the closet in the adjacent guest bedroom. This will provide them with an additional three-foot-deep space, and allow for the his-and-hers double-head shower they have always imagined.

As they take the sledgehammer to the tile and break through the wall, they accidently hit the hidden central air conditioning and heating duct. In the process of doing so, they dislodge a maroon-colored bag with a rope attached to it. When they open the bag and check the contents, they are surprised to discover a large amount of diamonds.

"Oh my gosh! There has got to be millions worth of diamonds here," announces Dwayne.

"What do we do … should we call the police?" asks a nervous Natalie.

"This is our miracle … our gift from the universe. I say we keep it. This will change our lives," replies Dwayne.

"We can travel, and do all the things we want … I can open my own dance studio!" replies Natalie.

The excited couple continues to play with their newfound treasure and discuss all the many things that they will do with the money.

"But how will we spend it? It's not like we can simply walk into a bank and say, 'Here is a bag of diamonds we found.' How much is it worth?" states Natalie as the reality of the situation sets in.

Dwayne thinks for a moment, and then shares his suggestion with his wife.

"No, we can't take this to a bank. We need to find a broker."

THE END

ABOUT THE AUTHOR

ALGERNON currently resides in New York City, where he was born and raised. When he was only ten years old, ALGERNON penned his very first story entitled: "The Coin" which was a mystery thriller about a group of children that found a rare coin, and the troubles that followed them when word of their discovery got out.

Mysteries and suspense thrillers were his favorite genre growing up. As an adult, ALGERNON enjoys all genres – From fiction to self-help and personal development.

After receiving a musical scholarship as a gifted jazz pianist, he went on to study music education. After obtaining his BA, ALGERNON went on to take creative writing classes and attended writing workshops conducted by award winning authors in New York City, Orlando FL and Los Angeles CA.

ALGERNON has also written stage plays and screenplays as well as unpublished motivational books.

Stage & Screen Plays include: Road To The Potter's House – Special Delivery I & II – Reality Check – Pick Of The Litter.

After teaching in private schools in NYC, ALGERNON has turned his ability and creativity of powerful story-telling towards Stories for Children which teaches valuable life lessons, as well as other educational tools. He donates his storybooks and coloring books to children's hospitals and government foster homes.

As a Motivational Speaker, ALGERNON has spoken to audiences on a variety of inspirational topics. In his signature message "Make It 'Till You Make It" ALGERNON shares his remarkable and courageous journey from being homeless and sleeping on the streets of New York City, to working on major television/film productions and creating the life of his dreams.

"I look forward to sharing all of the creative stories in my mind as well as real-life personal events in hopes that they will entertain, assist, motivate, inspire, and provoke change or improvement in the reader and in the world."

—ALGERNON

Website:
http://algernonwrites.com

Facebook:
https://www.facebook.com/ALGERNON-1623201117896471/

Twitter:
https://twitter.com/AlgernonWrites

Instagram:
https://www.instagram.com/algernonwrites/

OTHER WORKS BY
ALGERNON

J.A.I.L.
"JUST ANOTHER INNOCENT LIFE"

JUST ANOTHER INNOCENT LIFE: BLISTERING NOVEL, BASED ON LIFE OF THE AUTHOR. The death of a police detective's young daughter rocks a town and creates a scandal, which exposes many dark secrets as the lover of the cop's wife is charged in the unthinkable crime. Defense Attorney Michael Petagnas – a former Prosecutor who now practices on the other side of the aisle, represents the young man who claims to have no involvement in the first-degree murder. Preparing to go head-to-head  against his former understudies in this very high profile, David versus Goliath trial, Petagnas hires Private Investigator Nick McLean. The street savvy investigator believes that there is much more to the story, and begins to uncover levels of corruption and police misconduct. He vows to discover the truth and prevent the young minority defendant from becoming the second victim of a heartless cover up, and just another innocent life.

BASED ON ACTUAL EVENTS

Made in the USA
Lexington, KY
07 December 2016